GIRL, HUNTED

(An Ella Dark FBI Suspense Thriller —Book Three)

BLAKE PIERCE

Blake Pierce

Blake Pierce is the USA Today bestselling author of the RILEY PAGE mystery series, which includes seventeen books. Blake Pierce is also the author of the MACKENZIE WHITE mystery series, comprising fourteen books; of the AVERY BLACK mystery series, comprising six books; of the KERI LOCKE mystery series, comprising five books; of the MAKING OF RILEY PAIGE mystery series, comprising six books; of the KATE WISE mystery series, comprising seven books; of the CHLOE FINE psychological suspense mystery, comprising six books; of the JESSIE HUNT psychological suspense thriller series, comprising nineteen books; of the AU PAIR psychological suspense thriller series, comprising three books; of the ZOE PRIME mystery series, comprising six books; of the ADELE SHARP mystery series, comprising thirteen books; of the EUROPEAN VOYAGE cozy mystery series, comprising six books (and counting); of the new LAURA FROST FBI suspense thriller, comprising five books (and counting); of the new ELLA DARK FBI suspense thriller, comprising six books (and counting); of the A YEAR IN EUROPE cozy mystery series, comprising nine books (and counting); of the AVA GOLD mystery series, comprising three books (and counting); and of the RACHEL GIFT mystery series, comprising three books (and counting).

An avid reader and lifelong fan of the mystery and thriller genres, Blake loves to hear from you, so please feel free to visit www.blakepierceauthor.com to learn more and stay in touch.

BOOKS BY BLAKE PIERCE

RACHEL GIFT MYSTERY SERIES
HER LAST WISH (Book #1)
HER LAST CHANCE (Book #2)
HER LAST HOPE (Book #3)

AVA GOLD MYSTERY SERIES
CITY OF PREY (Book #1)
CITY OF FEAR (Book #2)
CITY OF BONES (Book #3)

A YEAR IN EUROPE
A MURDER IN PARIS (Book #1)
DEATH IN FLORENCE (Book #2)
VENGEANCE IN VIENNA (Book #3)
A FATALITY IN SPAIN (Book #4)
SCANDAL IN LONDON (Book #5)
AN IMPOSTOR IN DUBLIN (Book #6)
SEDUCTION IN BORDEAUX (Book #7)
JEALOUSY IN SWITZERLAND (Book #8)
A DEBACLE IN PRAGUE (Book #9)

ELLA DARK FBI SUSPENSE THRILLER
GIRL, ALONE (Book #1)
GIRL, TAKEN (Book #2)
GIRL, HUNTED (Book #3)
GIRL, SILENCED (Book #4)
GIRL, VANISHED (Book 5)
GIRL ERASED (Book #6)

LAURA FROST FBI SUSPENSE THRILLER
ALREADY GONE (Book #1)
ALREADY SEEN (Book #2)
ALREADY TRAPPED (Book #3)
ALREADY MISSING (Book #4)

ALREADY DEAD (Book #5)

EUROPEAN VOYAGE COZY MYSTERY SERIES
MURDER (AND BAKLAVA) (Book #1)
DEATH (AND APPLE STRUDEL) (Book #2)
CRIME (AND LAGER) (Book #3)
MISFORTUNE (AND GOUDA) (Book #4)
CALAMITY (AND A DANISH) (Book #5)
MAYHEM (AND HERRING) (Book #6)

ADELE SHARP MYSTERY SERIES
LEFT TO DIE (Book #1)
LEFT TO RUN (Book #2)
LEFT TO HIDE (Book #3)
LEFT TO KILL (Book #4)
LEFT TO MURDER (Book #5)
LEFT TO ENVY (Book #6)
LEFT TO LAPSE (Book #7)
LEFT TO VANISH (Book #8)
LEFT TO HUNT (Book #9)
LEFT TO FEAR (Book #10)
LEFT TO PREY (Book #11)
LEFT TO LURE (Book #12)
LEFT TO CRAVE (Book #13)

THE AU PAIR SERIES
ALMOST GONE (Book#1)
ALMOST LOST (Book #2)
ALMOST DEAD (Book #3)

ZOE PRIME MYSTERY SERIES
FACE OF DEATH (Book#1)
FACE OF MURDER (Book #2)
FACE OF FEAR (Book #3)
FACE OF MADNESS (Book #4)
FACE OF FURY (Book #5)
FACE OF DARKNESS (Book #6)

A JESSIE HUNT PSYCHOLOGICAL SUSPENSE SERIES
THE PERFECT WIFE (Book #1)

THE PERFECT BLOCK (Book #2)
THE PERFECT HOUSE (Book #3)
THE PERFECT SMILE (Book #4)
THE PERFECT LIE (Book #5)
THE PERFECT LOOK (Book #6)
THE PERFECT AFFAIR (Book #7)
THE PERFECT ALIBI (Book #8)
THE PERFECT NEIGHBOR (Book #9)
THE PERFECT DISGUISE (Book #10)
THE PERFECT SECRET (Book #11)
THE PERFECT FAÇADE (Book #12)
THE PERFECT IMPRESSION (Book #13)
THE PERFECT DECEIT (Book #14)
THE PERFECT MISTRESS (Book #15)
THE PERFECT IMAGE (Book #16)
THE PERFECT VEIL (Book #17)
THE PERFECT INDISCRETION (Book #18)
THE PERFECT RUMOR (Book #19)

CHLOE FINE PSYCHOLOGICAL SUSPENSE SERIES
NEXT DOOR (Book #1)
A NEIGHBOR'S LIE (Book #2)
CUL DE SAC (Book #3)
SILENT NEIGHBOR (Book #4)
HOMECOMING (Book #5)
TINTED WINDOWS (Book #6)

KATE WISE MYSTERY SERIES
IF SHE KNEW (Book #1)
IF SHE SAW (Book #2)
IF SHE RAN (Book #3)
IF SHE HID (Book #4)
IF SHE FLED (Book #5)
IF SHE FEARED (Book #6)
IF SHE HEARD (Book #7)

THE MAKING OF RILEY PAIGE SERIES
WATCHING (Book #1)
WAITING (Book #2)
LURING (Book #3)

TAKING (Book #4)
STALKING (Book #5)
KILLING (Book #6)

RILEY PAIGE MYSTERY SERIES
ONCE GONE (Book #1)
ONCE TAKEN (Book #2)
ONCE CRAVED (Book #3)
ONCE LURED (Book #4)
ONCE HUNTED (Book #5)
ONCE PINED (Book #6)
ONCE FORSAKEN (Book #7)
ONCE COLD (Book #8)
ONCE STALKED (Book #9)
ONCE LOST (Book #10)
ONCE BURIED (Book #11)
ONCE BOUND (Book #12)
ONCE TRAPPED (Book #13)
ONCE DORMANT (Book #14)
ONCE SHUNNED (Book #15)
ONCE MISSED (Book #16)
ONCE CHOSEN (Book #17)

MACKENZIE WHITE MYSTERY SERIES
BEFORE HE KILLS (Book #1)
BEFORE HE SEES (Book #2)
BEFORE HE COVETS (Book #3)
BEFORE HE TAKES (Book #4)
BEFORE HE NEEDS (Book #5)
BEFORE HE FEELS (Book #6)
BEFORE HE SINS (Book #7)
BEFORE HE HUNTS (Book #8)
BEFORE HE PREYS (Book #9)
BEFORE HE LONGS (Book #10)
BEFORE HE LAPSES (Book #11)
BEFORE HE ENVIES (Book #12)
BEFORE HE STALKS (Book #13)
BEFORE HE HARMS (Book #14)

AVERY BLACK MYSTERY SERIES

CAUSE TO KILL (Book #1)
CAUSE TO RUN (Book #2)
CAUSE TO HIDE (Book #3)
CAUSE TO FEAR (Book #4)
CAUSE TO SAVE (Book #5)
CAUSE TO DREAD (Book #6)

KERI LOCKE MYSTERY SERIES
A TRACE OF DEATH (Book #1)
A TRACE OF MURDER (Book #2)
A TRACE OF VICE (Book #3)
A TRACE OF CRIME (Book #4)
A TRACE OF HOPE (Book #5)

PROLOGUE

Amanda Huber swayed into the middle lane as she fiddled with the dials on her car stereo. She quickly jerked the car back straight and refocused. Finding a good driving song wasn't nearly as important as staying alive.

It was nearing midnight on a brisk March evening, and around thirty miles away, Amanda's young daughter was waiting for her mother to get home. Amanda's work had taken her to some shithole town just outside San Diego, meaning travel had taken up most of her day and all of her evening.

Even more concerning was the babysitter fee which was piling up by the hour – a fee that a single mother with a growing toddler could scarcely afford. Every time the clock ticked two zeros was another thirty-five dollars to the bill. Amanda turned up the music, opened the window and put her foot down on the gas. She was on a long stretch of country road and welcomed the freedom to drive above the speed limit. If she kept things at a steady 80 MPH, she could be home in twenty minutes. The chances were that Chloe was still awake, probably collapsed on the sofa with that grumpy-but-tired face. She never went into a deep sleep when someone other than her mother put her to bed.

The wind felt sharp on her face but it kept her alert. Amanda decided to stop clock-watching. It was 11:43. The chances of her being home before the hour were slim, so it was best to forget about it. Instead, she let her thoughts drift, falling into autopilot. What would she get Chloe for her birthday in a few weeks? When would that gym guy text her back? If she showed up late to work tomorrow, could she blame the exhausting journey and get away with it?

Clunk.

A sudden scraping sound jolted Amanda from her thoughts. She instinctively pushed the brake. *What the hell was that?* It sounded like it came from underneath the car. She checked her rear view mirror but couldn't see anything on the darkened road. The lack of streetlamps didn't help.

Slowing down to a moderate 50 MPH, something didn't feel quite right. The power steering had seemingly been disabled. There was a

1

scraping sound coming from the rear passenger side. Amanda slammed her palms on the wheel.

"For God's sake. Just what I need."

She pulled into a small dirt alcove on the roadside and stepped out. The problem was obvious right away. Her back wheel had a huge rip along it. A small plume of smoke bellowed out.

Amanda didn't know a whole lot about cars, but she knew she couldn't get back on the road with that.

What were people supposed to do in situations like this? Call a breakdown company? Did she even have breakdown insurance? Was it going to be another chunk of cash she couldn't afford? Whatever, she had no choice. Amanda grabbed her phone from the dashboard and opened up her Internet browser.

The screen loaded. Then loaded some more. A minute later, Amanda was still staring at a white screen.

"Oh, you gotta be kidding me," she said. "No signal. Great."

She collapsed against the car and surveyed the street in both directions. Since getting on this country lane, she'd only seen one other car pass by. It wasn't exactly teeming with life. Her thoughts jumped to the extremes. What if Chloe had been tantrum-ing all night? What if she was confused that her mom wasn't there? Amanda locked her car up, and almost by instinct, began to walk down the country road, keeping herself perched on the small strip of grass that stretched parallel with it. Worst case scenario, she'd just have to walk home and pick up her piece of junk car another day. She didn't care anymore. Besides, it gave her an excuse to blow off work tomorrow and enjoy some rest.

Amanda kept her eye on her phone. Surely the signal must come back soon? She cursed into the air, damning anyone who chose to live in such secluded areas. As a lifelong city girl, the idea of living anywhere other than a major urban area was alien to her. In the city, you had everything you needed. If you broke down in Los Angeles, someone would be there to help you within seconds.

The cold began to seep in. Amanda pulled up the hood on her jacket. She looked back, her car having now vanished from sight. Maybe when she returned another day, the car fairy might have fixed it, she laughed. If only. Such luck would never rain down on someone like her.

Then a car horn made her jump back in fright. She'd been so lost in her thoughts that she hadn't heard any car approach behind her. She turned around, startled to see a pair of headlights coming towards her.

Amanda stepped back onto the grass and waved her arms around. She pulled down her head to appear less threatening to a potential savior. A silver Volkswagen pulled up in front of her. An old model, more ancient than hers. She couldn't make out the driver in the darkness.

His window rolled down and a head peered out.

"You okay, miss?" a voice asked. "Don't see many people wandering alone out here."

The man seemed nice, pleasant enough. Probably in his thirties. He was wearing a brown jacket with a red baseball cap. An odd choice, she thought, but she was in no position to be critique the man's fashion sense. He might just save her an arduous journey.

"Car broke down," she said. "I just decided to walk the rest of the way."

The man laughed. "You're gonna be walking a long way, sweetheart. Is that your Ford Focus back there?"

"Yep, that's mine," Amanda said, not wanting to ask the inevitable question just yet.

"I saw it. That's what's called a tire blowout. When did you last pump those wheels up?"

Amanda thought. "The last time I blew those tires up was… never," she laughed. Unfortunately, the newcomer didn't see the funny side. He shook his head.

"You gotta throw some compressed air in there every couple o' months. Or else, well, that happens." He jerked his head in the direction of Amanda's broken vehicle. "You made the right choice. Driving that would be a death sentence."

Amanda nodded and stuffed her hands into her pockets. She wasn't in the mood for a vehicle education.

"Where are you headed?" he asked.

"La Mesa. What about you?"

"I'm going a little bit further than that myself, but I can drop you off closer to home if you like. As long as you promise me you'll get AAA out to fix that wreck behind us," he smiled.

"Would you? That would be fantastic, thank you."

The man leaned over to his passenger side and pushed the door open. He revved the engine. "No problem at all. Jump in."

Amanda sauntered towards the passenger side, and while the prospect of a free ride was attractive, she quickly felt the crushing weight of reality upon her. It was midnight, and she was getting into a stranger's car. Wasn't this how those horror stories began, with a naïve young woman desperate for help? She pulled open the car door, hoping that once she was in here, she'd find some relief among the commonplace nature of two people sharing a car ride. Perhaps they'd have something in common, she thought.

The man's car was unexpectedly filthy. Amanda had to contort herself in the passenger seat to avoid stepping in litter. She tried to steal a few glances at the man to get an idea of his character but didn't want him to catch her staring. She caught a glimpse of her Ford in the wing mirror, disappearing like a sinking ship. Now, they were alone, and she struggled to contain her mounting heart rate. She breathed slowly and thought of Chloe.

A mile down the road, the man turned his radio down. "So, what brings a young lady like you out here at this time of night?"

"I've been on a training semester for work. Total waste of time."

"Sounds fancy."

"I wish. I'm just an admin worker for a school." Amanda looked out of the window and watched the tree clusters pass by. The rickety old Volkswagen bounced as it reached 80 MPH. It seemed that he was as lenient with the traffic laws as she was. "What about you?" she asked.

He took a deep breath and adjusted his cap. He waited a few seconds before replying. "They don't let people like me near schools."

Amanda wasn't sure she heard him right. She looked at him, expecting a wry smile to follow. Maybe he had a dark sense of humor. "Very funny. What do you do?"

He picked up speed, pushing the 90 MPH mark. "I'm serious," he said.

Amanda shifted her seat. Her neck hairs stood on end. The air in the car blew hot, but Amanda felt a chill in lieu of the blasts. "Why?" she asked.

"They think I'm trouble, those blue meanies."

What's wrong with this guy? Amanda asked herself. They arrived at a stretch of road that she recognized, bringing her a little comfort. She checked her phone and the signal was full. Relief washed over her.

"What's your name, by the way?" she asked.

Another long silence, like he was thinking of the answer. He held the wheel loosely in one hand and sat back in his seat. He pushed the lock down on his door.

Amanda felt a surge of panic. A few minutes before, this guy had seemed genuine, wholesome. Suddenly, he'd become a socially awkward freak. Amanda clutched her door handle. She clenched her fists. God knows enough men had made unwanted advances on her in her thirty years of life, so she knew how to handle such a situation. Maybe he was one of those guys who got uncomfortable once women were in close proximity. She saw it from the school dads all the time. They were all talk from afar, but once they got face-to-face, it was a different story.

"Arthur," he said.

Amanda just nodded and turned to stare at the familiar terrain. The closer she got to home, the more reassured she felt. She checked the time on the dashboard. Four past midnight. Another thirty-five dollars gone, but it didn't bother her. She just wanted to get home and cuddle her little girl – and get the hell away from this creep.

The turn-off was barely a mile ahead. The country lane turned into a stretch of road with intersections and crossings. Their car slowed down to a reasonable 70 MPH as they approached the turning for La Mesa.

"Anywhere up here is fine," Amanda said.

Arthur said nothing. The turning came into view, and before Amanda make comment, the turning was behind her.

The tiny hairs on her arms stood on end. She felt sudden nausea. She looked at her driver, focused intently on the road ahead.

"How's Chloe?" he asked.

Amanda retraced their conversation, trying to recall when she mentioned her daughter's name to this stranger.

She hadn't. Something wasn't right.

"Excuse me?" she asked, clutching the door handle to the point her fingers hurt.

"Chloe. How is she?"

Amanda felt her stomach tighten. The warm air suffocated her, and all she could see in her mind's eye was her little girl waiting for her at home. Then suddenly came the terrifying possibility that she might never see her again.

"How do you know her name?"

"You told me. Well, your possessions told me." He threw her purse on the dashboard. "You should be more careful."

"Oh my God." Amanda realized her error. "I left that in my car?"

"Yes. And I know what you're thinking. We didn't miss your turning."

"What are you talking about?" she spat.

"We're not going there."

"Come again?"

Amanda reached out to grab her purse, but the man's hand stopped her. He clutched her wrist, sending a spike of adrenaline through Amanda's veins. He forcefully threw her arm away. "Leave that there. You won't be needing it."

Amanda's survival instinct kicked in. Every fibre in her body told her that this man had no intention of delivering her home safely, or delivering her anywhere safely. She prepared herself, tensed her muscles and brought up her forearms in front of her chest. "What? Who the fuck do you think you are? Stop the car. I'm getting out," she screamed.

Arthur pushed down on the gas and picked up speed. "You're not going anywhere."

Amanda wasn't a fighter. She couldn't remember the last time she'd gotten into a scrape, if ever in her adult life. She knew that she couldn't best a man of his stature in a physical competition and that brought on a new wave of dread.

Amanda grabbed her phone, but the man reached over and knocked it from her grasp. It fell down the side of the chair.

"Don't think about calling the police," he laughed. "If the blue meanies are going to get me, they'd better get off their asses and do something."

"What do you want with me, you creep?" she shouted. "Let me out of here!"

Ideas ran through her head. Freedom was her first thought, attacking was second. Amanda tugged on the door handle, unconcerned with the fact the car was speeding along. A few scars were preferable to any more time with this lunatic.

But the door wouldn't budge.

Amanda yanked harder, then tried the windows. Nothing. She slammed her hands on the glass, praying that they'd somehow shatter to pieces under her force. They didn't. Suddenly, the man's hands were around her throat, the car swerving along the empty road as he tightened his grip.

Amanda contorted herself to push him away with her legs while she clawed at the door. She kicked him in the ribs, breaking his grip for a few milliseconds.

His foot fell off the gas and the car coasted, swerving across all three lanes. He fell against the driver's door and quickly grabbed the wheel to keep the car from smashing into a rest stop.

Amanda heard a click. She grabbed the door handle again and yanked. The door swung open with the force of the wind, almost ripping off its hinges. The air hit her like a block of ice.

Without hesitation, Amanda leaped from the car onto the road, the tow dragging her along the rough concrete. It tore away the flesh on her hands and ankles, but Amanda didn't have time to register the pain. She jumped to her feet and ran across the expressway, leaping over a metal railing into an expanse of grass. A farm, maybe. She didn't care. She ran towards a distant building and didn't stop to look back.

CHAPTER ONE

Ella Dark stopped her car at the entrance to the prison grounds. Suddenly, it all felt very real. Inside the building up ahead was a collection of some of the most heinous men in the country.

Maine State Prison was a maximum-security facility that held over nine hundred inmates, including many of the East Coast's high profile serial killers, mass murderers, terrorists, and school shooters. Those charged with life sentences were banished to Maine prison to live out their remaining years.

Ella hadn't told anyone about this secret rendezvous. When Ben had asked her what she was doing with her day off, she'd told him she was catching up on *work stuff*. She was seeing him later tonight too, so she'd give him the rest of the details then. She hadn't heard from Agent Ripley all week, and so the opportunity to tell her never arose. Or at least, that was what Ella told herself. It was a convenient lie that protected them both.

The nerves had almost crippled her, to the point that she thought that maybe it was all a bad idea. But a chance like this only came once in a lifetime. She'd dreamt of a moment like this for longer than she could remember. If she didn't take it, she'd regret it for the rest of her life.

She arrived at the barbed wire fences, rolled down her window and pushed the buzzer.

In the small cabin to her left, a uniformed guard appeared. "Yes, Miss?" he asked.

"Agent Dark here for visitation. Inmate number two-seven-six-one."

The guard flipped over the pages on his clipboard. "Campbell?" he asked with a surprised look. "Are you sure?"

Ella reached over to her passenger seat and pulled out her documentation. She passed it to the guard. Despite her invitation, her meeting needed to be approved by the US Department of Corrections. Most visitations were approved by the local prison management, but any contact with Tobias Campbell required consent from the highest authority. Fortunately, Ella's status within the FBI fast-tracked the process.

"Doesn't get many visitors, that one." The guard handed back Ella's papers and returned to his cabin. The mesh gates whirred open slowly.

Ella drove along the one-way path towards the building. Now that she was closer to it, she could scarcely believe its size. It seemed to stretch on for miles, with four huge towers on each corner almost piercing the sky. Ella saw a number of armed guards atop each one, keeping an eye on her.

At the parking area, another guard came over to her and told her where to stash her vehicle. Ella did, then met the same man at the prison entrance. The guard swiped his keycard on the door and held it open for her.

Inside was nothing like Ella expected. Two service desks were sitting on a polished marble floor. The air smelled fresh and clean. Awards for outstanding service decorated one of the far walls. "Please take a seat and the warden will be here to escort you through to the cells."

"The cells?" Ella asked. "I'm here for visitation."

"I know, Miss, but Tobias isn't allowed out of his designated area. He's confined to the Red Zone. Conjugal and regular visitations are off limits to him."

"How come?" she asked.

"The warden will explain everything." The guard left, leaving Ella alone on a white leather seat. She'd spent the past week researching Tobias Campbell to obsessive levels. She knew everything about his life and crimes, from his early farm life to the five young women he killed. Parts of his story had stuck with her to the point she'd dreamt about them, like the fact that Tobias's father once made him stomp a burlap sack of puppies to death. As a teenager, Tobias's favorite game was to point a rifle at a horse's head, pleasure himself and then pull the trigger at the point of climax. It was no surprise that he had acted out similar scenes in his adult life, only with women in the place of animals.

Then there was Agent Ripley's story. Ella's partner in the FBI had been the one to apprehend Tobias fifteen years prior, and when she found his rural shack, she'd found a number of personal possessions that suggested Tobias Campbell had killed much more than the FBI believed. Children's shoes, bloody nooses, jewelry, clothing, ID cards.

But the FBI could prove none of this, since Tobias captured Agent Ripley and made her burn the whole thing down. To this day, Ripley claimed she saw it, but the officials didn't see it that way. They said Ripley was suffering from post-traumatic delusions.

But now, Tobias was willing to talk. Ella had no idea what to expect from him, and the prospect of seeing this monster in the flesh was daunting. But since his letter had arrived at the FBI offices, Ella had thought of nothing else but meeting him, getting inside his head, learning how he thought. An opportunity like this could not only improve her knowledge of lust killers, but it was a rare chance to dig into Campbell's other crimes. There were still a lot of unsolved murders out there attributed to Campbell, with plenty of circumstantial evidence placing him at the scene of various murders throughout Chicago. Unresolved murders grieved millions of families the world over, and this was a rare chance to bring closure to some of them. Not many, but even one was better than none.

Ella heard a buzz and looked up. A well-dressed gentleman appeared from beyond the glass door.

"Miss Dark?" he asked, extending his hand. He was fairly large, bald and bearded with sun-kissed skin. He wore an all-black suit with a white shirt and carried himself with confidence. Ex-military, Ella thought.

"Yes, that's me." Jumping out of her seat and returning the gesture.

"I'm Derrick Banks, the warden here. Have you been briefed?" He took a seat beside her.

"No, I haven't, sir. What do I need to know?"

"Please, less of the sir, especially from an agent. Regular visitation rules apply, but since you're here to meet Mr. Campbell, there are a few extra precautions we need to take."

Ella nodded. "I'm listening."

"First of all, your meeting will take place outside of Campbell's cell. Don't worry, he'll be safely locked behind. We keep him in an area of the prison known as the Red Zone. For the past ten years, Campbell has been the only inmate in there."

Ella had heard the rumors of Tobias's solitude but had no concrete evidence of it. Some true crime enthusiasts claimed that Campbell was kept in the basement away from the general population. Others claimed that they sometimes fed the disruptive prisoners to him.

"I understand, but why is he so isolated?"

"His notoriety does him no favors. Every time he's mixed with the general pop, he finds himself on the end of beatings. A lady killer like that? The gang-bangers want him crucified. Secondly, there's the fact we have to limit Campbell's interaction with the other prisoners. You probably know that Campbell is well-connected, both inside and out. We do our best to keep him inaccessible but he still finds a way to communicate. Truth be told, we don't know how he does it."

Ella had an idea how he did it. Informants within the prison. She decided not to mention it. "Right. Well, I'm ready. I won't reveal any information to him."

"Good. But before we go, there's one last thing you need to know about Tobias Campbell."

Ella waited for the warden to continue. She pulled out her mobile phone and placed it beside her. The warden took it.

"The other reason we don't let Campbell communicate with other inmates is that he likes to… play games."

Ella had heard these stories too. In fact, in her research, she'd already pieced certain things together. During Campbell's incarceration, three inmates inside had died under suspicious circumstances. The details were kept from the public, but Ella had a feeling Campbell had something to do with them.

"Games?" she asked.

"Yes. Over the years, Campbell has had a number of cellmates. Well, not in the same cell, but next door. Close enough to communicate. All of those prisoners ended up killing themselves. Campbell talked them into suicide."

"Oh, Christ," Ella said, her suspicions confirmed. "Do you know how he did it?"

"We don't. But Tobias is a master manipulator. He's a predator who lives in people's heads. I've talked with him enough to know how he works. He gets off on traumatizing people. Miss Dark, do not tell Tobias Campbell *anything* about your personal life. He'll dig his claws in and won't ever let go. Do you understand?"

Ella complied. She rested her hand on her knee and only now realizing she'd been jigging it up and down out of anxiousness. She needed to talk to this man *now*. She couldn't wait any longer.

CHAPTER TWO

The warden led Ella through the twisting hallways of Maine State Prison. The cells were modernized, so all that was visible were the doors with a little glass panel in the center. Long gone were the iron bars of yesteryear. Every time Ella sneaked a peek, someone was staring at her through the glass. It made her feel observed, on show.

They descended a spiral staircase down to the bottom floor, then another staircase below ground level. Ella heard shouts and cries from the cells, piercing, shrill, booming. Prisoners hammered on the cell doors. She felt an instant sense of vulnerability, like these monsters could escape and attack at a moment's notice. Living here must be hell on earth, she thought.

Everything darkened in the new hallway. Gone were the overhead fluorescent lights and instead were a series of low bulbs. The warden keyed open a steel door and the first thing Ella saw was a sign declaring *RED ZONE BEGINS HERE*. They walked the length of the corridor, probably some fifty feet in length. By the time Ella reached the end, she could no longer hear the disturbances from the general population. Things were quiet in here, even peaceful. They arrived at a final locked door.

Banks turned to her in the narrow hallway. "Ready?"

"In there?" she asked.

"Yes. He's expecting you. Just knock when you're ready to leave."

Ella summoned up the courage she needed. She told herself how rare an opportunity this was. Few people, even those in law enforcement, got the chance to meet Tobias Campbell. He was a golden-age serial killer living in the modern world. In years to come, they'd mention his name alongside Bundy, Dahmer, and Gacy. The day he died would be celebrated the world over.

"I'm ready," Ella said. "Let's go." She pulled back her hair and took a few deep breaths.

"Remember what I told you," Banks said before swiping open the door. Ella nodded and walked through, into the dragon's lair. The room inside was vast, boasting two cages made of iron and glass. These weren't the modern cells she'd just passed; they were entirely traditional. The cell to her right was empty, but in the cell to her left stood a man dressed in a crisp white jumpsuit.

Inside was Tobias Campbell, leaning up against the glass.

"I'm so glad you came, Agent Dark."

Few pictures of Tobias had made their way to the public, and the ones that did showed him in his prime. But standing in front of her was someone she didn't recognize. Tobias had a shaved head, sharp cheekbones and incredibly pale skin. He smiled at Ella, showing two rows of jagged teeth. He was on the short side, around five-foot-eight, and his once-muscular frame had clearly deteriorated over the years. All that was left was a skinny male with sagging shoulders.

"Thank you for inviting me," she said, keeping her distance. Iron bars surrounded the outside of the glass box. Double protection.

"Come closer so I can hear you better. Don't be scared."

Even though Tobias was caged, Ella still felt vulnerable. She eyed him up and down, taking in his stature and his posture. He held himself upright with an undeserved confidence. His eyes glittered piercing green. Behind him, she saw the basic prisoner necessities. Sink, toilet, a white mattress on a metal frame. A pile of leather-bound books sat beside a wooden chair on the opposite side of the cell. But among these basic provisions were objects surely to Campbell's preference: a chessboard with its pieces neatly arranged, a deck of well-worn playing cards, a small bronze statue of an armored horse. In the opposite corner of his cell stood a wooden easel with a half-finished painting attached. The outline of a horse leaping over a fence had been messily etched. Ella thought back to Tobias's childhood and felt her blood turn to ice.

"I'm fine right here," Ella said, keeping her voice strong and firm. She was fascinated by this creature, but he needed to understand that she was in charge.

"Good. I trust you found me easily enough."

"No. I live in Virginia. It was a long journey, so the least you can do is tell me what you want from me."

"I'm surprised you showed up. Most people, even those in your profession, would jump at the chance to refuse me."

Tobias began to walk slowly around his cell, turning his back to her. He reminded Ella of an exotic tiger in a zoo or a historical artifact in a museum. In either case, she played the part of the gawping spectator.

He was soft spoken, even eloquent, thought Ella. She expected someone rough, trashy, a blue collar career criminal. Tobias was the opposite.

"Because you said you have information."

Tobias ceased his pacing. He turned to Ella and smiled. "I've seen you. You've been around. William Edis thinks highly of you, doesn't he?"

She cast a sideways glance at Tobias. "I believe so." She recalled what Warden Banks told her. Reveal as little information as possible.

"Sending a trainee out into the field with no experience. Doesn't it strike you as odd?"

Ella shrugged. "At first, but not anymore. I have a partner. A good one."

"Oh yes, that old sweetheart. How is Agent Ripley? Still desperate to prove her dominance? Still angry at the world for leaving her behind? I bet she loves imparting her wisdom on you, as misguided as it may be."

"She's fine," Ella said. If Ripley knew Ella was here, talking *about her* to the man who nearly killed her, she dreaded to think how she'd react. Explosively, she imagined. "Are you going to tell me about your new information, Mr. Campbell?"

"Not so fast," he said. "I saw you on the TV last week. You caught that pesky little killer down in Seattle. If you'd have asked me, I could have told you who the culprit was immediately. And those copycat murders down in Louisiana. Pretty obvious *modus operandi* right from day one, wasn't it? Although I admit, it helps that the pesky Louisiana killer had contact with me before he began his operation, too."

Ella waited a second before replying. She itched with curiosity but was desperate to keep an emotional distance. "You were in contact with that killer?"

Tobias smirked. "I wouldn't call him a friend, but I might have advised him on a thing or two. My point still stands regarding the *modus operandi*. And those Seattle killings? I could have told you who the culprit was within twenty-four hours."

"Not obvious at all. It took a while to piece things together."

Tobias moved closer to the glass box. He spoke through three circular holes. "Oh, how embarrassing for you," he said. "Agent Dark, you and Agent Ripley look at these scenes with a clinical eye, but there's nothing systematic about the act of murder. Killing is the rope across the spiritual abyss, between man and his failed aspirations. Psychological profiling is much less a learnable skill as it is something inherent, despite what hacks like Ressler and Ripley might tell you."

Ella didn't quite know what to say. She thought about it for a moment. "How do you mean? I've learned it just fine."

"Don't mistake fortune for ability." Tobias beamed his crooked smile. "Only creators understand other creators. There isn't a textbook in the world that can make you feel what we feel during the act of killing. FBI profilers are the art critics of law enforcement. Criticizing others yet they themselves are unable to draw a straight line."

Ella held Tobias's stare. Barely a few minutes in his presence and he was already divulging his vile censure. He must have been waiting a while to let this frustration out.

"I'm guessing you don't get many visitors down here, Mr. Campbell."

"I do not."

"It shows. Unfortunately, I'm not here to listen to you berate my profession. I'm here at your request. Either divulge what you know, or I'll be on my way."

"We both know that's not true," Tobias said. "You're here because you want to be."

"Is that right?"

"You've dreamt of a moment like this your whole life. It's why you chose law enforcement over an easier profession. You didn't fall into your job by accident, did you?"

Ella surveyed the room, trying to imagine what it must be like to live in this place twenty-four-seven. Gray walls, sterile surroundings, total silence. It would be enough to drive anyone insane.

"No, I worked hard to get here."

"That's why you agreed to meet me. You think that by understanding the psychopathic mind you can avenge some perceived wrong in your life. You think it will keep you safe. What is it for you? A childhood trauma? Did a bad man stamp on your dog? Did your old man pay nightly visits to your bedroom while your mother was at the casino?"

"No, nothing like that."

Tobias rested his hands atop his head, caressing the bones in his skull. "One more try," he said, "and if I guess correctly, you have to tell me everything that happened. Deal?"

Ella didn't want to go down this route, but she was fascinated to hear his thoughts. "Deal."

"You flinched a little when I mentioned your old man. Let me guess, you lost him at a young age. Did he die in a car accident when you were a sprightly little kid? Did he owe money to the wrong people? Did you wake up and find him dead in his armchair?"

She had to use all of her willpower to keep from lashing out, from screaming at Tobias to shut his mouth. There was no way he could know this. Hell, even Ella wasn't sure what happened to her dad. She wasn't going to give Tobias the satisfaction of a positive response, but even so, how was it possible he knew? A lucky guess?

"You said one try, Mr. Campbell. That was three."

"Didn't get the justice you felt you deserved, so now you're desperate to get it for others. Correct?"

Ella shook her head, putting on the best mask she could. "I'm afraid not. Not quite." Ella wanted to get away from this topic immediately. Any further prying and this maniac might actually get close to the truth. "What are you painting back there?"

Tobias moved to his easel and traced the outline of his drawing with his finger. "I'm painting the Winged Hussars," he said, his smirk emerging once again.

"What might one of those be?" Ella asked. Judging by Tobias's grin, he enjoyed the fact that Ella didn't know what he was talking about.

"The Winged Hussars were unstoppable killing machines from the sixteenth century. The deadliest cavalry in humankind, stopping at nothing to completely obliterate the opposing forces. Their horses were decked with steel armor and giant feathery wings to intimidate whoever stood opposite them on the battlefield. Years later, they became mercenaries, selling their deadly skills to the highest bidders. Isn't it funny how the more things change, the more they stay the same?"

Ella didn't quite know what Tobias was talking about, but she was just glad they were away from the subject of her dad. "How do you mean?" she asked.

"Do you like horses, Agent Dark? You look the type. I could see you in an equestrian getup: a sleeveless jacket and riding boots."

"Never had the interest. I was always a cat person."

"Pet choices can reveal a lot about the owners. What drew you to cats? Passivity, social sensitivity, a distrust of authority?"

Ella just shook her head, not wanting to give Tobias anything to work with. "Mr. Campbell, you said you could have recognized the culprit from the Seattle artist murders immediately. Care to explain how?"

"You don't believe me?" Tobias said, returning to the front glass and tracing his index finger around the holes.

"It's a bold claim, I'm sure you'll agree."

"The burgeoning psychopathology was predictable fantasy-fulfilment of the most extreme nature. Each murder was an act free of moral restraints, committed under the prying eyes of the general public. Quite clearly, the murders were being controlled by a woman, but a man was doing the handiwork. It was all right in front of you from the start."

Ella heard the words but didn't quite take them in. Maybe Tobias was lying. Maybe he was just trying to belittle her. "Sure, it's easy to identify the killer after the case is solved," she said.

"You don't believe me, and it stuns me you can't see it for yourself. You must remember that for most serial killers, the act of murder is an afterthought, a necessity, a conclusion of the ritual, a precautionary measure to erase the only witness who has been subject to the killer's true nature. In the case of your so-called artist killer, none of this was present, meaning the chances of the mastermind being a man were almost zero. They were murders of convenience, vanity. The fact that you or Agent Ripley didn't immediately suspect a woman's touch shows why criminal profiling is nothing more than a buzzword thrown around by those too afraid to get their hands dirty."

Could Tobias really see things so easily? Was this a part of his game, to make her doubt her own skills? She began to feel like this visit was a mistake. She eyed the exit, wondering if she should leave now or push him further.

"Agent Ripley caught you, didn't she?"

Ella saw a quick change in his demeanor. He tensed up, bringing his shoulders higher. "No, actually. Her partner caught me. And tell me, Miss Dark, I might be locked in this cage until the day I die, but my mental faculties are pristine. I live in peace and acceptance, never having to worry about what tomorrow might bring. Agent Ripley might live a free life, but she's trapped in a cerebral prison. I know she thinks about me constantly. I made her doubt the most sacred thing: her own perception. Next time you see her, ask her if she enjoyed the gifts."

Ella said nothing, waiting to see if Tobias followed up. He moved closer to the glass and looked Ella from top to bottom.

"Oh, I see," he continued, as if reading her next thought. "Agent Ripley doesn't know you're here, does she?

Ella shifted her weight to one side. She felt a tremor run through her legs. If she told Tobias the truth, he might exploit it. If she lied, he might recognize she was lying. "Not yet," she said, hoping a middle-of-the-road approach would satisfy his curiosity.

"Well, let's hope she doesn't find out, eh? I imagine that wouldn't do much good for your career, would it?"

Ella wanted to reach out, rattle the iron bars and scream at the man in the cage, but she quickly realized it was her own fault. She'd been warned he'd do this. By Mia, by the authorities. They said he'd do everything within his power to toy with her, and she foolishly believed she could keep him at bay. Now, he'd seen a weakness and pounced like a waiting predator, and acknowledging it would only give him what he wanted. Mia couldn't find out about this, least of all from Tobias himself.

"Are you ready to tell me your information yet? I can't stay down here all day." She hoped it would be enough to steer Tobias away from the thought.

"I'm afraid not, Miss Dark. You see, I was expecting someone capable, someone on my level. Every time a rising star crops up in the FBI, I can't help but scope them out. I yearn for the day I meet an agent who doesn't bore me, but I've decided that you fall in line with the rest of them. I was looking for the person to share my story with, my *real* story, not the rehashed biographies I read in sensationalist publications. Maybe if you can impress me, I'll change my mind, but until then, my secrets stay inside this cell." Tobias Campbell sunk into the depths of his cage and turned his back to Ella. "You're free to leave."

Ella realized her fists were clenched. Her forearms were trembling. Had this man – this monster – really just said she needed to impress him?

"I came all the way out here to talk to you, and this is what you tell me?" Ella asked, her voice raised.

Tobias dropped into the rear of his cell and picked up the deck of cards perched on the shelf. He fanned them out with enviable grace, swooped them back together and cut the deck with one hand. "I know, it's amazing isn't it? For someone who studies the so-called criminal mind, you certainly made some bad deductions today. I believe they call it the Dunning-Kruger Effect."

Ella wanted to continue, wanted to pry further, but was determined not to give Tobias what he wanted. If she pleaded for more, that would be validating his perceived status as a figure of importance. No words would form on her lips. She found herself backtracking towards the door.

"Take care, Miss Dark. I have a feeling we'll talk again," Tobias said, his voice barely audible. Ella reached the door and took one last glimpse at the beast in the cage, living his life in comfort and tranquillity. She felt the rage building. She'd come all this way, expecting to learn something the rest of the world didn't know. Something that could bring comfort to grieving family members still seeking closure. His real victim count, his true motivations.

But nothing.

Ella pushed the buzzer and waited.

"Give my love to Agent Ripley," Tobias said. Ella didn't acknowledge him. The door opened from the other side revealing the corridor leading back into the main prison area.

"On second thought, I might just tell her myself," he shouted as Ella took her leave.

CHAPTER THREE

The Cuckoo Oak Bar was the perfect place for a quiet drink, but Ella's mind wasn't on drinking, nor was it on the gentleman sitting opposite her. She clenched the single whiskey-and-Coke in front of her and felt the condensation run down her palm. All she could think about was her meeting with the man in the cage earlier that day. The whole incident felt surreal, like she wasn't sure if it really happened.

"Are you sure you want to know?" Ben asked, leaning forward. This was only the third time they'd met in the flesh, but every time she saw Ben, she liked him that little bit more. He was dressed in a t-shirt and jeans, with his black hair gelled to one side. She couldn't remember the last time she'd seen gelled hair on a man, not in this decade at least, but there was something cute about it on him.

"Yes, I want to know. Everything," Ella said, hopefully prompting him to take the conversational reigns.

"Well, I'm what's known as a *professional wrestler,* but the title is quite misleading. *Amateur wrestling* is also a professional sport but there are some big differences between the two. First off, amateur wrestling is a real combat sport. Professional wrestling is...well..."

"Fake?" Ella asked.

Ben laughed. "No. Well, yes. When I step into the ring with a guy, we both know what's going to happen. The moves we're gonna do to each other, the winner and so forth. But you can't fake landing on your back. There's no safe way to take an elbow to the head. That's all real, and let me tell you, it hurts sometimes."

Ella loved his energy and his enthusiasm. When Ben spoke, he did it with a smile. He waved his arms around a lot, something Ella thought made him more inviting.

"So why do it?" she asked. "Not criticizing, I'm genuinely curious."

Ben scratched his stubble. A three-day growth. "When I was a kid, I wanted to be an actor. My parents pushed me towards being an athlete though, and pro wrestling is kind of a middle ground between them both. The wrestling ring is my stage, I guess. And my moves are my dialogue. Does that make me sound pretentious?"

Ella kept her gaze on him and nodded along gradually. "No, not at all. It's really cool. I'd love to come and see you one time."

"Is that an excuse to see me in spandex? Because I'll be honest, I don't look that good, especially compared to some of the body guys I work with. There are some real muscle-heads in my business. It's lucky our promotion doesn't enforce steroid tests because those guys would melt the cup."

Ella stifled a laugh and took a gulp of her drink. The alcohol hit her straight away. "I'm sure you look a treat."

"It might be a shock the first time you see me like that, but please don't be put off. Just think of it as my work uniform."

Ella's gaze drifted beyond Ben to the orange lamps behind him. The light consumed her vision, taking her out of the conversation. The next image that jumped into her mind was Tobias Campbell, sitting in his prison cell, plotting his next manipulation effort. How much did he know about her already? Was it possible he would contact Agent Ripley directly? He knew her address, given he'd sent her gifts over the years, but how likely was it he'd write her a letter? Or, given his number of informants on the outside, he could easily pass the information along to her through them. And how would Ripley react knowing she'd been to see the man who broke her? She'd already warned Ella not to go, borderline pleaded with her.

"Everything okay?" Ben asked. "You don't seem yourself. Is it something I said?"

Ella suddenly snapped back into the room. She realized she'd drifted into a stupor. "Sorry, I've just had a stressful day. I've been on the road all day. I only got back an hour ago."

"Oh, you should have said. We could have rearranged."

"No, no, I wanted to see you. Really, I did."

"Work travel? Anywhere nice?" Ben asked.

"Yes and no," Ella said. "I've been to a prison in Maine. I met this guy, and he was… something." Ella didn't want to reveal too much, but maybe talking about it would make her feel better.

"Shit me, a prison? In Maine? That's cool as hell. Who was the guy?"

"A lowly criminal. No one special," Ella lied. "He said he had some information about his case. New information. I was sent to check it out."

"And?" asked Ben.

"He didn't. Or at least, he didn't reveal anything. He just spoke badly about FBI agents. Said I'd never be able to think as he does, or like any criminal does."

Ben dropped back in his chair. Ella saw a look of concern on his face. A look she hadn't seen before. "And you believe him? You're taking a murderer's words to heart?" Ben asked.

"I know. I shouldn't. It's just hard not to. I had all these ideas about what I was going to talk to him about and none of it happened."

"There's a pretty simple solution to your problem, don't you think?" said Ben.

Ella pursed her lips. She suddenly regretted bringing up this topic of conversation. It didn't make her feel better about what happened. Besides, could Ben really know what she was going through? Not that he was inexperienced, but his job was worlds apart from hers. The two didn't overlap in the slightest. "A solution?"

Ben gulped down the rest of his drink and planted the glass on the table. "About a year ago, I had a match against this wrestling veteran. He used to be one of the biggest names in the industry, and I was lucky enough to land a headline match with him in some shitty indie show. I thought it was going to be a real banger, a barn-burner. It was gonna be the making of me. But we went out there and our match sucked. Dead crowd. Me and the guy didn't connect. Totally forgettable. It really got me down for months."

Ella wasn't sure where he was going with this. "I'm sorry to hear that," she said.

"Don't be, because you know what we did? We had another match, and this time we tore the house down. That same week I got picked up by one of the biggest promotions in the country."

She felt her phone vibrate in her pocket. A short vibration. Probably her roommate asking her how the date was going.

"So, you're saying I should visit him again?"

Ben nodded. "Absolutely. Why not? What have you got to lose?"

Ella would be lying if she said she hadn't already entertained the idea, but it would be exactly what Tobias wanted. She knew that he wanted to get inside her head, just like he'd done to Ripley fifteen years ago. "It's not as easy as that. There's bureaucratic red tape to cross. Meetings with prisoners need to be approved beforehand. You can't just walk in whenever you feel like it."

"I don't know," Ben said, "I'm just saying, get back out there and try again."

She knew he was trying to be supportive, but his oversimplification of the situation wasn't really helping. She was about to change the subject when she felt another pulsation in her pocket. A longer one. Someone was calling her.

"I think your phone's vibrating," Ben said. "At least, I hope it's your phone."

Hints of a smile spread across her face, but she quickly quenched it when she realized there was only one person who might call her at 8pm on a Saturday. "Do you mind if I see who it is? I hate pulling my phone out when I'm with people."

"Of course. It could be important."

Ella did and recognized the number. It was HQ. "Can I take this? I won't be a moment."

Ben nodded and turned away, giving her a glimmer of privacy. "Hello?" she said, picking it up one ring before it went to voicemail.

"Miss Dark?" the voice asked. "It's William. I hope I didn't interrupt your evening."

William Edis was the FBI director. The man at the top of the pile.

"Good evening, sir. No, it's fine. Is everything okay?"

"Not really. Can you get to the office in the next hour?"

Ella looked at Ben who was staring across the room. She didn't want to leave him so abruptly, especially as this would be the second time it happened. But what if it was another serial case? Was the opportunity to jump into another investigation preferable than spending time with Ben? She always cursed herself when she chose work over matters of the heart.

"I can try, sir. What is this regarding?"

"I'll explain everything when you get here. Agent Ripley is on her way too. See you soon."

Edis hung up. Ella placed her phone down and sighed.

Ben turned back to her. His persistent smile showed signs of fading. "You've gotta go, haven't you?"

Ella nodded reluctantly. "I'm sorry. Maybe we could rearrange? I hate having to do this to you."

"Don't sweat it. I know you have a stressful job. I'm in no rush to jump into anything, so don't feel bad about it."

Not many guys would be so understanding, Ella thought, but that made her feel even worse.

"I'll text you when I can?" she said.

Ben stood up and gave her a hug. Ella collected her things, said her goodbyes and left the bar. Out in the brisk spring air, she put aside her disappointment and thought about Edis's request. Excitement overcame her at the idea of taking on a new case alongside Ripley. Who knew where they were headed, or what deranged unsub they might be chasing?

But then she remembered what Tobias Campbell had said.

CHAPTER FOUR

Ella arrived at the Washington, D.C., FBI headquarters just after 9pm and made her way to the top floor of the building. The 45-minute drive was helped by a lack of Saturday night traffic.

The offices were as deserted as they could ever be. While the bureau machine operated continuously, there were certain hours when only the most crucial cogs continued turning. From what Ella could tell, FBI director William Edis never left the building. Everyone had heard rumors of Edis's impressive real estate résumé, but he never seemed to spend any time at his luxury properties.

Ella knocked on Edis's office door and waited for the invitation. The voice came from the other side. "Come in."

She entered and saw two bodies. William Edis hunched over a pile of papers on his desk, his gray hair an inch receded from the last time they met. Edis was dressed in his trademark black suit which he wore like a second skin against his stocky frame. Agent Mia Ripley was sitting opposite him.

"Miss Dark, thank you for coming. Please, take a seat," Edis said. He gestured next to Mia.

"Well, if it isn't the rising star," Mia said. "Welcome back, rookie."

Mia's choice of words struck Ella as a little odd. Didn't Tobias use that same term? *Every time a rising star crops up in the FBI, I can't help but scope them out.*

Ella took a seat beside Mia and felt her palms begin to sweat. Did she already know? She decided not to address it. Not now. Not ever. Ripley was dressed in casual jeans and a brown jacket. Her dyed red hair had been pulled back tight. Her eyes looked heavy, but even at the ripe age of fifty-five, she'd kept the wrinkles at bay. "Good to see you, Agent Ripley. How was your birthday?"

"As good as it can be. If you're not getting older, you're dead," Ripley said.

"Miss Dark," Edis interrupted, "we've called you in here because we have a situation down in California. Given your work on the last two serial cases, I'd love to get you out there and see what you think. We think this one will play to your strengths."

Relief washed over her. This wasn't anything to do with Tobias Campbell. If either Edis or Ripley knew about her meeting, surely one of them would be quick to mention it.

"Of course, sir, I'd love to get out there again. What do you have?"

It had only been a week since she'd caught the artist killer down in Seattle, and she still hadn't fully recovered, at least physically. The lacerations on her shoulder and forearm still stung and an FBI physician had advised her to avoid any strenuous activity for at least two weeks. But since returning to D.C., all Ella wanted to do was get back out there and do it again. This job brought a rush that her Intelligence job – or any job for that matter - just didn't.

"Four victims in total. Three dead, one alive."

"One escaped?" Ella asked. She turned to Mia. "That should make things easier. We can get a good description of the unsub from the victim."

"It might not be that easy, but everything you need to know is in these files," Edis said. He passed Ella a brown folder with the case designation number in the top right. "We didn't think it was related at first, but we discovered something this morning that connected them all."

"What was it?" asked Ella.

"Agent Ripley will fill you in. You don't need me to tell you how important it is that we clear this mess up immediately," Edis directed his comment at Mia. "The Governor has already chewed me out over this so we need it stamped out pronto. With the California election next year, the last thing we need right now is a serial killer raining hell down on the city. The press will twist it and turn it into a political shitshow, so get out there, do what you have to and don't call me until it's done."

"Understood, sir. We'll do everything we can," Mia said.

"You're on the next flight to San Diego International." Edis checked his watch. "If my Rolex is on the ball, that gives you 90 minutes to get to the airport. Better get moving. Call me from the road if you need anything."

The agents took their leave and found themselves out in the hallway. "I'll just get my bag from my locker," Ella said. "I keep some stuff here now just in case this kind of situation crops up. Proactive is better than reactive, right?"

Mia had a stern look on her face. "Rookie, I'll meet you at the terminal. When we get there, I think we need to have a little talk."

***

Ella was first to arrive on the 10:40pm flight from Reagan National to San Diego International Airport. She was alone in the first class area but wasn't able to relax on the leather recliner seats. Mia knew about her meeting with Tobias Campbell. She had to. Ella was stupid to think Tobias wouldn't immediately spread the word about it. Tobias had seen a weakness in Ella's eyes – the fact that she was visiting him without Mia's knowledge – and was going to exploit it to appease his power fantasies.

But had she really done anything wrong? She'd visited a notorious serial killer, albeit one who played a part in her partner's mental destruction. Ella reassured herself that Mia wasn't her boss. She had no say in what she did, whether it was under the FBI umbrella or not. Besides, she visited Tobias on her personal time. Sure, Ella could have told her about the meeting herself, but she kept it a secret for Mia's own good. She didn't want to cause her unnecessary mental anguish.

Boots clinked down the aisle. Ella looked up and saw Mia arrive, still with the same formidable look on her face. Mia threw her bag down and dropped into the chair. Ella waited a few seconds before speaking.

"Everything okay?" Ella asked.

Mia waved over one of the stewardesses and ordered two whiskey miniatures. Only when that was done did she address Ella.

"No, not really, Dark."

This was it. She was about to get her head torn off. She'd prepared her excuses but wasn't sure if they'd fly. "What's wrong?"

"Two things," Mia said. "First, I hate California. Busy. Overcrowded. Hot as hell and smells like a taint."

"I've never been before. I'm sure it's not that bad."

"Just wait. You'll see. But more importantly, I'm worried about you, Dark."

This was it. A scolding disguised as affection. "Worried about me?"

Mia plugged in her laptop to the outlet beside her chair. "Yes. It's barely been a week since we caught the Seattle unsub. You took a serious lashing that day. The physician advised you no hard labor, right? I'm worried you're breaking your back to do this."

The pressure eased. Ella waited a little longer in case Mia had anything else to add but nothing came.

"I feel fine," Ella said. "Wait a second, how did you know what the physician advised me?"

"You think I don't check up on you to make sure you're okay? I advised Edis to keep you back on this one, but he was adamant he wanted you out here with me. Unfortunately, I didn't fight him. I knew you'd say yes the moment he asked you."

"So much for confidentiality," Ella said, masking her guilt with a wry chuckle. She had no idea Mia actually followed up on things like that and was touched that she did, but the sudden wave of affection was thinned by remorse for her deceit. "But seriously, I'm healthy as a horse. What about you? You got knocked out cold. How are you feeling?"

The stewardess dropped two whiskeys on the table, assuming they wanted one each. Mia pulled them both over to her side. "Don't worry about me, I've been doing this a lot longer than you. You know Keith Richards can only play guitar when he's hammered? Drunk is his default state. Constant exhaustion is mine."

"That doesn't sound good," Ella said, relieved that Mia was acting more like herself. Maybe the combination of worry and California hatred was all that was plaguing her. Ella placed the case file on the table in front of her and opened it up. "I haven't had a chance to look through these yet."

"Right, this one is a little weird, so keep up," Mia said. "Check photo number one."

Ella pulled out a picture of a body lying on a roadside. From what she could tell, it was a young girl, early twenties. It was a sorry sight. A beautiful woman who clearly looked after herself, left to rot in a ditch. "Got it. Oh, Jesus Christ. This is horrible."

"Victim number one. Her name is Amy Evans. She was stabbed to death while she walked home along Point Loma four nights ago. A total of forty-two stab wounds to her torso. Her killer also slashed her throat nearly to the point of decapitation."

"Holy smokes. Complete overkill, so it was likely a targeted attack?" Ella asked. "Maybe there was a personal connection between Amy and her killer?"

"Maybe," Mia said, "but it's impossible to say right now. But check out the next photograph. This is where it gets interesting."

Ella pulled out photograph number two and this time, there were two bodies. A young woman lying dead in the passenger side of a car and a man on the ground outside. Both doors were left open. Again, she saw the multiple stab wounds immediately. "A couple?"

"Uh huh. Max Westbrook and Zoe Cousins, a couple from San Diego. They were found outside Black's Beach in a lovers' lane, both stabbed multiple times."

Such a tragic loss, Ella thought. A young couple, probably on a date, enjoying the privacy of a secluded lane. And then this. "That's bold. He managed to kill them both without the use of a gun?"

"Certainly looks that way," Mia said. "What do you think?"

"It's difficult. The male is outside the car, meaning he might have tried to escape. Perhaps he blitz-attacked Zoe, then Max jumped out of the car to attack him. Maybe they got into a scuffle there and Max lost."

"It's a strange scene, and you're right. I'm not sure exactly how he managed to pull it off. It either requires a lot of luck or a lot of skill. We'll know more when we see the crime scene for ourselves."

Ella dropped back in her chair and looked at the overhead lights. An instructional safety video appeared on the giant screen hanging from the ceiling. She checked the time and realized she was watching the video for the third time in a single day.

"But there's more," Mia said. "In addition to these three bodies, a woman was abducted from a country lane outside San Diego last night. She was hitching along the road and a white male picked her up. As they were driving, he attacked her, but she managed to break free and escape."

Ella tried to piece everything together but some things weren't making sense. "So, we've got a single victim attacked on a roadside. We've got a couple attacked in their car, and a woman abducted from a country lane. These are all massively different operandi. How do we even know this is the same unsub?"

"Now you're asking the real question," Mia said, unscrewing her whiskey and taking a gulp. "We know it's the same perp who committed these murders because he took credit for them. Both of them. The abduction is a different story."

Ella began to make the connections. She scanned her memory bank for historical serial killers who had carried out similar attacks, and it didn't take her long to land on a particularly infamous name. It was all there. The stabbing, the lovers' lane, the abduction, the targeting of young couples.

"Don't say what I think you're going to say," Ella said. The plane rumbled to life and slowly made its way to its take-off position.

"What do you think I'm going to say?" Mia asked.

"Our unsub sent a letter to the press."

29

Mia mimed a tick in the air. "Bingo. He did exactly that. But it doesn't stop there."

Ella squeezed her eyes shut and took herself to 1969. She ran through the information in her head and saw it all. Dates, times, locations, methods of operation. "It wasn't just an ordinary letter. It was a cipher. A cryptic clue written with symbols and strange characters," said Ella.

"Ten out of ten," said Mia. She turned her laptop around to show Ella her screen. "This was received by the San Diego Union Tribune this morning."

The screen showed a ten-by-sixteen grid, each square filled with symbols. Ella recognized some of them, but most were completely alien. Beneath the grid, there was a hand-written message. "Someone solved it already?"

"It wasn't too difficult," said Mia. "A member of staff at the Tribune was able to translate it with software."

Ella leaner closer and read it aloud.

Dear Editor, I am the one who killed the bitch along Point Loma. I stabbed her about 40 times, something you forgot to mention in your news report. I also killed those naïve lovers in their Toyota in Black's Beach. Print this message in your next issue or I will go on a kill rampage tomorrow night. Your whole city is going to be terrorized with fear.

And then there was the symbol that put the final stamp on everything. Just below the cryptogram was a symbol not associated with the others. A jagged T on top of an X, like some kind of bizarre signature.

Ella was quick to make the connection. It all reminded her of the Zodiac killer.

CHAPTER FIVE

In the parking lot of San Diego International, Mia spotted the officer waiting for them. He waved them over when Mia made eye contact. She didn't believe in anything that resembled a sixth sense, or anything supernatural, but one thing she'd discovered in her career was that law enforcement could always recognize one of their own.

"Agent Ripley?" the man asked. He was around Ripley's age, she thought. Balding at the front with wisps of grey at the back. He looked in good shape with a pair of stocky shoulders on an athletic frame. He was dressed in standard uniform with the San Diego PD badge on the breast.

"The very same," she said. "This is my partner Agent Dark. Thank you for meeting us."

"Don't mention it. I'm Officer Denton, but please call me Ray. I'm in charge of the ongoing investigation."

Mia and Ella loaded their bags into the squad car. "We'd like to start by interviewing the most recent victim," Mia said.

"Can do," said Denton. "Jump in. I'll take you right to her."

Both agents took a seat in the back. Ella had been unusually quiet since they met up on the plane, Mia thought. Usually, Ella was quick to throw out her theories and ideas but so far she'd kept everything to herself. Judging by her body language, something was on her mind. Last week in Seattle, Ella had mentioned something about a new guy she was seeing. Given that Ella was wearing Maison Francis perfume when she showed up in Edis's office, chances are she was out somewhere before she got the call. Mia knew too well the personal sacrifices an agent had to make, especially in regard to the dating game. Although maybe not so much these days.

"Have you already questioned her?" Mia asked.

"Only the basics. We knew you'd be arriving pretty soon so we kept her comfortable back at the precinct until you arrived," Denton said. The car rolled out into San Diego streets and within a few minutes they were on the I-405. Mia saw Ella scribbling something in her notepad.

"What are you thinking, Dark?" she asked.

Ella peered out the window and tapped her knuckles against the glass. She scrunched up her face and bit her lip. "I don't know. This one is all over the place."

"I agree. Each attack has been different, meaning it's going to be difficult to predict his next move. But there's been one consistent in each of the crimes. What is it?"

Mia discreetly watched Ella's micro-signals after she asked the question. She wanted to gauge her reactions. In truth, there was no consistency to the crimes, and if Ella was paying attention she'd be quick to dispute it.

"Uhm," Ella said, scrolling back through her notebook pages. "He used a knife. He was probably going to use a knife on the victim who escaped." She phrased it more like a question than a statement.

"No, we don't know that for sure. It was also possible he used a gun to subdue his victims before attacking them with a blade. The consistent is the victimology. He purposely targeted at least two women, possibly three. The male in the second scenario could have been a murder of convenience."

"Oh, right. Of course. I can't believe I missed that."

In actual fact, the age ranges were wide enough that no consistent victimology could be established. The first victim was 23, victims two and three were both 19, and the recent abductee was 35. When combined with the versatile range of the methods of operation, there were no consistencies between either of the three incidents. It was quite clear that Ella's mind was somewhere else. Maybe it was personal issues or maybe it was mental exhaustion. Even the most experienced field agents waited two or three weeks between cases, usually spending that time catching up on admin work at home or at HQ. Mia was used to jumping between active cases so quickly, but to a newcomer like Ella, it was bound to take its toll.

Mia decided to let it slide for now. Give her time to come around. "How was the abductee when you questioned her, officer?" she asked Denton.

"Damn shook up. Once she got out of the car, she ran straight towards our precinct. Didn't have her phone or nothing on her. She must have hauled ass like the wind because she could barely stand up when she arrived."

"And that was last night?"

"Sure was. About one o'clock in the morning. I wasn't on duty myself but one of the other officers filled me in."

"She hasn't left your building at all since she arrived"

"No ma'am," Denton said, leaning his head towards the back seat. "We offered to take her home and stay with her but the poor girl said she couldn't bring herself to get in a vehicle with a stranger."

"Understandable. She's still in shock."

"We sent an officer to pick up her daughter and bring the kid to the station."

Ella suddenly perked up. "She has a daughter?"

"Sure does."

"How old?" Ella asked.

"Just gone twelve months."

Mia could see the cogs were turning in Ella's head, but she didn't inquire any further. When she was ready to reveal her thoughts, she would. Ella went back to jotting something down in her notepad.

"Apparently her tire blew out somewhere along Lakeside Road. I've got some guys on their way to retrieve it right now."

Mia still wasn't sure if this recent abductee was related to the other murders, but it was the third incident within a week inside the same five-mile stretch. Additionally, there was every chance that the first victim had also been abducted in the same way. Regardless, she had a lot of questions on her mind.

***

The San Diego Police Department Headquarters was a six-story building located on West Broadway. It was an odd-looking structure, like a flight of stairs had been tipped on its side. Rectangular blacked-out windows ran from corner to corner on every level. Mia had been here more times than she could remember, but the place had modernized since her last visit.

Officer Denton led her and Ella to the second floor where the recent abductee was waiting in one of the side rooms. "Victim's name's Amanda Huber, 35 years old. I'll leave you ladies to it. If you need anything, be it coffee or a hand setting up, I'll be at my desk." Denton pointed to the corner of the open-plan room. "That's me over there."

The place was full of gray desks set out in no particular arrangement. Around fifty officers inhabited the office, some leaning over paperwork, some with their phones glued to their ears. Only a few had stared at the new arrivals for any longer than a few seconds, much different than how things had been last time Mia was here. The officers most likely knew that Mia and Ella were Feds, but the more overworked police departments in the country welcomed outside help for their investigations. It meant a smaller workload for them.

"Thank you, officer. We'll call you if you need anything," Mia said as Denton took his leave.

Mia opened the door into the room and Ella followed behind. Amanda Huber sat on a plastic seat in the corner of the room, a pile of Styrofoam coffee cups lying at her feet and another one in her quivering hands. She looked up at the agents but didn't say a word. However, the other person in the room made enough noise for all of them.

A toddler sat not far from Amanda, cross legged, shaking a toy shaped like a bumblebee. The toy chimed and sang and the infant laughed along with every sound. When the little girl saw the newcomers, she flapped her arm around in a waving gesture.

"Good day, Miss Huber," Mia said, "and your beautiful little girl. It makes a nice surprise seeing someone so cute in these kinds of places."

Amanda nodded and sighed. She finished the last of her coffee and put her cup with the pile. "Tell me about it. How can I help you?"

"I'm Agent Ripley and this Agent Dark. We're with the FBI. We're trying to locate the man who did this to you. Would you be able to run us through your story?"

"The FBI?" Amanda asked. Chloe crawled over to Amanda's feet and picked at her shoelaces.

Mia pulled up two chairs. She and Ella took a seat opposite Amanda. "Yes, we have reason to believe that whoever did this is also responsible for other crimes in the area. That's why we've been called in to assist."

Amanda ran a hand through her hair then pinched the base of her nose between the eyes. She jittered her legs furiously. "I already told the other officers everything I know. To be honest, there's not much I can tell you. I barely got a chance to look at him, and I'm not even sure I can recall everything in detail." Amanda kept her gaze firmly on her daughter as she spoke.

Chloe crawled over to Ella's feet and tugged on her trouser leg. Ella leaned down and stuck her tongue out at the child, causing an explosion of laughter and drool from Chloe's mouth.

"I think she likes you," Amanda said.

Ella laughed. "At least someone does." Chloe pulled herself up and started patting her hands on Ella's knees. Ella tapped her on the nose with her finger.

"There might be something in your story that will give us a hint at this person's identity," Mia said. "Clothes, accent, vehicle model. You might be surprised at the little things that give these culprits away."

Amanda fell back in her chair and looked towards the ceiling. "I was driving back from a seminar outside San Diego. My tire blew out when I was driving along Lakeside Road. You know that country road that stretches on forever?"

"I do."

"I got out of the car to call a breakdown service but I had no signal. That's when I just decided to hitch down the road and hope for the best. I knew there was a town a few miles down so I thought *what the hell.*"

"Understandable," Mia said. She quickly imagined herself in the same situation and thought she'd probably have done the same thing.

"That's when a car pulls up beside me. A guy sticks his head out the window and offers me a ride. A silver Volkswagen, before you ask. No, I don't remember the license plate."

"Do you remember his exact words?" Mia asked.

"Something like, 'don't see many people out here at night,'" Amanda said. "He seemed genuine. Approachable. Non-threatening."

"Can you describe his appearance?"

Chloe crawled back to her collection of toys against the far wall. She picked up a toy horse and rolled around on the floor with it.

"White. Thirties. Average height. He was wearing a red baseball cap but I saw some dark hair peeking out. He spoke with a Californian accent. That's all I know." Amanda rubbed her temples, looking like she was upset with herself for not being able to recall more.

Mia jotted down the description on her pad. Ella did the same. Up until now, Ella hadn't asked anything. She'd simply observed. It was very unlike her, Mia thought.

"And what happened when you stepped in the car?"

"His car was real dirty. Lots of junk, food boxes, tons of cigarette lighters. We drove a few miles down the road. Everything was normal. But when I started talking to him, he got… strange."

"How so?"

"He drove like crazy. Like, close to a hundred miles per hour. That's when I started getting a bit worried. Then out of the blue, he says to me, 'how's Chloe?'"

"He knew you?" Mia asked.

"No. At least, I don't think so. He said he found my purse in my car. He must have looked through my belongings."

Mia thought about it for a second. "How could he get Chloe's name from your purse?"

"That's another thing. I don't know. I mean, it's possible, but I left my purse and phone in his car when I escaped, so I can't check."

Mia and Ella swapped a glance of concern. Mia was thinking that perhaps Amanda had been purposely targeted by this unsub. She was certain Ella was thinking the same thing.

"What came next?"

"We went past the turn for my town, and he told me we weren't going there. That's when I threatened to call the cops. He got angry and attacked me. I tugged on the door but it wouldn't open, but I kicked him into the control panel on the driver side and managed to unlock it. Then I just dived out of the car onto the road." Amanda held up her palms to show the cuts. "I ran like hell into some farmland. Somewhere where he couldn't follow me, at least by car."

Amanda was right, Mia thought. There wasn't much to go on here. They could inspect the camera footage along the expressway but most of them were just visual deterrents.

"Thank you, Miss Huber. Is there anything else that sticks out about this perpetrator? Any identifying marks or particular phrases he used?"

Amanda moved her gaze towards the ceiling, then hesitated for a second. Mia saw a look that said she'd remembered something important.

"What is it?" Mia asked. "No matter how insignificant you might think it is."

"Well," Amanda said, moving her eyes to her daughter. "He said a couple of very odd things. I just thought it was his attempt at humor."

"What did he say?" Mia said, readying her pen to take notes.

"When I told him I worked in a school, he said 'they don't let people like me near schools.' I remember brushing it off as a joke, but there might have been something to it."

Mia jotted it down. That could mean the perpetrator was a registered sex offender. "Excellent. That really helps," she said. "What else?"

"He had a really specific name for police, but I can't remember what it was. I just remember thinking it was weird as hell."

Mia had heard them all. "Pigs? Filth? Popos?"

"No, I've honestly never heard it before. Blue, blues… something."

"Blue meanies." The words came from Ella this time, surprising both Mia and Amanda. Mia glanced at her.

36

"Yes!" Amanda said. "That was it. Blue meanies. It sounded really odd, like something a child would say."

"We'll look into it," said Mia. "Agent Dark, is there anything you'd like to add?"

Ella shook her head. "No, but could I speak to you privately outside Agent Ripley? There's something I think you need to know."

CHAPTER SIX

Ella only had one thought on her mind.

She and Mia thanked Amanda for the information, then Ella ushered Mia into the room that doubled as their new office. It was a rectangular room decorated with a row of desks, a few plug sockets and not much else. Their view overlooked a construction site and some high-rise apartments to the west.

"What is it, Dark?" Mia asked.

Ella shut the door. "Doesn't all this remind you of something?" she asked. While Ella was the expert on historical serial killers, the parallels between these crimes and the Zodiac were obvious even to the layperson.

"You mean a previous case?"

"I mean a very famous case. The Zodiac killer. This unsub is copycatting the Zodiac."

Ella had used the word that Mia hated the most: *copycat.* But there was no other term to use. All of the evidence pointed towards it.

"Yes," Mia said. "The cipher reminded me of the Zodiac too, but honestly, the press and police receive cryptic notes all the time. You'd be surprised at how many so-called ciphers I've seen over the years. And right now, we don't even know if Amanda's abduction had anything to do with the recent murders. Nothing links them other than the fact they occurred around the same time."

"But it's not just the ciphers," Ella said, pulling out the case file from her bag. She laid out the victim's photographs on one of the desks. "Victim number one. Amy Evans. She was a young college student who suffered forty-two stab wounds. *Forty-two.*" Ella emphasized the numbers.

"And?" Mia asked, looking confused. "What's the stab count got to do with anything? And wasn't the Zodiac's first victim a couple?"

"It depends who you ask. A lot of researchers think that Zodiac's first victim was an 18-year-old student who he killed two years before his first confirmed murder of the couple. And guess what? He stabbed her forty-two times. What if our unsub believes that theory and he's copying it?"

Mia looked like she was considering it. Truthfully, Ella expected to be cut down, but the look on Mia's face said she might have gotten through to her.

"What else? You're not basing it on that fact alone, are you?"

"God no," Ella said excitedly. She felt her heart thumping against her chest. "Next up are victims two and three. If this unsub *was* following the theory I mentioned, then the next victims in line were a couple who he attacked in their car. The only difference is that the Zodiac shot these victims. He didn't stab them."

Mia sat down and scrutinized the crime scene photos of victims two and three. "Well, if I was entertaining your theory, I could attribute his use of a knife to a personal preference. If he's doing this for a sexual thrill, stabbing makes much more sense. But what else? I'm listening."

"Then there's Amanda's abduction. Admittedly, this one throws me because Zodiac's confirmed murders ended in 1969, and he didn't carry out his own abduction until 1970. But the whole situation is identical. Zodiac flashed down a female driver and said her tire was loose. He fixed it, but when she drove off the tire collapsed. She was left with no choice but to hitch a ride with the guy who helped her."

Mia pondered it for a second. "Something bugged me about that in Amanda's story. Are we supposed to believe this guy stopped, looked around Amanda's abandoned car, got her daughter's name and then picked Amanda up along the road? It's possible, just implausible."

Ella looked through the office window at the San Diego streets. The blacked-out windows did a good job of keeping out the heavy sun. "I agree. I think it's possible this suspect was tailing Amanda from the beginning. I think he damaged her wheel before she even began driving. What were his intentions with her? That I don't know."

Mia joined her at the window. Ella saw the look of distaste on her face as she surveyed San Diego. She didn't know why Mia hated California so much but she wasn't going to ask – at least not yet. "I think he's escalating," Mia said. "Natural progression of the serial killer. First, he kills three people in public arenas, and now he's got a taste for it, he craves privacy. He wants to enjoy it, savor it."

Ella was surprised Mia was going along with everything, so she used the momentum to her advantage. "Then there's the cipher. I'm not sure exactly where all the characters come from, and some of them are probably made up, but he's even used some of the Zodiac's same symbols."

"Has he?" Mia asked.

Ella rushed to her bag and pulled her laptop out. She ran her fingers along the keyboard to get it out of standby mode. She pulled up the cipher picture Mia had forwarded her during their plane ride. "Look, this triangle with a line through it, that's one of Zodiac's. This backward *p* and *k*, he used them too. And of course, his little signature at the end. Zodiac's signature was a crosshair, but this guy has used a variation of it. Oh, and Zodiac used the term *kill rampage* in his own letters too."

"The similarities are pretty clear," said Mia. "I have to say, some of the parallels are interesting. There's definitely something there, I'm just reluctant to base this whole investigation on an unsolved murder from fifty years ago. As we've seen before, it can lead us down the wrong path. Right now, let's look at this as a brand new unsub. If the Zodiac's shoe fits, we'll look into it, but we can't make it the primary focus."

"But it doesn't stop there," Ella said. She knew Mia was right, but she wanted to get all of the information out while Mia was being responsive. "Sure, all of these could be a coincidence, but there are two other things that are way too specific to be coincidences."

Mia closed the window blinds, casting the room a dark orange. "Go on," she insisted.

"Amanda said that her abductor said he wasn't allowed near schools. One of the Zodiac's main suspects was a school teacher – but one that got fired for sexual misconduct with his students. Strange, yes?"

Mia pulled out a pen and tapped it against the desk. "That stood out to me too. It's a very bizarre thing to say, unless he was just trying to instill terror in Amanda. Perhaps he was just trying to make her uncomfortable. Besides, if he was telling the truth, it would have been very revealing."

"He didn't think Amanda would escape. Murder is a precautionary measure to erase the only witness who has been subject to the killer's true nature. This was his true nature. He didn't think Amanda would be alive by the next morning, so it didn't matter what he told her."

Ella had to pause. Tobias's words were coming out of her mouth. Since her theory had been flowing, she'd all but forgotten about her meeting with the monster.

"Very profound," Mia said, scratching her head. "Hold on a second, where have I heard that before?"

Ella clasped her lips shut, as though it might somehow erase what she'd said. "Huh? You've heard it before?"

"Yeah. Sounds oddly familiar."

Ella thought on her feet. "It's from a textbook. The Art of Profiling. Mandatory reading."

Mia didn't look convinced but she shook the thought off. "That must be it. And yes, I agree with what you're saying. Our first point of call should be to pull up a list of people in the area with a history of sexual misconduct."

"Agreed, but there's one last thing. The real kicker. Amanda said this guy referred to the police as 'blue meanies'. Have you ever heard that term in your life?"

Mia thought for a second. "Yes, actually. It was a popular term back in the early seventies. Long before your time, obviously. It was a slang term for the police, but I haven't heard it used in... God knows... fifty years."

"Right, so our killer was either consuming pop culture fifty years ago, putting him somewhere between the ages of sixty to seventy now, or..." Ella pulled up a webpage on her laptop. "Or he was referencing a letter the Zodiac sent in 1971. A very obscure letter. Everyone knows about the ciphers and cryptic messages, but this one was sent to the L.A. Times two years after the Zodiac stopped killing."

Mia leaned closer to the screen to read it. There was a scan of a badly-written letter above a transcription. She read aloud. "This is the Zodiac speaking. Like I have always said, I am crack proof. If the blue meanies are ever going to catch me, they had best get off their asses and do something. The longer they fiddle around, the more slaves I collect for my afterlife."

"See?" asked Ella.

Mia nodded her head a few times in succession. She read the transcription a few times. "Good spot, Dark. Did you know that from memory?"

Ella shrugged. "I went through a Zodiac phase a few years back. I just remembered his language and some of the odd words he used. I was one of those obsessive people who tried to crack his unsolved codes."

Mia smiled. "Any luck?"

"Nope. The unsolved ones are all so short they're basically impossible to solve."

"But you had a go, that's what matters." Mia knocked her hand against the desk. "Damn, I wish we had a definite link between the murders and Amanda's abduction. I'm just worried we're looking at two unrelated events and imagining connections."

Officer Denton knocked on the door. Both agents turned to him.

"Everything go okay with the interview?" he asked.

"All good, thank you," Mia said. "While we have you Ray, could you get some of your officers to search your local database for possible suspects? We have a good starting point."

"Sure, what do you need?"

"Search your records for white males who live within ten miles of the first crime scene. Aged twenty-eight to thirty-five with a history of sexual misconduct. Doesn't matter if it's against legal aged victims or minors. Including everything from sexual assault to public exposure. Please also include anyone with a history of minor offenses like assault, battery, or kidnapping. If any of them have handwriting or signature samples on file, that would be a major plus."

Denton's phone rang in his pocket. He held up a finger to Mia. "One second. This is one of my guys on the case." He answered the call and moved out into the corridor.

"We'll go and see the second crime scene, Dark," Mia said. "If we can figure out his method of attack, it might give us some insight into how he operates."

"Sounds good. Let's go." Ella grabbed some essentials out of her bag and stuffed them into her pockets, but before they could go, Officer Denton ran back into the room. He looked flustered.

"Agents, that was one of my officers who's been to retrieve Amanda's car."

"Right. Is everything okay with it?" Mia asked.

"Sort of. He's sending me a picture now." Denton's phone pinged. He tapped the screen. "Wow. That's odd."

"Let's see," said Mia. Denton held out his phone screen. They leaned closer.

When Ella saw it, her theory was all but confirmed. She clenched her fists with excitement. This was the feeling she loved. Never in her life did she think she'd have the chance to hunt down a Zodiac killer, but every new piece of evidence made it more and more likely that was the case.

"Well," she said, turning to Mia. "Looks you've got confirmation that they're connected after all."

CHAPTER SEVEN

Ella thought about the picture Officer Denton showed them. Amanda Huber's abandoned car, but scrawled on the driver's door was the unsub's signature – the T shape on top of an X. Once again, a reference to the Zodiac killer. He'd done the same thing at one of his crime scenes too.

The discreet lovers' lane overlooked San Diego's famous Black's Beach, one of the largest beaches in the whole United States. Mia parked their vehicle around twenty feet from the cordoned-off zone. Two officers, each in a patrol car, kept curious onlookers away from the crime scene.

"Do you think he went back and did it?" Ella asked Mia as they stepped out of the vehicle.

"Almost certainly," said Mia, speaking over the car. "He wouldn't have done it prior to abducting Amanda. He must have gone back after she escaped and put his mark on it then. My only question is why he'd take credit for a failed abduction."

Up above, the mountains blocked out most of the afternoon sun, casting a gray shadow over the whole overlook. Ella welcomed it. Surviving through many Virginia summers had given her a preference for the cold.

"Same. I mean, the Zodiac's abduction failed too, but surely no unsub would risk giving themselves away like that."

They made their way towards the yellow tape and flashed their badges to the waiting police officers. They both replied with a thumbs-up out their car windows. Unfortunately, everything had been removed from the crime scene so they needed to use their imaginations to fill in the blanks. All that remained were the blood stains.

"Max Westbrook and Zoe Cousins. Both 19 years old. Students at San Diego State. Both new to the area, so there's no family we can speak to around here," Mia said.

Ella stepped over the tape while Mia glanced out at Black's Beach below them. Ella knelt down and inspected the blood splatter. There were two pools, about six feet apart from each other. She crossed back over the tape to get a wide-angle look at the scene.

"If you were going to do this, how would you do it?" Mia shouted to her.

Ella thought about it. She scanned the area, arriving at several conclusions. The lane was quite small in comparison to some of the mountainous roads, and the actual entrance to the beach was a good ten minutes away.

"First of all, no one comes to this part of the road by accident. You're either here to make out, or you're here to assault someone. It's a dead end here, so it's not like all the beach-goers would be passing through."

"True. There are no real vantage points either, though. It's not like he could scope anyone out. Chances are he took a gamble on this area and it paid off. Does this beach have any connection to the Zodiac?" Mia shouted. Her voice echoed through the mountains.

Ella moved closer to her to save her voice. She ran through everything she knew about the Zodiac in her head. Victims, crime scenes, dates, letters. Nowhere did a beach crop up. "Nothing. The Zodiac operated closer to San Francisco. And he favored lakes, not beaches."

"Chances are our unsub stumbled upon this couple by chance and seized the opportunity. Who knows how many lovers' lanes he perused before stopping here?"

Ella put herself in the killer's shoes. She imagined the car, the position of the passengers and how a potential attacker might approach them. "So, if I was our guy, I'd want to take out the biggest threat first – the man. Did the autopsies uncover the order they were killed?" Ella asked.

"Unfortunately not," Mia said. "They were most likely killed within minutes of each other, making it near-impossible to determine the order they died. The only indicator we have is the blood flow but even then it's difficult." Mia photographed the reddish-brown stains on the asphalt with her phone. She shook her head.

"What are you thinking?" Ella asked.

"The male was almost certainly killed outside the car. I'm just trying to work out how our killer could have coaxed him out."

Ella followed the path away from the lovers' lane. Once the asphalt ended, a dirt path led off in three different directions. When it all converged into a single lane, the lane narrowed significantly. She recalled the original Zodiac's method of operation and applied it.

"This lane is pretty tight, right?" Ella shouted up to Mia. "What if he drove up here and then just blocked their exit? The real Zodiac killer did exactly that."

Mia joined her down near the dirt road. "Well, I'm seeing some tire tracks, but plenty of cars have come and gone in the past two days. These tracks could belong to anyone. Plus Cali had one of its famous flash floods yesterday so it's washed most of them away."

In between the bricks and clumps of mud, Ella spotted something nestled in the dirt. She reached down and pulled it out. It was a red plastic cigarette lighter, but one with a crack right down the middle.

Tobias's words rang in her ears: *psychological profiling is much less a learnable skill as it is something inherent.* Her first instinct was to discard the lighter as it could have belonged to anyone, but something in her gut told her to persevere. As she let her mind wander, a connection sparked.

"Didn't Amanda say the guy had a bunch of lighters in his car?" Ella blurted out.

"She did."

Ella moved a few feet further down. She picked up another one. Suddenly, she realized something. "Ripley, could he have used these lighters to coax his victims out?"

Mia looked bemused. "A lighter?"

Ella had that creeping doubt that she was mistaking mist for smoke, but decided to run her idea by Mia regardless.

"The original Zodiac used to pull up behind his victims and make a commotion. He'd flash his lights, making banging sounds, anything to get the male driver out of the car. But of course, this was fifty years ago when people were a lot more trusting. Now, he'd need to do something different."

"Like offer them a cigarette?" Mia asked.

"No. Did you never throw plastic lighters on the ground when you were a kid?"

Mia didn't look any less confused than she had a minute ago. "We didn't have plastic lighters when I was a kid."

Ella mimed the action with the broken one in her hand. "If you throw a plastic lighter hard enough, it makes a pretty loud boom. The exploding plastic causes a tiny spark, then the flammable liquid mixes with the oxygen and bang, explosion. I think that's what our unsub did here."

Mia's eyes darted from the dirt path to the area where the victims had been killed. "How would that draw out the victim?" she asked. "I'm not saying you're wrong, I'm just trying to cover every base."

Ella put herself in the female victim's shoes. She took in a deep breath and ran through the whole events in a linear fashion. "Societal pressure," Ella said. "I'm sure you've been out with a guy and they've been desperate to impress you in the past."

Mia pulled out a pair of gloves from her pocket and put them on. She took the lighters from Ella and looked them over. "It's been a while, but I see what you mean. Max would have been in default protector mode. He and Zoe are sitting in the car and a strange vehicle pulls up behind them. Suddenly, they hear a few loud bangs. Max's instinct is to check it out."

"Exactly," Ella said. "It's not like they could just drive off if this other car was blocking the way, so Max was forced to step up and be the guardian. He didn't want his date to think he was weak. And the explosion sounds could have been anything, like someone struggling with their vehicle. The immediate masculine response is to help out."

She saw Mia was coming round to the idea. Ella was surprised at how little she was rebutting her theories this time. Maybe she'd finally earned her place as a field agent, she thought.

"You could be onto something, Dark. Once Max is out of the car, our killer storms him and stabs him frenziedly. By this point, Zoe is in shock. She panics. Max is out of the picture so she becomes an easy target."

Both agents walked back up to the taped-off area. Mia handed the lighters to one of the waiting officers and told him to get them to the forensic technicians assigned to the case. The officer gave her a hearty nod.

Ella took a last look at the blood spatter and forced herself to imagine how these young lovers felt in their last moments. Max had tried to be the protector but had been cruelly taken down. Zoe lived her last moments in confused terror, succumbing to the killer's urges after watching her date get dismantled in the same way. It knotted her stomach to think that two innocent lives had ended in the exact spot she stood.

But she knew this killer. He was a copycat, an obsessive, someone who lived vicariously through the original Zodiac. If she knew the Zodiac like she thought she did, there was nothing this killer could do that would escape her. The idea of catching someone with such bizarre psychopathology filled her with an excitement nothing else could ever provide. What would he be like in person?

"Let's get going, Dark. There's not much else here to look at," Mia said, checking her phone. They returned to the car.

"What do you make of this perp, Ripley?" Ella asked.

Mia started up the engine and reversed back onto the pathway. "He's not stupid. He knows what he's doing. I remember having to profile the Zodiac as a mental exercise back when I started in eighty-nine. My memory might be a bit hazy, but I remember profiling him as a chancer who lucked his way to infamy. If the Zodiac cropped up today, he'd get caught within a month. He was a disorganized offender who craved attention. He didn't kill for sexual gratification. Am I along the right lines?"

Ella watched the mountains roll by. "I'd say so. I don't think the Zodiac was particularly skilled, just fortunate when it came to avoiding detection. Not to mention the police slip-ups that happened. But I think this unsub is a little more capable."

"He's confident enough to gain someone's trust without restraining them. He understands human psychology. He gets a sexual thrill from these kills."

"That means we're dealing with a very dangerous, very proficient offender," Ella said as the mountains smothered them once again. "Where are we headed?"

"Victim number one. Her mother is ready to speak to us."

CHAPTER EIGHT

Ella looked over the apartment block and saw a number of boarded-up windows, clothes hanging over balconies and a shirtless man smoking drugs on his balcony. When he noticed the two unfamiliar women heading towards the complex, he quickly retreated inside.

This was Carter Avenue, one of San Diego's more impoverished areas. Inside the apartment block lived Terri Evans, mother of the first victim.

At the entrance, Mia pushed the buzzer to apartment 113. A few seconds later, a tired voice answered. "Hello?"

"Miss Evans, we're with the FBI. Do you have a few minutes to speak with us?"

There was no response. The line disconnected and the door to the apartment complex clicked open. Ella understood. She hated this part of the job. No amount of emotional detachment could help when faced with someone who'd lost the most precious thing to them, especially when they'd lost them in such a violent way. Ella composed herself and remembered that the only people who could bring this woman comfort was them when they eventually caught this unsub.

They headed up the stone steps to the first floor and found Terri's apartment. There was a distinct smell of dirt and rust throughout the whole building, along with a brief hint of marijuana hidden somewhere in there too. Mia knocked on the door and Terri opened up instantly. Mia held up her badge.

"Thank you for meeting with us, Miss Evans. I'm Agent Ripley and this is Agent Dark. We're investigating the circumstances around your daughter's murder."

For the mother of a 23-year-old, Terri was on the young side. She was supermodel skinny with luminous blonde hair down to her chin. She wore an oversized white t-shirt and grey sweatpants. She barely looked forty years old, but it was difficult to tell given the deep red marks under her eyes.

"Come in," Terri said, walking away and leaving the door open for them. Mia and Ella stepped into the tiny apartment. The lounge and kitchen were one and the same. There was a small blue sofa nestled in the corner opposite a TV. Terri dropped down onto it. "Sorry, we don't get many visitors. There are some chairs in the kitchen."

"Don't worry, we'll stand," Mia said. "We're very sorry to hear what happened. We're doing everything we can to find whoever did this and with your help, we can get a little closer."

"Catch him. Don't catch him. I don't care. Nothing's going to bring Amy back. I don't know what I can tell you." Terri held back the tears. She dropped her head into her hands. Mia went to speak but Ella held out her hand in a *stop* gesture. She couldn't help herself. What this woman needed was compassion, not protocol.

Ella moved over to the sofa and sat next to Terri. She heard her sobs from behind her hands. "You're right, Terri. Nothing we can do can bring Amy back. We've looked into her and honestly, she sounds fantastic. Working through her hospitality degree. A part-time waitress. She sounds like someone I'd want to be friends with."

Terri nodded, still cupping her face. She removed her hands and took a sharp inhale of breath. "That's right. She was working hard to get us out of this shit hole. It's just been me and Amy since day one. Lived here since I was 17. Looked after her, raised her, only for some piece of shit to do this to her." Tears flooded again. Ella knew this kind of living took its toll. She had no doubt Terri and Amy were both clean but they probably didn't bring in much money, and California wasn't a cheap place to live.

In her FBI training, Ella had been taught never to overly-sympathize with a grieving interviewee. She'd also been told never to make physical contact outside of handshakes if necessary. But looking at Terri and imagining the pain she was in, she decided protocol could shove itself. Ella leaned over and embraced Terri tight. She looked back at Mia, expecting a cold stare, but she just nodded in approval.

Terri welcomed it, it seemed. The sobbing ceased and she returned to a sitting position after a few seconds. She wiped her face. "Thank you. It's nice to have some affection. Don't get much of it anymore."

Ella was only five years older than Amy Evans, and no doubt Terri would see her daughter every time she saw a similarly aged woman from this moment forward. But now, her first memory of projection would be a show of sympathy. It might not be much, but it was better than nothing.

Ella stayed sitting on the sofa. "What can you tell us about Amy?" she asked. "Doesn't matter how small or insignificant you think it might be."

"Like you say, she was a waitress at Skeeter's in town. She'd gone back to school last year after we finally saved the tuition fees. Everyone loved her. She had no problems with work, friends, school, anything. I don't know who'd want to do this to my girl."

"Given what we know so far, it's unlikely that Amy was purposely targeted. She just ended up in the wrong place at the wrong time. The person who did this has also taken two other lives. Once again, two people who were in the wrong place. Nothing more." Ella knew she shouldn't be divulging details of the ongoing investigation, but there was some reassurance to be found in the fact that others were enduring the same hell as you.

Terri shot up. "A serial killer?" she asked. "Oh, fuck."

"It's too early to say," Mia intervened. "The incidents may or may not be connected. We don't know for sure." That was when Ella received Mia's harsh stare. These murders were definitely connected but the general public couldn't know this yet.

"Did she walk the same route home every evening?" Ella asked.

"Yes. Well, four nights a week. It's a straight road from here to her restaurant."

"Was she seeing anyone?"

"No, Amy wasn't the type. She was more into books, writing, drawing. If she wasn't working or studying, she was in her bedroom."

Ella felt her heart sink. She instinctively saw a little bit of herself in Amy, and now she knew why. Same upbringing, same hobbies. "She sounds like a great girl. We're going to find whoever did this to her, whether it takes us a week or a decade, okay?" Once again, Ella knew she shouldn't make such promises, but it was like she couldn't control the words coming out of her mouth. There was a fire in her. This perpetrator was going to get caught by her own hand, and when she had him at her mercy, she was going to make him pay for what he did.

"I think that's all we need to know, Miss Evans," said Mia. "If you think of anything else that might be useful, please call the San Diego PD and ask for me or Agent Dark."

"I will, thank you," Terri said. The agents thanked her and prepared to take their leave. Terri accompanied them to the door. Just as they were past the threshold, Terri spoke up again.

"Is it true, agents? What it said in the paper?"

They turned around. "Is what true, Miss Evans?" asked Mia.

"His message in the Tribune. He said he stabbed her forty times. Is it true?"

Ella felt her stomach churn. She didn't know what to say.

"Yes," Mia said with a heavy sigh. "I'm sorry to say that it is."

Terri cupped her hands with her mouth. Her eyes welled up again. Ella consoled her. "We'll catch this person and I'll make sure he never sees the light of day again, okay?"

Terri nodded her goodbyes. Ella and Mia made their way back down the stairwell and out onto the street. "That was tough," Ella said.

"It never gets any easier."

"I'm sorry for revealing information like that," Ella said as Mia unlocked the car. They got inside. "I just had to say something to make her feel better, anything. It kills me to see people in that state."

"It's fine. You did good. Keep it up. I'm just really pissed off that the Tribune actually printed his note," said Mia. She pulled out her vibrating phone from her pocket. "Hold on. Denton's calling me."

Mia answered the call while Ella took a last glance at the run-down apartments in front of her. She thought about the attack on Amy Evans. What was the likelihood that Amy was purposely targeted, stalked, and then attacked? Small, she thought. This unsub saw a woman walking alone late at night and he struck while he had the chance. Amy and the couple were both victims of opportunity, just like the original Zodiac victims.

"So anyone could be a victim," Ella said aloud just as Mia ended her call.

"What was that?" Mia asked.

"Sorry, thinking out loud," said Ella. "If these victims are opportunistic kills, that means anyone is a potential target. Any young woman or couple prowling the streets at the wrong time could be targeted."

"I'm not sure," Mia said, turning on the ignition. "I agree Amy, Max, and Zoe were targeted at random, but Amanda's abduction was too clean. Not to mention that he knew some info about her personal life."

"I guess. Maybe he wanted to try something different? Maybe he wanted that personal connection this time?"

"Yeah, but does that mean he's only going to target specific people from now on, or will he go back to randomizing his victims? It's impossible to predict right now, meaning this is one volatile son of a bitch we're dealing with."

"There's another possibility," Ella said as Mia backed out of the compact parking lot. "One that also links to the original Zodiac."

"Go on," Mia said.

"He might be swerving us on purpose. What if he *wants* us to think he knew Amanda? He could have mentioned her personal details in his newspaper cipher, leading us to think there was a personal connection? There are theories that the original Zodiac knew a couple of his victims, and Zodiac himself fanned the flames of those theories. What if this unsub is following that line of thinking?"

They found themselves back on the San Diego streets. "Your guess is as good as mine there, Dark. But that was Denton on the phone. He said they've rounded up a few suspects for us to check out. They're all back at PD in person. Amanda is there too so we can see if she recognizes any of them."

"That's gonna be hard for her, putting herself through the whole experience again," Ella said.

"It will, but that's what it's gonna take to catch this guy."

CHAPTER NINE

Ella, Mia and Officer Denton stood behind the two-way glass in the precinct. On the other side, six men stood in a row, all of them with a look of disdain on their faces. Ella was surprised how quickly the SDPD got to work.

"That was fast," Mia said.

"No time to dawdle around here. West coast, best coast," Denton said. "We rounded up everyone we could on such short notice. There are a few we couldn't track down right away but some of these guys fit the bill quite well."

"They're all previous offenders?" Mia asked.

"They all have a history of sexual misconduct as well as minor offenses. Battery, arson, you name it."

Ella checked them out. They were all white males around the age of thirty, nondescript, unremarkable. None immediately stood out to her. She eyeballed the gentleman on the left, a short man in a wool jacket despite it being scorching hot outside. She tried to imagine him as the person responsible for furiously attacking Amy, Max, Zoe, Amanda. She tried to imagine him standing over their bodies and savoring the sexual high that came from the act of murder.

She couldn't. Her imagination wouldn't take her there. She sighed, suddenly seeing Tobias Campbell's face in her mind's eye. If he were standing beside her, he'd no doubt have something to say about the whole thing. What would he think? Would he be able to see the perpetrator immediately?

"Are we ready to bring in Amanda?" Denton asked, knocking Ella out of her daydream.

"Ready," Mia said. She turned to Ella. "Keep an eye on her, rookie. This is going to be hard for her. If she gets upset, use that magic you did back at Terri's place."

Ella nodded. "I'm on it."

The door opened and Amanda stepped in. She stayed near the entrance as she looked at the suspect line-up through the glass. She hesitated to step any further.

"Is Chloe okay?" Ella asked, trying to reassure her.

"She's fine. I didn't want to bring her in here. Don't want her anywhere near these scumbags."

"Understandable," Mia said. "Miss Huber, do you recognize any of these men?"

Amanda slowly approached the glass and eyed the men one by one. Ella watched her reactions closely. There was a look of frustration on her face. A brief glimmer of rage. She rubbed her right shoulder with her left hand, a sign that she was becoming defensive.

"No, I don't recognize any of them. But like I said, I didn't get a good look at his face. The man on the right has the same height and build, but I'm sorry, I don't know."

"Don't worry," Mia said. "Let's try the line."

Officer Denton pushed in a silver button and spoke into a microphone beside the glass. "Number one, please step forward and say the line."

The man on the left hand side stepped off the platform and stared straight ahead at the glass. "You okay, miss? Don't see many people wandering alone out here," he said.

All eyes turned to Amanda. She shook her head. Officer Denton returned to the mic. "Thank you. Please step back. Number two, same request."

The second man stepped forward and repeated the line. Amanda again shook her head.

"Definitely not. Way too husky. It's not either of them."

Suspect three and four followed and Amanda dismissed them. Too tall, too gravelly-voiced. Only when suspect five stepped forward and spoke did Ella notice something change in her. There was a look of hopefulness like she desperately wanted number five to be the correct one.

But Amanda waved him off. Number six followed, and while Amanda took a minute to respond, she eventually dismissed him too.

"Anything?" Mia asked. "Any resemble the man who abducted you at all?"

Amanda breathed heavily. She grabbed a clump of her hair and moved it around to her mouth. Ella could see there was an idea running around her head.

"Number five," she said.

"Something stands about number five?" Denton asked.

"No. Everything stands out about him. Number five is the man who abducted me."

***

His name was Jim Mallon. Six feet tall, nicotine-stained teeth and dark hair on top of what Ella called a weasel face. Tight cheekbones, pert lips. As he sat across the table opposite Ella and Mia, he stuffed his hands into the pocket of his brown jacket. From outside the interrogation room, Amanda and Officer Denton watched on behind the tinted glass.

"Mr. Mallon, do you know why you're here?" Mia asked.

"Nope," he said. Abrupt, cautious. Ella could see that getting through to this man wasn't going to be a simple task. His body language screamed defensive, from his pocketed hands to the way he was speaking directly to the table.

"You're here under suspicion of abduction. Can you clarify your whereabouts between 11pm and midnight on the night of Friday, March twelve?"

Jim shrugged. "Poker."

"Poker? Where at?" Ella asked.

"Chameleons. It's a little club in town."

Mia made a note of it. "Right, and can anyone else confirm you were there?"

Jim removed his hands from his pockets and folded his arms. "Doubt it. I went there alone. Spoke to a few people but they won't remember me."

"Why won't anyone remember you?" Mia asked.

Jim shrugged again. "Would you remember me?"

Ella and Mia exchanged a look. "Well, the woman behind that glass remembered you." She nodded to the other side of the room.

"Remembered me from where?"

"Mr. Mallon, our victim claims that you abducted her in a silver Volkswagen alongside Lakeside Road last night. Do you have anything to say about that?"

The color vanished from his face. "What the hell? Are you kidding me? I thought this was some stupid drug bust or something. I didn't abduct no one. I was at poker last night. I wasn't driving along no road, alright?"

Ella scanned him up and down. The sudden outburst was a surprise. Human psychology said that guilty perpetrators usually gave short answers and refused to acknowledge the act they were guilty of. It was always *I didn't do it* rather than *I didn't murder that woman*. Ella was in two-minds.

"We'll check the CCTV of this so-called poker club," Mia said.

Jim shook his head. "No, you won't. Doesn't have any. It's not that kind of place."

Ella raised her eyebrows. "What kind of gambling club doesn't have CCTV?"

"One that's not really a gambling club," Mia added. "Some gambling goes on there, but it's not exactly a licensed establishment."

Jim smirked. Ella wanted nothing more than to wipe it off his face.

"Mr. Mallon, I'll be honest, I don't believe for a second you were gambling last night, so unless you can give us a reason to let you go, we'll be keeping you here for further questioning," said Mia.

"How's this for a reason? I don't own no Volkswagen. Shouldn't you detectives check that out before dragging me here?"

"Just because you don't own one, doesn't mean you couldn't get hold of one," Ella said.

Jim reached into his jacket pocket and pulled out his wallet. From the inside, he pulled out a small receipt, handwritten. "Here, this is from last night. My winnings slip. Now find a problem with that why don't you?"

Ella pulled it across to her side of the table. It was written in blue ink, with the date, time and the amount of Jim's wager. One hundred dollars.

"You expect us to take a handwritten receipt as proof?" Mia asked. "You could have scribbled all that down yourself."

"Knew it. You cops get more corrupt by the day. This is evidence of where I was and you won't accept it. Makes me sick."

Mia sighed. "I'll ask another question. Where were you on the night of Wednesday, March tenth?"

"Work. Night shift. Six p.m. until two a.m. Check my clock card, ask my supervisor. Do whatever you have to. I wasn't stabbing a bitch or killing no teenagers, alright?"

Ella glanced over at Mia, knowing she was thinking the same thing. "Mr. Mallon, why did you mention killing? We never mentioned that."

Jim laughed and tapped his hands on the table. "Oh please. Everyone knows. I might look like an idiot but I can read a newspaper. This is about them murders. Well, you're looking in the wrong place. I'm no saint but I'm no killer, either."

A long silence followed. Ella watched Jim's body language closely and while the defensive characteristics were still there, she heard a tone of authenticity in his voice.

"Okay, Mr. Mallon. You're free to leave. We'll be confirming your alibis shortly and if there are any discrepancies, we'll be back in touch." Mia stood up and opened the interrogation room door. The suspect left without looking back. Ella watched an officer escort him out of the precinct and out of sight. Mia peered her head out of the door and asked Officer Denton to take Amanda to another room. She returned to Ella.

"Thoughts?" she asked.

Ella ran through everything in her head and started from the beginning. "First of all, Amanda didn't even seem sure that he was the right guy. She said she was sure, but did you see the look on her face?"

"I know. Pure uncertainty. I've seen it before. Some victims are so desperate, be it for justice or closure, that they'll pick anyone as long as it vaguely resembles their attacker. It's a kind of subconscious projection."

"Right? And then there's the suspect. Amanda said he was friendly and approachable when they first met, but that guy was the total opposite. Most women would run a mile if that guy offered them a ride. He was cold and abrupt. It's obvious just from his face."

Mia folded up her notes on the table. "Tell me about it. He was a real sleaze. I think he was telling the truth about his whereabouts too. He looks exactly the kind of person you'd find in an illegal gambling den, not to mention he's a heroin addict."

That took Ella by surprise. "Was he?"

"The tips of his fingers were scabbed and they had marks from where he'd tested the needle. He had muscle cramps in his shoulders too, probably from withdrawal. No heroin addict is capable of pulling off these murders, especially without leaving any traces."

Ella thought about it for a second. She recalled what she knew about drug addiction. "I guess. I suppose if he's a drug addict, his primary focus will be finding a hit. Sexually motivated murder probably isn't on his list of priorities right now."

Mia led the way out of the interrogation room and back into their office. "Exactly that. And heroin makes people physically weak. No way would he be confident enough to abduct someone."

"Then there's the car. Our unsub definitely owns a silver Volkswagen. We can be pretty certain of that."

"More like owned. That car is in a compound somewhere by now. But you're right, he definitely owned a VW prior to today."

Ella sat down at her desk and pulled the case file in front of her. She eyed the crime scene photo of Amy Evans, dead and discarded on the road side. It made her stomach knot. Even if Jim Mallon didn't do this, someone did, and that someone was still out there. She wasn't going to rest until she'd found out who.

CHAPTER TEN

They'd been going through the list of potential suspects for six hours. Ella had extracted the files of anyone with a history of criminal activity who matched Amanda's vague description and had amassed a list of almost a hundred people. She looked up from her desk and peered beyond the closed window blinds, only now realizing that it was pitch black outside. Opposite her, Mia gulped down her coffee. Their desk now had more coffee cups than paperwork.

"Something's bugging me," Ella said.

"Out with it," Mia said without looking up from her laptop.

"Our unsub isn't following any kind of pattern. He's mimicking the Zodiac's crimes, but he's doing them out of order. If we're going on the Zodiac's canonical victims, he killed three couples and then a lone male. Why is this guy doing things differently?"

Mia tapped on her keyboard and then sat back in her seat. "Experimentation or a lack of confidence. Killing one person is hard, but killing two people is even harder. Aside from the Zodiac, do you know many other serial killers who took two victims on their first kill?"

Ella thought about it. "Three, out of about six hundred."

"Exactly. He went with what he was comfortable with."

"That makes it really hard to predict what he's going to do next, but if Amy Evans's murder shows one thing, it's that our unsub doesn't subscribe to the regular beliefs about the Zodiac. It means he believes he took more victims than what he claimed." Ella pulled off her glasses and threw them on the table. She rubbed her eyes with her thumb and middle finger.

"Dark, stop with the Zodiac stuff. Stop treating this like it's a historical case. It's not. It's a brand new case that could go in any direction. We already know this killer isn't following Zodiac's timeline exactly so it doesn't matter. If we can't predict his next move based on historical events then there's no point even thinking about those events, capiche?"

Ella knew Mia was right, but there was something else playing on her mind. Something she'd only just thought about. "Alright, I get that, but there's one more thing. The last thing, I promise."

"Okay, hit me, then we're getting out of here. I've had enough for one day."

"Right, well, the night after the Zodiac's failed abduction, there was another coupled murdered not far away from the abduction site. The Zodiac took credit for it, but it was never officially linked to him."

"And? What's your point?" Mia asked.

"Tonight is the night after our guy's abduction. What if he tries the same thing?"

"Is there any reason why he would, other than this tenuous connection? Right now, it's more important to focus on the facts rather than the theories, Dark."

Ella grabbed her laptop and clicked three times. She brought up a webpage she'd stumbled upon a few minutes earlier, but it had taken a few minutes to connect the dots. "In the original case, the couple were killed as they were overlooking a carnival celebration." She turned her laptop screen to show Mia, basking in the adrenaline rush her revelation provided. Finally, a lead that followed a logical pattern. "Look. Beach party, five miles from here, tonight."

Mia arched her eyebrows. She leaned closer to the screen and read it out. "Coronado Beach party extravaganza. Join the fun at 9pm, March thirteenth."

"Another beach," Ella said. "Paid entry, which means there's going to be a lot of people watching from afar. Perfect opportunity to find a secluded couple." For the first time, Ella felt like she'd gotten into this unsub's head. The addictive high she chased came in sudden and sharp waves.

Mia jumped out of her seat. She peered out the office door and signaled to Officer Denton who was also burning the midnight oil. He joined them right away.

"You ladies still here?"

"We are, and we might have something. How many officers can you get on patrol tonight?" Mia asked.

"For a potential serial killer? As many as you like. What do we have?"

"Beach party, could be a place for our unsub to find easy victims. Can you get a patrol on the area? Squad cars around the perimeter, some plain clothes officers on the inside?"

Denton smirked. "No problem at all." He opened the door and shouted into the open-plan room. "Boys, who wants to patrol a beach party tonight?"

The voices came thick and fast. Ella looked out the office window and saw about fifteen officers with their hands raised. Denton came back.

"See that? I'll get every inch of that place covered."

"Great," Mia said. "And a two-mile radius around the outside too. Our guy might target stragglers leaving the party."

"You got it. Send me the details and I'll make it happen."

"Just follow us," Mia said. "Ready to go to a beach party, Dark?"

Ella relished the irony. Under social circumstances, a beach party would drive her to insanity with its noise and blinding lights and intoxicated attendees. But if there was a murderer amongst the party-goers, she wouldn't miss it for the world.

"Ready as I'll ever be. Let's go."

***

Ella perched herself against the wall, took off her boot and emptied the sand out. It had only taken a few minutes for the sand's unwelcome intrusion, and given how much beach there was to cover, there was no doubt more to come.

The place was awash with bodies, both lively and tranquil. Groups of half-naked youngsters were scattered as far as Ella could see, some dancing around campfires, some flirting with the incoming tide. Rows of floodlights cast the beach and its pop-up stalls various neon shades. Music had been omnipresent since she arrived, like it was being pumped directly into her ear canal by some invisible force. Given that there was plenty of ground to cover, Mia had stayed around the outskirts to catch anyone who might be leaving the party alone. Ella had dived into the heart of the operation, and her approach was to single-out anyone who fit Amanda's description of her abductor. White, thirties, medium athletic build. It wasn't an easy task with such a vague description, but the one advantage she had was that most of the party-goers were on the younger side.

Ella stood as far back from the action as she could, keeping her wits about her. Two shirtless guys walked past, one of them engaging her in casual banter, but Ella smiled and waved them off. Now wasn't the time for distractions.

She walked across the beach, finally spotting someone who fit the bill. An older male, alone, standing with his hands planted firmly in his pockets. Ella stood in the shadow of a taco stall and kept a watchful eye, only for a new woman to tap him on the shoulder seconds later. They both drifted off towards the sea together.

Amongst the frolicking and the color overload, Ella's thoughts turned back to Tobias Campbell. Every time she tried to clear her mind, his face manifested and his soft tones invaded her ears. He was like a living virus and her thoughts were the host, only she didn't yet know quite what the cure was. She thought that maybe it would fade with time, like most afflictions. Or the other alternative was to find this perpetrator and prove that Campbell had been wrong about what he'd said.

FBI profilers are the art critics of law enforcement. Criticizing others yet they themselves are unable to draw a straight line.

Down here was a waste of time, Ella soon realized. There were no loners or stragglers on the beach, only congregations of young souls enjoying their primes, and what few singles appeared soon converged with groups. There was only a small chance that this unsub might be amongst them, but the higher likelihood was that he'd scope out the quieter areas. Judging by the last double homicide at least, this killer was as opportunistic as they came. Vengeful and determined, but opportunistic nonetheless. It didn't matter who was on the receiving end of his wrath as long as someone was.

Ella made her way off the beach and up the stone ramp to the perimeters. The surrounding mountains dulled the music and sprung some energy back into her other senses. Up here, groups still congregated but in lower numbers, and while it wasn't an ideal place to commit murder, it was better than the beach front. Rows of cars overlooked the party below, a lot of which still had gamblers inside them. Ella passed them by and caught a whiff of cheap alcohol and marijuana smoke, and almost felt sorry for them given that the heavy hand of the San Diego PD was doing a thorough border patrol tonight.

She found a vantage point and surveyed the scene below her, and among the social dances and camaraderie saw something that looked out of place.

A vehicle sat in the shadows, far away from the others. It was perched up against the mountainside in a small area, offering no views of the events or scenery a hundred feet to the right.

And what drew Ella the most was that it was a silver Volkswagen.

Ella descended from her perch, down the stone rampway towards the road. She kept her eyes on the prize, fearing that the driver might scuttle away any second. She committed the licence plate to memory and hurried towards its location while keeping a casual air about herself. The tinted windows made it impossible to determine if anyone was inside.

Beside the row of cars, someone called to her. Ella looked and saw a man offering her a can of beer from his car window.

"No thank you," she said, instead choosing to loiter a few feet away. Then she realized that her singular presence could be construed as odd, and if that *was* the unsub in the Volkswagen, he'd no doubt pick up on it.

"But I appreciate the offer," Ella continued, turning back to the driver. Every seat in his car was occupied by another drinker.

"You all alone?" the man asked, swigging his own can through gritted teeth. He had a shaved head and a black vest on. That was all Ella could see.

"I'm not. Just waiting for my friends to arrive."

"Well, you're welcome to party with us if you want."

Ella barely registered what he said, instead locked on the lone vehicle. Suddenly, the Volkswagen door swung open.

A woman stepped out, waved goodbye to whoever else was inside, then headed towards the beach. Another woman stepped out of the passenger seat and assumed the driving position.

Ella sighed, part frustration, part something else she didn't quite know what. A tap on her back made her jump.

"Had the same thoughts as me, didn't you?" the voice said. Mia appeared with a plastic beer cup in her hand, empty. It was the first thing Ella spotted. "Don't worry, it was empty when I got it. I just wanted to look the part."

"Sure," Ella said.

"Who's your friend?" the guy in the car said. He offered her the same drink Ella declined. "You want a can?"

Mia looked him up and down before accepting the can graciously. She took it from him, popped it open and tipped the contents into her cup. "Thanks buddy, but we need to make a move."

Mia put her arm around Ella and they began to walk away. The man in the car said a defeated goodbye, followed by something inaudible.

"Guess this was a dud," Ella said.

"Not at all. We needed to check it out to be sure. But if you ask me, this is way too lively an event for our guy to strike. Too many moving parts, too many uncontrollable variables. Even if he showed up to stake it out, he'd change his mind straight away."

Ella thought the same. "I guess. But it's probably a good idea for a few cops to stay here just in case."

"Yeah, but right now we gotta head out of here. I'm starving and I refuse to eat the crap they serve here."

"Good call. Where do you want to go?"

"If there's one thing Cali has going for it, it's the food. If we have to spend time here, we're eating at the best restaurants. Come on, I know a great place not far from here," Mia said.

They found their car and headed away from the beach party. Ella wasn't completely sure, but all signs pointed to this being a night without death.

CHAPTER ELEVEN

For a San Diego restaurant on a weekend night, the La Palma was unusually quiet. When Ella opened the menu and saw the prices, she realized why.

"Jesus, three-hundred dollars for a steak? What's it made from, gold?"

"Wagyu beef. It's the most expensive steak in the world. They have to import it from Japan," Mia said.

They sat at a small booth in the back of the restaurant with only two other diners within earshot. The place had a warm red glow to it, with soft jazz music filling the air. "You're not kidding. They could fly that cow first class for that much."

Mia laughed. A waitress appeared at their table with an electronic device to take their order. "Drinks?" she asked.

"Hibiki and Coke, please. Double," said Mia. Ella scoured the drinks menu, only really wanting something light but realizing she couldn't in a place like this. Peer pressure won this round.

"And I'll have the same, but single."

"No problem. I'll be back to take your food order shortly," said the waitress and left.

"Are you sure you want to eat here?" Ella asked. "Don't the accountants at the office put limits on what you can spend?"

"Dark, I've been at the Bureau thirty-five years. If I haven't earned an expensive steak, no one has. But yeah, they cap us at two hundred dollars a day. I have to justify everything I've spent – on both of us. I bet you didn't know that, did you?"

"I did not. I assumed you just swiped and left it to the accountants to sort out."

"Ha. I wish. But don't worry, I don't think you've ever broken the twenty-dollar barrier during any of our trips so far."

Ella nodded. "I'm a cheap date."

"Speaking of that, how's that new guy in your life? You told me about him last week, if I remember rightly."

Since arriving, Ella had been too distracted to think about Ben. Suddenly, she felt a pang of guilt for abandoning him the way she had.

She also realized she hadn't messaged him since she arrived. Another broken promise.

"Oh, Ben? I mean, he's great. A bit too great, you know?"

"Too great? No, I don't know what you mean."

"He's this energetic, excitable young thing. Super cute. Full of life. Never has a bad word to say about anything. And he's a professional athlete. It's just all a bit... wow."

"Okay?" Mia said with a confused face. "And why haven't you snapped him up like a trout? He sounds like a catch."

"I've met him three times, and two of those times I had to bail on him because of work. I don't know, I feel like if he was my boyfriend, it would be like having an exotic tiger and never letting it out of its cage."

The waitress arrived with their drinks and placed them down. "Food?" she asked.

"Steak for me," Mia said. "Medium, with potatoes and peppercorn sauce."

"Carbonara, please" Ella said.

"Good choice," said the waitress, taking their orders on her device.

"I know, I'm committing carbicide."

"Should be about twenty minutes," the waitress said before disappearing.

Mia took a big drink. "So you *were* on a date when Edis called you to his office. I knew it because you were wearing fancy perfume, and you looked a little bit down. I know that look when I see it. I've been in that position many times in the past."

Ella's guilt amplified. While she was upset about leaving Ben, the bigger concern was her meeting with Tobias Campbell. What had become clear was that Tobias hadn't yet divulged the details of their meeting to anyone in his circle, at least not yet. But what if it took a few days for the information to trickle down? How would Mia react, knowing that she'd kept a secret from her when she had ample opportunity to tell her?

The words almost fell out of her mouth. *I went to see Tobias Campbell.* She imagined herself saying them, but there was no scenario Ella could picture that didn't result in Mia being upset. Even worse was that the longer she left it, the more hurt Mia would be. This woman who'd done so much for her, who'd plucked her from a desk job and allowed her to live out her childhood dream of chasing down predators.

Ella couldn't think about it. It was too overwhelming. Surely a solution would present itself someday so that she could let Mia down gently. "Yeah, I was out with him. But I had to leave him high and dry."

"You know you don't *have* to agree to Edis's requests? You're technically still an intelligence analyst. I can do some of these cases on my own if you ever need a break."

Ella knew this, but she'd rather be out in the field than anywhere else. "No, I love being out here. I want to speak to Edis about doing this full time."

"He'd absolutely let you do that, but this job doesn't translate well to relationships. You'd be on the road at least one week per month, probably a lot more. Poor Ben would be sitting at home wondering what you were up to, and vice versa."

"Yeah, it would be hard. I don't know. I've got decision fatigue."

"If it was me, I'd snap him up in a heartbeat. A pro athlete? That's the dream. Put in a few years and retire at 35. Not to mention he must have stamina for days."

Ella laughed. "Well, I wouldn't know. I just feel bad that I can't give him what he deserves. It sometimes feels like he and I are from two different worlds. He's a performer, out in the open, playing a character. Meanwhile I'm working in secret. It feels too different." She sipped her whiskey and Coke, which seemed to be a lot heavier on the whiskey side. "Christ, that's got a kick."

"Sure has." Mia checked her phone. "Nothing from Denton yet."

Ella looked at a painting beside their table. A cat, made from colorful swirls. Not exactly high art but attractive enough to look at. Almost unconsciously, she remembered what she'd told Tobias about being a cat person. It had been an off-hand remark to segue into a subject change, but for some reason she could still remember every word of the conversation she had with him, as she'd mentally recorded it and was constantly playing it back.

The urge to spill the details to Mia came again. Maybe it was the influx of alcohol. She looked at her partner, still with her phone in hand and decided to speak up.

"Mia, there's something I have to tell you. Something you need to know." Her palms began to itch. Her appetite suddenly vanished. Was this a good idea? Right now, of all times?

"You know you can tell me anything. I don't judge."

"Remember last week? When I had that letter?"

Mia quickly glanced up from her phone. Her eyes widened so much that her pupils looked minute. "You didn't?" she asked. "Did you really?"

Ella nodded. "I did."

"Oh, wow. Who is she?"

Ella refocused. "Huh? She?"

Mia nodded excitedly. "Yeah, the letter to your dad, from that woman."

Then it clicked. In Ella's dad's old storage unit, she'd found some strange letters written to her father by a woman named Samantha. Ella had run the handwriting through some graphology software and located the writer. It was a woman in Virginia. She'd mentioned it to Mia during their case in Seattle.

"Oh, yeah, sorry. I misheard you. Yes, I found the woman who wrote them. I'm thinking of paying her a visit."

Mia summoned a waitress over. "You absolutely should. Closure is good. You might learn a few things about your old man. You want another drink?"

"No… thank you." The moment had passed. Her courage disappeared. Now wasn't the time to tell her. Since arriving in California, Mia had been usually receptive to her. Ella didn't want to ruin this good thing they had.

And hopefully, no one else would either.

CHAPTER TWELVE

The man hovered his fingers near the candle flame and dipped his fingertips in the wax one by one. Once the wax hardened, he slipped on a pair of thick latex gloves and pulled out a piece of paper from the middle of the ream.

With the paper on his desk, he drew out his ten-by-sixteen grid. Stapled to the wooden board in front of him was his cipher code. He put the pen to paper, ensuring none of his bare skin came into contact with the materials.

Dear Editor, this is...

He needed a name. All of the best serial killers assigned their own monikers, including the one and only Zodiac. The Zodiac knew this fifty years ago, and he knew it now. Only a select few did. He never expected his crimes would gain so much exposure, but the whole country was abuzz with speculation already. Within a few days, he was a phenomenon, much more widespread than his counterpart was back in his day.

He looked around his den for inspiration. On the walls were reproductions of all of the Zodiac's letters. By now, he knew all of the contents by heart, but using one of the Zodiac's own terms would make things too easy. Original newspaper clippings from the San Francisco Chronicle in the 1960s were framed beside them. *MANHUNT FOR ZODIAC CONTINUES, A MURDER CODE BROKEN* were the stand-out headlines. Above them was the bullet, displayed in a black shadow box to showcase all its glory. It had cost a pretty penny from the retired detective who claimed it was from the Zodiac's first murder, but it was worth it.

The man placed his pen down and moved to his computer on the other side of his den. For five days, he'd done nothing but refresh news sites and scour articles for his name. He did the same again, now seeing a new breaking headline on the San Diego Union Tribune website.

POLICE URGE PARTY GOERS TO BE VIGILANT.

He couldn't help but laugh, but he was surprised they caught this possibility. Clearly, someone on the task force knows their Zodiac lore, and that made things a lot more interesting for him. He read the first paragraph.

In light of a recent span of homicides, San Diego Police have advised those attending the annual Beach Party Celebration on Coronado Beach to be cautious. As an event that attracts thousands of teenagers and young adults, police believe it could be an attractive spot for the culprit behind the recent killings to scope out.

He shook his head disapprovingly. Firstly, someone on the opposite side of the moral spectrum had put two and two together. They sensed he was a Zodiac connoisseur and that person also knew about the more farfetched Zodiac theories too. It took a capable mind to put those elements together so quickly. It wasn't something that a quick Wikipedia read could determine. Someone had either spent the past few days brushing up on Zodiac theories or they already knew them. Either way, it meant he was going to have some fun.

His reflection stared back at him in the screen's glare. "If you think I'm going to hit the lanes around that beach tonight, you're sadly mistaken, detectives." He had no intentions of being there. Too many people, too many uncontrollable variables. There was a possibility he'd find a secluded couple hoping to get lucky, but the chances were slim. He much preferred the solitude of a late weekday evening. Just when those poor souls thought it was safe to enjoy some explicit activity… boom. He loved seeing the terror on their faces, the heart-rending knowledge that their life was about to end. Beside his laptop, he picked up his Royal Marine hunting knife, still coated with the blood of the last two unfortunate lovers. He took in its scent and was instantly transported back to the crime scene, ambushing those poor kids and gutting them like fish.

Oh, how that woman screamed. He'd never heard anything like it. The others had died so quickly that he hadn't had time to really savor the sexual high, but that girl…Zoe, according to the newspapers, was a special kind of fun.

He returned the knife down and searched online for 'San Diego murders,' finding endless news pieces discussing the incidents. Finally, infamy. For over thirty years he'd been a nobody, unforgettable, a face in the crowd. All he had to show for a life of hard work was a tiny apartment that barely had working electricity. Now it was time to rise to the top and strike terror into the hearts of millions. It was a power-rush like nothing else he'd felt in his life. At last, others were at his mercy rather than the other way around.

If this news had reached the whole world, maybe the actual Zodiac might hear about them? He must be out there somewhere, eighty years old, living out of his days in a San Francisco retirement home. Maybe he read this news and smiled, knowing that his legacy had transcended generations.

Now, it was time to put a name to these murders and live forever, just like his idol had.

He stood up and moved over to his trophy wall. There, he scanned the framed newspaper articles. One particular piece in the San Francisco Chronicle mentioned that it was possible the Zodiac had acquired his nickname from the Zodiac watch brand.

The man looked at his wrist. Suddenly, it hit him. Why had it taken so long to think of it? The original Zodiac was obsessed with the numbers two and three, and this word referenced them both.

"Perfect," he said with a grin. He went back to his desk and picked up his pen.

Dear Editor, this is the Gemini speaking...

CHAPTER THIRTEEN

Ella sat at her motel dressing table staring at her laptop. She glanced at the time. 01:10. She knew she should be sleeping but her thoughts were racing too fast to tune them out. The bright glare of the laptop screen didn't help either. Her motel room was a double, for reasons she could only attribute to Mia's innate dislike of California and thus the desire to live comfortably while here.

Since arriving back here, she'd recalled everything she could about the Zodiac killer. She had all the details stored in her brain, but she wanted to shape them in a linear format to organize her thoughts. With any luck, it could clue her in on this unsub's next move.

Between 1968 and 1969, the Zodiac attacked six victims in the form of three couples. Four died, two survived. All of them were either shot or stabbed and all three attacks took place near bodies of water. Zodiac's last confirmed murder took place in October 1969, but this time he shot and killed a lone male taxi driver who'd given him a ride. So far, her unsub hadn't followed this linear pattern at all, something that didn't sit right with her.

Following the first murders in 1968, the Zodiac began taunting the press and police with letters and cryptic messages. The killer used a series of bizarre symbols, some of which were present on runes in the middle ages, some extracted from military coding, and some which had he'd simply invented himself.

It took a long time for some of the Zodiac's ciphers to be cracked by code experts or puzzle enthusiasts. His letters were made available to the public for their help. In most cases, the letters took credit for murders around San Francisco and made threats to carry out more kills. In one note, Zodiac stated that he'd blow up a school bus full of children if his letters weren't printed in the newspapers. The unsub had already done something similar by threatening to go on a 'kill rampage,' the same term used by the Zodiac in his first ever letter too.

In many of his ciphers, Zodiac made strange references to 'slaves for the afterlife,' believing that every victim he killed would become a servant of his, post-death. This fell in line with various religious beliefs, particularly Islamic terrorist beliefs, prompting theories that perhaps the Zodiac was a fundamentalist exacting terror on a smaller scale.

However, a sighting of the Zodiac by eyewitnesses just after his final murder stated that he was a middle-aged white male with a crew cut, around five feet nine inches tall. Throughout the entirety of the Zodiac's reign of terror, this was the only eyewitness sighting of his face ever recorded. Zodiac was also seen by one of his surviving victims, but during the attack he wore a strange executioner's hood

In addition to the confirmed murders, many others were rumored to be attributed the Zodiac, with the Zodiac even taking credit for many more in his letters to the press. In his final ever contact with the press in 1974, he claimed he'd taken a total of 37 lives, but the authenticity of this was a matter of personal opinion. Ella didn't think so, since such a number would make Zodiac one of the most prolific serial killers to ever walk the earth.

Speculation around the Zodiac's identity continues to the present day, with more theories and possibilities put forward than perhaps any other case in history. It wasn't until December 2020, fifty-one years after Zodiac sent a particular cipher, that it was finally solved by an amateur researcher.

The most prominent theory is that the Zodiac was a San Francisco school teacher, a man with a history of sexual misconduct and a deep hatred of women. Plenty of circumstantial evidence pointed towards him being responsible for the Zodiac murders, including the fact he wore a Zodiac-brand wristwatch; however, his DNA wasn't a match for the samples found on the letters.

Outside of this primary suspect, some researchers believed that Zodiac was another infamous serial killer who'd migrated to New York. The Unabomber, the Black Dahlia Murderer, and Bruce Davies of the Manson Family were all considered to be viable suspects.

Ella closed her laptop and sat back in her chair. Did any of this information matter? Or was Mia right and that it would be impossible to predict his moves based on historical events? So far, there'd been no word from Denton regarding incidents at the beach event, so chances were he wasn't going to strike tonight. Or maybe he'd been prowling the area, seen the police cars and fled. As long as lives were spared, that's what mattered the most.

Everything suddenly felt very familiar. Scouring through historical archives looking for connections, trying to guess next steps based on old cases. Only four months ago, Ella had been summoned to Louisiana for her first case, a case now known among true crime researchers as the Mimicker.

Tobias Campbell had said that he and the Mimicker had been in contact prior to commencing his killing spree, but given what she knew about Campbell, she had no idea how true it was. Was it possible this killer had been inspired by the Mimicker, or perhaps even contacted him directly? Art imitating life and life imitating art.

There was no way to find out. She vowed she wouldn't ever see the Mimicker again, given that she came within inches of death during her last altercation with him. She promised him that the next time she saw him would be at his execution and she planned on keeping it that way.

Ella turned out the lights and lay on one of the single beds. She stared at the ceiling, her tired eyes conjuring up odd shapes, some of the killer's symbols, black and white squares. It was almost one-thirty in the morning and no doubt Mia would be knocking on her door in about six hours. She closed her eyes and tried to empty her head of the recurring thoughts about this killer. How would I feel to finally catch him? To elicit a confession from him? Was he a disorganized, blue collar offender or was he a fully competent predator, maybe the CEO of a finance firm looking for that next high?

She didn't know, but moments before she drifted to sleep, she realized there was one person out there who might already know.

CHAPTER FOURTEEN

Ava stepped out of the tent and grabbed a can of beer from the pile. She zipped up her hoodie and cracked open her drink. She walked a few yards down the dirt path and took in the forest air. It was cleaner down here, much better than the city smog she was used to.

Just down below was Dixon Reservoir, a gorgeous body of water full of exotic fishes. During the day it was a fishing hotspot, but there was a much nicer ambiance at night. It was the perfect place to get some alone time with her new boy toy.

"Boo," a voice said. Peter's hand appeared on her shoulder. "What you doing out here? It's colder than a witch's tit."

"Gross. I just wanted to see the woods at night. It's a nice feeling," Ava said.

"True that. Everything else feels like a million years away. We should do this more often."

"Hell yeah. You know what we should do right now?"

Peter scrunched up his face. "What? Again? Men can't just keep going like women can."

Ava slapped him on the chest. "Not that, dingus. We should go down to the lake. You sometimes get fireflies over the water. Want to head down?" she asked.

"Sure. I'll just grab a beverage."

They'd only been seeing each other a few weeks, but Ava always found that camping out together was a great way to test the foundations of a relationship. Just the two of you and minimal distractions. It helped that the phone signal down here was non-existent.

"Let's go," Peter said, beer in hand. "You can lead the way."

"Because you're scared?"

"No, because I don't know where I'm going. Also, I'm scared."

"Knew it," Ava said. "God forbid I ask you to start a fire again." She led the way down the path and between the trees.

Peter laughed. "Fire is the great equalizer. Nothing embarrasses a man more than the inability to start a fire, so I play it safe and avoid it."

"Sound reasoning," Ava said. "Look, you can see the lake already."

The trees became denser as the shore came into view. Broken branches and dead leaves crunched under their feet. Ava hopped over a row of nettles. Peter did the same, slipping as he landed.

"I saw that," Ava said.

"I did it on purpose. What's the plan down here anyway? Don't say you want to skinny dip."

"Out here? This water is gonna be freezing. But it could be fun."

Peter grabbed her arm. "Hold up."

Ava spun around. "Oh God, please don't say you're scared of skinny dipping."

"No, did you hear that?" There was a look in Peter's eyes, one she hadn't seen before.

"Hear what?"

"It sounded like rustling, and then a zip," Peter said.

"Pete, we're in the woods. Of course you're gonna hear rustling."

Peter looked back towards the direction they came. "It sounded like someone was messing with our tent. Didn't you hear it?"

"You heard someone messing with our tent? From here? Don't be ridiculous." Ava grabbed his hand and tried to continue on but he stopped her.

"I'm serious. I know that zip. My wallet is in there. What if there's someone there? Just let me check and then I'll meet you back here. I'll be thirty seconds, tops."

Ava flung her arms up. "Alright. Make it quick."

Peter rushed back up the dirt path, hopping over the nettles and disappearing between the trees. Ava turned back towards the lake and took in the view. She could hear its water droplets even from a hundred feet away. Up above her, nocturnal birds chirped their early morning songs. Ava dropped down onto the soil and crossed her legs, thinking that she could happily spend the rest of her life here. How did one go about getting a cabin in the woods, she thought?

Then Ava shot up.

She heard Peter shouting behind her.

But he was nowhere to be seen.

"Pete?" she shouted, squinting her eyes to see further up the path. She could barely make out ten feet in front of her before it dissolved into absolute darkness. "Pete? Did you call me?"

A chill came on the wind. Ava stood between a cluster of trees, praying that this was another of Peter's little jokes. Since the day they'd met, he was always doing stupid little things like this. On their first date, he'd texted her saying he couldn't make it minutes before they were due to meet. After Ava cursed him blind, he popped up behind her. She remembered finding it funny at the time, but the more she thought about it, the more she thought it was a dick move.

Ava went up the path back to the tent. She adjusted her vision to the darkness, and when she did, she almost tripped up in shock. "Pete, what the fuck...?"

The tent was open. Peter was lying inside with only his feet poking out. One of his shoes was missing. Just beyond the tent, a flurry of footsteps caused the sea of dead leaves to crisp and crackle. Ava jumped back in fear, noticing a blurry figure had manifested in front of her.

Small. Four legged.

Then laughing. Peter jumped out of the tent. "Boo!" he screamed.

Ava's heart almost thumped out of her chest. Her arms and shoulders froze in place from the sudden confusion and adrenaline and dread. Up ahead, a small fox scuttled away from them, brushing up leaves in the process.

"You bastard!" Ava screamed, kicking Peter in the shin. He recoiled back. "What was the point of that, you asshole?"

Peter's grin beamed. "Got you! Now who's scared?" he asked.

"Of course I was scared. I thought you were dead, you prick."

"Dead? What's gonna kill me out here?"

"I don't know. Wild animals. Heart attack. Anything."

Peter held his arms out for a hug. "I don't think you get wild animals out here, Ava. And I'm twenty-three. I don't plan on having a heart attack until I'm at least twenty-five."

Ava pushed him away. "No. I don't want to hug you. You messed me up. I don't know if you've noticed, but little tricks like this aren't my idea of fun. You need to learn to read the room." She threw her beer at his feet. Peter jumped back.

"I'm sorry, babe. Really, I just wanted to play a joke. You know? The woods, at night. Perfect time to get spooky."

"Shut up. I'm going back to the lake and I don't want you with me. Stay here."

Peter narrowed his eyes. "Seriously? I thought you'd laugh."

"Do I look like I'm laughing?"

"I don't know. I can't see you very well in this light."

Ava flung her arms out and turned around. Peter went to follow. Ava threw her palm in his face. "Don't bother. Stay right here. I'll be back in twenty minutes, and then you can find a way to make it up to me."

Peter sank back onto one of their camping chairs. "Oh yeah?" he asked.

"Keep dreaming," said Ava and walked away.

"I won't move out of this chair until you're back," he shouted. "Pinky swear."

Ava ignored him. She crossed the plants and vegetation and headed towards the lake again. Once Peter was out of sight, she breathed in and out deeply, consuming the crisp air and calming her nervousness. It was a shame, she thought. Peter was decent in every other way; she'd even go as far as to say he was perfect boyfriend material. But why did every guy she dated have some weird immature crutch? Why wouldn't they just be normal?

The serenity cleared her head and soothed her. Ava thought about the guy before Peter, the one who had a compulsion to scratch himself and make her sniff it. Yeah, that was a bad one. By comparison, she guessed Peter wasn't too bad, but there was no way she was putting up with these pranks, however harmless he thought they were.

A minute later, Ava realized she didn't have a drink because she'd launched it at her so-called boyfriend. "Damn it," she said, retracing her steps. A few sips of alcohol would greatly complement the lake view, she thought. She trod over the same ground again, back to the tent, quickly finding the dirt patches annoyingly familiar now.

Once there, Peter was no longer in his chair. Oh well, he'd probably gone to take a leak or something. She was sure he'd be back.

As Ava leaned down to grab another beer from the pile, she caught something in her peripheral vision.

Peter was inside the tent.

Moving. Convulsing.

"For God's sake. What now?"

He moved like a mouse trying to escape a trap. He rolled from side to side, clutching his stomach, unable to gain any momentum with his movements.

When Ava stepped closer, she saw the blood, black beneath the moonlight. Her beer exploded as it fell to the floor.

"Peter!" she screamed rushing into the tent. She knelt at his side, seeing now the deep laceration across his neck. Blood followed out in a thick stream, rendering Peter unable to speak or scream. All that came from his mouth were inhuman gargles. "What the fuck? What happened?"

Ava frantically searched around for her phone. She landed on her bag, ripped it open and furiously pulled everything out. "Where the fuck is my phone?"

Peter's legs violently shook. Ava turned to him, crying. She reached down and hugged him, smearing herself in his blood.

"Behind...you..."

Ava sprung up. Peter had whispered something to her with his last breaths.

"Talk to me, baby. Please talk to me." She let him go, grabbed her bag and tipped it upside down.

Nothing.

Peter's arm shot up. His index finger outstretched. Ava followed his line of sight.

That's when she saw the figure standing outside the tent. In one hand, her phone. In the other, a butcher's knife.

He threw the phone inside the tent, landing between Peter's legs. "No signal out here, anyway," he said.

CHAPTER FIFTEEN

She was back in Maine State Prison, back in the Red Zone. She stood between two glass cages, both of them occupied this time. To her right, she saw Ken Dark, but stripped of everything that made him her father. He wore an orange jumpsuit, resting against the cell bars with tears fit to burst from his eyes. He had that thick mane of hair but there was no soul to his presence, like someone had torn off his shell and removed the things made him real.

To her left was Tobias Campbell, grinning that crooked smirk that she'd been unable to cleanse from her mind's eye since the first time she saw it.

"I'm so glad you came, Agent Dark. Come closer so I can hear you better," he said.

Ella reached out and touched the iron bars, the first line of defense between her and the monster. As her fingertips caressed them, the bars disintegrated to nothingness. Suddenly, there was no protection between her and the man dressed in white.

"Closer still, Miss Dark, I have something for you."

Behind Tobias, Ella saw a small table with two chairs on either side. Tobias motioned with his finger for her to join him at the desk.

"Ella, don't go anywhere near him," her dad shouted from his cell. "He's going to kill you."

Ella jerked back. That voice, deep but soft, that she hadn't heard for over twenty years. But like an android programmed to do someone else's bidding, Ella disobeyed her father's command and continued onwards towards the fiend in the opposite cell. Ken retreated, accepting the defeat. Ella and Tobias took a seat opposite each other.

Between them, a chessboard appeared, already with Staunton pieces lined up at either end. She was whites, Tobias was blacks. "Tell me what's on your mind, Miss Dark," Tobias said. He kept his stare on her, not deviating for a second. "And please, ladies first."

She hadn't played chess in years but she used to be pretty good. She dangled her hand over the pieces, landing on the bishop. She moved it diagonally. It was a sacrificial move, something that would give her the advantage in three moves' time. "I'm dealing with a copycat," Ella said. "Of the Zodiac killer."

"Are you sure about that?" Tobias asked, bringing forward his first pawn.

"Positive," she said. "It's all there. The victims, the methods, the letters, the symbols. It must be." She took another glance at her dad who was fixated on them with penetrating eyes. She made her next move.

"There's a certain flattery in imitation, and yes, you're probably right. Your unknown subject is obsessed with the Zodiac killer, likely believing himself to his natural successor. Your father taught you to play chess, didn't he?" Tobias took his turn.

"Yes, he did. When I was 5. What do you mean, his natural successor? How do I find him?" Ella moved her queen.

"Judging by your bold bishop move, your father taught you to be immediately aggressive, didn't he? He taught you to open strong because he believed it provided better defense in the long run."

"What? I don't know. Tell me about this killer," Ella barked.

"Old habits die hard, as they say." Tobias moved his pawn, capturing Ella's unmoved king. "Checkmated by a pawn. How does that feel?"

Ella glanced at the chessboard in shock. Tobias's pieces were placed strategically across the board while hers had barely got out of the starting position. "What the…?"

"Not to worry. Chess clearly isn't your thing. How about poker?" A deck of cards appeared in Tobias's hand. The chessboard vanished. He threw the cards to Ella. "It's your deal."

Ella reluctantly handled the cards. She shuffled them, dropping several as she did. "Tobias, I don't want to play games. What can you tell me that will help me?"

"Miss Dark, we know the same information, yet I'm able to arrive at conclusions that you never could. Why do you think that is?"

Ella picked up the last slipped card and moved it held it between her thumb and palm. It was a natural reaction whenever she held a card, the side-effects of a magic trick she'd learned as a kid. "Because you and he think the same way. You have the same compulsions, the same need for power and sexual gratification. To you, it's natural. To me, it's something I have to think about."

"Your father taught you a magic trick, did he?" Tobias asked, nodding at the card in her hand.

"What? Yes. How did you…?"

"Show me," he interrupted.

Ella fiddled with the card. Her hands were shaking. Not ideal conditions to perform magic. "No."

Tobias placed his hands behind his neck. "Understood. In that case, I'll be keeping my thoughts to myself."

Without thinking, Ella placed the card between her index and middle finger and pretended to throw the card across the room. As she drew the card in, she clutched it with her thumb, hiding it from Tobias's view behind the back of her hand. She caught his gaze, hoping it would momentarily avert to the other side of the room.

It didn't. His stare was planted firmly on her hand, giving her no opportunity to knock the card into her lap.

"A simple palm and a failed lap," Tobias said with a disapproving shake of the head. "Pass the deck here."

Ella didn't want to but she was unable to control herself. She pushed the deck to Tobias's side of the table. He plucked one card out and held it between his thumb and forefinger, then took it into his other hand. The card vanished from sight, then appeared again in his original hand.

"The human brain is very simple to fool. We're predisposed to linear events, patterns, repetition. While you're looking at one hand, you miss what's going on in the other."

From Ella's side of the table, it looked like Tobias was vanishing a card and then plucking another one out of thin air. In actual fact, it was the same card every time. Tobias stopped and pointed to the card with his left hand. "It's called pattern recognition exploitation, and once you've established that pattern, the only way to fool onlookers is to break it."

"I know this. I know about misdirection," Ella said. "It's a core principle of psychology. You think I don't understand how you're doing that?"

"Of course you do," Tobias said, "it's very simple. But what happens next is where things get interesting." The card in his right hand vanished, then he opened up his palm showing it empty. The same card appeared in his other hand.

It caught Ella off-guard. She didn't know how he did that, but she wasn't going to admit it.

"Your unknown subject has already established a pattern. He's the Zodiac, and by now, he knows that *you know* that too. So, what do you think he'll do next?"

Ella didn't know. She'd asked herself that question countless times already. "It's impossible to know. How can anyone know? He's killed a lone woman, a couple, and abducted someone. How could I possibly predict what he'd do next?"

Tobias sighed and closed his eyes. He slammed his cardless hand on the table and made Ella jump back in fright. "Because I just told you," he said calmly. In his other hand, the card vanished again. When he lifted up his palm off the table, the card had returned. "The closer you look, the less you see, and that makes things *very* easy for this unknown subject. Do you understand?"

Ella had had enough. She hammered her fists down. "No, I don't!" she shouted. "Why don't you stop messing around and just tell me! I don't have time for your shit. People are dying out there and all you can do is talk about stupid magic tricks. Just tell me what I need to know so I can get the hell out of here!"

Tobias began to laugh. "Oh dear, have I upset you?"

Ella jumped up, knocking the table and the chair over.

"I told you, Miss Dark," Tobias continued. "While you're looking in one hand, you miss what's going on in the other. Misdirection is one thing, but pattern exploitation is completely different. You already know this subject understands the human condition to a high degree. He's established his pattern by mimicking the Zodiac, directing your attention exactly where he wants it. Then what?"

It took her a few seconds, then it hit her. "He's going to swerve us," Ella said. "He's going to strike somewhere we never expected him to. He's directed all the police officers to one area while he attacks somewhere else."

"Oh yes. And whose fault's that? What genius directed all those officers to that confined area?"

How did he do it? How did Tobias Campbell just know this information? She began to realize that she was in a realm beyond reality, lucid dreaming, perhaps. And even in here, this crooked monster was still able to make her feel more inadequate than anyone else had in her life. Years, no, decades of research to obsessive levels and she still couldn't out-think him. If only she could harness his skills for her own use, there was a chance she could solve this case before any more lives were lost.

Ella looked over at her father, still peering helplessly through the bars.

"Oh, and don't worry about your little friend over there," Tobias said. "I'll look after him. They haven't given me a cellmate in years."

She rushed to the Red Zone exit and hammered on the door for someone to let her out. No one came. Behind her, Tobias's footsteps sounded across the stone floor. She pressed herself into the wall to keep her distance, but Tobias moved over to Ken's cell instead.

He turned to Ella, still with the playing card in his hand. He made it disappear and in its place, a box of matches appeared. Ella banged on the door again, pushing the button, hoping it would someone jolt her from this dream state.

"Did you give Agent Ripley my love?" Tobias asked, now holding a flaming box in his hand.

Ella said nothing.

"No? Well, this is for her." He reached through the iron bars and pushed the box through the holes in the glass, sending Ken's cell into a fiery inferno. For the second time in her life, her father's dead body lay in front of her.

CHAPTER SIXTEEN

Ella awoke to the sound of banging. She shot up on her motel bed, still in the same clothes as the day before. The clock said it was 07:11.

This wasn't the Red Zone, nor was it Maine State Prison. She was safe in a secure building, far away from Tobias Campbell, but after that dream, she felt more vulnerable than ever before. She pushed herself off the bed and scraped the hair from her face. She tied it back with the scrunchy from her wrist. It took a few seconds for the details of her dream to come soaring into her consciousness. She couldn't remember it in full detail, only that Tobias had mentioned something about misdirection and pattern exploitation.

Bang bang bang.

Ella shook herself awake and moved to the door. She peered through the spyglass. Mia. She opened up.

"Ripley, good morning," rubbing the sleep from her eyes.

Mia was already dressed and make-upped. She had black suit pants and a jacket on with a white top underneath. "Morning, Dark, but I'm afraid it's not a good one."

"Don't say what I think you're going to say."

Mia walked past Ella into her room. She sat down at the dressing table chair. "You were right about one thing; our killer struck again last night."

Ella shut the door and followed, sitting on the edge of the second bed. "Oh God. Do you have the details? Was it at the beach?" she asked.

"No, it wasn't. He killed a couple out camping in the woods near Dixon Reservoir, about five miles away."

Ella dropped her head into her hands. Suddenly, Tobias's words rang clear in her mind. It all came surging back like a lost memory recovered through hypnosis. "Shit, I should have known. I should have guessed."

"A young guy and girl, both 23-years-old. He hunted them down in the middle of the woods and stabbed them both. According to the officer on the scene, it's a bloodbath."

Ella sat up straight and clenched her hands together. "Ripley, how could we not see this coming? This guy has us by the balls. With our expertise, how could we not have predicted this?"

Mia looked confused. "Dark, you always do this. You constantly blame yourself for the actions of unhinged psychopaths. No one on this earth could have predicted he'd strike in that location on that date. Murder is random. Serial killing is random."

If her subconscious was anything to go by, there's one person who knows, Ella thought. She wanted to reveal what she'd dreamt about but didn't want Mia to think she was crazy.

"He's playing us. He purposely misdirected us. I looked too closely and couldn't see the forest through the trees."

"What are you talking about?" Mia asked, checking her phone. "Denton is about to send me the coordinates for the crime scene then we'll make a move."

"This killer is obviously inspired by the Zodiac, and by now, he knows that we're aware of that fact. So he knew that we'd be scoping out that carnival based on the original Zodiac's crimes. All he had to do was strike elsewhere while we were so focused on that one location. I thought I was being smart by predicting his next step but he just swerved me, and so easily too."

Mia's face was a look of exhaustion, and Ella could help but match it through sheer frustration.

"Rookie, are you being serious? What were we supposed to do? Stake out every beach, lake and woods in California? There aren't enough cops in the world for that. Nothing that I, you, or anyone else could have done could have stopped this. How many times have I told you to stop blaming yourself for every single victim that falls into our laps?"

"I dreamt I was talking to someone," Ella blurted out. She didn't want to say his name to Mia. Quickly, she came up with a white lie. "You remember the copycat killer in Louisiana? The Mimicker? He told me that our unsub would misdirect us. He laid it all out for me. Why could he see it but I couldn't?"

Mia's phoned pinged. She checked it. "We're on. And rookie, dreams are your neural pathways making connections. They're a manifestation of your subconscious thoughts. It wasn't the Mimicker who told you that. You already knew it. You were probably just so exhausted that your rational mind didn't make the connection. You don't need me to tell you that."

Ella did know that but it didn't make the facts any easier to digest. She picked herself up, needing to see this new crime scene for herself. Somehow, she thought, it might bring her closer to understanding this unsub. "Give me a few minutes and I'll be ready," she said.

"Alright. I'll wait downstairs."

***

They drove as far as they could into the Dixon forestry and walked the rest of the way. At just after 08:30, they arrived at a nightmare scene that looked like something from a bad acid trip. Ella could see the blood and the organs from fifty feet away, quickly summoning a stream of bile into her throat.

Two uniformed officers stood before a string of yellow tape wrapped around a group of trees. Mia flashed her badge and one of the officers held up the tape for her and Ella to pass through. At the base of a redwood tree, the whole scene came to life in all its hideous glory. Ella's hand instinctively cupped her mouth and nose to keep out the foul odor.

"You'll be needing these," Officer Denton said, appearing from within a group of masked technicians. He handed them masks and latex gloves. "It's pretty bad, agents."

Ella decked herself in the protective equipment before seeing Mia pocketing her mask with a latex-covered hand.

"Not using it?" Ella asked.

"Don't need it. Death smells the same every time. What have we got?" Mia asked Denton.

They put on the equipment and made their way towards the bodies.

"Ava Jones and Peter Cromwell. Both twenty-three years old. We found their IDs in their wallets. They were camping out here last night. According to forensics, they've been dead for about seven hours. That puts the time of deaths between one and two AM."

"Who called it in?" Mia asked. "Pretty isolated out here."

"A dog walker found them this morning. We've checked him out. He's clear."

The gray tent was torn to shreds. Inside lay two bodies side-by-side, both mutilated beyond recognition. At Ella's feet lay a pile of beer cans beside some camping chairs. These brief glimpses into the couple's life filled Ella with a combination of frustration and despair. They were probably just young lovers searching for adventure, only to find themselves at the mercy of a sadistic maniac looking for his next high. It was a crushing thought.

Ella shut her eyes and tried to brush the feelings aside. She leaned down to inspect the first victim, Ava Jones, lying with jeans removed and hoodie zipped open. Out of the hole where her stomach should be, intestines draped out, reaching down to her knees. Her throat had been lacerated and the dried blood drenched her entire top-half. In her open mouth, Ella saw a pool of blood, still watery, sparkling in the sunlight.

"Shit in a flaming pile," Mia said, appearing at her side. "He's evolving. Fewer stab wounds but more brutality. And an obvious sexual motive given he's removed some of Ava's clothes. I can't imagine what these two went through."

Ella turned her attention to Peter. Still dressed, but the intense lacerations were visible through his jeans and t-shirt. Ella counted six stab wounds to his thighs and four to his stomach. The most significant cut, however, was to Peter's throat. There was an abyss-sized hole, with his throat having been torn from inside.

"You gotta be kidding me," Ella said. "He pulled the victim's throat out through his neck. This is sheer overkill. Way more brutal than anything the Zodiac did. What's happening to this guy?"

"Progression. Experimentation. He's got a taste for killing now. He's realized how much he enjoys it so he's pushing things a little further. What concerns me isn't the brutality, it's how he pulled this off."

"Agents," Denton interrupted, "we found something quite strange when we first arrived on the scene."

Ella and Mia stood up and stepped away from the tent. "No shit," Mia said. "This whole thing is strange."

Denton seemed to ignore her remark. He held up a plastic bag with a pair of scissors inside them. Beneath the dried blood was a hint of stainless steel on top of black handles.

"Scissors?" Ella asked. "That's new. Completely unique to this killer."

Mia took the evidence back from Denton and held it up to the sunlight. "These are garden scissors. Sharp as hell, but he'd have a hard time causing all this damage with just these. They were left inside the tent?"

Denton brushed back what little hair he had left. "Not quite. We found them in the female victim's hands."

"What? She was holding them?" Mia asked.

"Uh huh. The techs checked them out and there were traces of polyester on them. Bit odd, yes?"

Ella turned back to the bodies, trying to imagine a scenario that involved the victim's use of a pair of scissors. "Ava tried to escape the tent by cutting through it, maybe? He could have held her hostage in there? We know he incapacitates the male first, so maybe once Peter was out of the way, he toyed with her before killing her?" The thought of it made her sick with dread.

"According to the technicians, those wounds were almost certainly inflicted with a butcher's knife," Denton said.

"Judging by the jagged cuts and the blood spatter, I can't see it being anything less," Mia said. "I'm just trying to piece together how this whole thing occurred. How did he even find this couple?"

"Sheer luck, I'm guessing," said Denton. "People camp out here all the time."

Ella moved away from the tent and looked out at the distant lake, but all she could see in her mind's eye was the two dead lovers. She reconstructed the scene, imagining the torment they were put through simply because they dared to venture outside. Once again, the feeling of failure fell on her. Maybe if they hadn't been so focussed on one area, some patrolling officers might have caught whoever did this in the act. If they didn't find this unsub soon, who knew what he was capable of next?

"Stop thinking it was your fault, rookie," Mia said. She put her hand on her shoulder. "There's nothing we could have done to stop this. We're not responsible for the actions of these monsters. We just have to react to their madness. Unless you're a mind reader, this was unavoidable."

Ella had heard it a hundred times but even so, it never helped. "But we *are* mind readers, Ripley. We're supposed to get in their heads, figure them out, intervene and stop tragedies like this. Every time a new corpse falls into our laps, it's on us, right?"

Mia exhaled deeply out of her nose. "No, Dark. That's not how this works. If you can't understand that, then you need to decide whether or not you really want to do this job. And if you ask me, you're doing great; you just need to get it into your head that you can't save the world." She walked off, leaving Ella staring out at the lake. She glanced back, seeing the forensic technicians had returned to the dead bodies.

Two new victims. Still no closer to catching this unsub, or even understanding him. Ella only hoped that there was something here that hinted at who was doing this. The Zodiac evaded detection for five decades, and this perp was everything the Zodiac was and more. What if his legacy went the same way?

There was an infestation in her brain, of words and condemnations.

Criminal profiling is nothing more than a buzzword thrown around by those too afraid to get their hands dirty.

For someone who studies the so-called criminal mind, you certainly made some bad deductions.

A ringing phone echoed through the woods and briefly quenched the disparagements terrorizing her thoughts. Denton fiddled around in his pockets and found the source. He answered and stepped away from the scene.

"Dark, get over here," Mia called. Ella trudged back up the path. "We're missing something. What is it?" Mia asked.

Ella thought the whole thing through. Two victims. Sheer overkill. What else? "A clear M.O.?"

Mia put her hands on her hips and looked up and down the forest pathway. "No. He hasn't left his mark. For all we know, this could be an act of random violence by a different unsub entirely."

Then it clicked. "He needs to take credit for this," Ella said. "He was alone here. He didn't need to rush. Surely he should have left his signature?"

"Right."

Denton returned from amidst the trees still mid-conversation. He said a quick goodbye and returned to the agents. The look on his face said there was an advancement.

"Ladies, this isn't all. We got something else."

"We're all ears," Mia said.

"The San Diego Tribune just got something in the mail. Another letter. And a parcel."

Ella caught a quick glimpse of the male victim. The killer's frenzied attacks had cut his t-shirt to ribbons. Instinctively, she knew what Denton was about to say.

"He mailed some of Peter's bloody clothes, didn't he?" Ella asked.

"Got it in one. Come on, we need to speak to the journalists at the Tribune."

CHAPTER SEVENTEEN

Ella was astounded to find that not only had the newspaper offices received a letter from the killer, but it had been published online immediately. Ella glanced at her phone and read the news piece again. Minimal copywriting, just a picture of the bloody clothing, letter, and a full transcript.

"Are they expecting us?" Ella asked from the passenger seat.

"No, but that's not going to stop us," said Mia.

Dear Editor, this is the Gemini speaking. Thank you for printing my previous message in full, and now I trust we have a mutual understanding. Every time you receive a letter from me, you will publish the contents immediately. Failure to do so will result in excessive bodies for the blue meanies to clean up. My nightly bloodlust now overflows into my days and stopping myself is now impossible. No longer a sport for me, the act of killing is now a compulsion I cannot control. I will take more lives tonight, although I don't yet know who or where.

Below was another cipher, using many of the same symbols but a few additional ones, Ella noticed. At just after 10am, they pulled into a parking bay opposite the San Diego Union Tribune offices. A towering crystal skyscraper deep in the heart of San Diego, or the heart of darkness as Mia had called it multiple times on the drive over. Before stepping out, Mia withdrew her pistol, unclipped the magazine and placed it in her pocket.

"The hell are you doing?" Ella asked. Mia's face had fury written all over it.

"Two things I hate, rookie. California and journalists. One of the fucks inside that building has just given a serial killer a nationwide platform to peddle his shit, *without* consulting us first. When I meet him, I'll be tempted to put a bullet in him."

Ella nodded a gesture of understanding. "Makes sense. He's calling himself the Gemini. Another reference to the Zodiac. First, it's a-,"

"Forget that for now. We need to find the shithead who approved this for publication," Mia interrupted. They crossed the busy street and entered the newspaper offices through a gigantic revolving door. The foyer consisted of blinding white marble walls and floors, polished to gleaming perfection. "Jesus, looks like the sun is only the second brightest thing in the universe," Mia said as they approached the reception desk.

Under any other circumstances, Ella might have laughed. A blonde-haired receptionist rushed from polishing a glass cabinet and took her position behind the desk. "Yes, how can I help you?"

"FBI. We need to speak to the editor right now." Mia flashed her badge and Ella followed suit.

The receptionist checked something on her computer. "Sorry, Mr. Carter's in a meeting until midday. Would you like to come back-,"

"No, I wouldn't like to come back later. I'm sorry, sweetheart, but we're with the FBI. This is more important than anything your editor has to concern himself with."

The receptionist held Mia's stare for a moment. "Okay. Let me check. He's just in a side office down here." She skipped over to a glass door behind them and swiped a keyfob to open it. Ella watched where she went.

"Can you believe this moron?" Mia asked. "This is why I unclipped my mag."

A few seconds later the receptionist popped her head around the glass door, clearly trying to keep a safe distance. "I'm really sorry, but he says he-,"

"Screw this," Ella said, inheriting Mia's frustration. She stormed towards the receptionist, pulled open the door and walked into the corridor. Mia followed behind her.

"Excuse me? You can't go in there! I'm calling security," the receptionist yelled behind them. They ignored her. On either side, multiple doors led into spacious offices, and the glass partitions revealed their occupants without the need for intrusion. Ella peered into the room where the receptionist had dipped her head.

"In here," Ella said. Inside, about fifteen men and women in suits sat around a long white table, all peering at a gigantic monitor at the far end of the room.

Mia burst through the door without concern. Naturally, all eyes in the room preyed upon her. "Which one of you is Carter?" she asked with vigor in her tone.

The stares of the spectators gave away the man's identity as many of them glanced at the man at the foot of the table.

"I am," the man said, pulling up the sleeves on his shirt. He was of small stature, greased hair, shaped eyebrows. "Excuse me, but who are you to come barging in here? We're in a meeting."

"Not anymore you're not." Mia flashed her FBI badge. "Come with us. You have some explaining to do."

***

Raymond Carter's face shone bright red. Even behind the fake tan, his embarrassment was evident to even the most casual onlooker.

Ella and Mia had taken Raymond to the adjacent meeting room, away from the befuddled looks of the strangers in suits. However, Ella was certain some of them were trying to listen through the wall. The agents sat opposite him on a small white desk.

"Do you have any idea how much you've embarrassed me? Those men in there were executives from Apple. I'm going to sue the backsides off you."

Raymond Carter was the definition of sleaze, Ella thought. He had slicked brown hair, beady little eyes and two buttons undone on his striped shirt. The arrogance dripped off him like the sweat on his forehead. There was a British twang to his voice. Born in England, raised in California, she thought.

"Yeah, that's what they all say. You can't sue the FBI, champ. Our needs outweigh whatever bullshit you were talking about in there," Mia said.

Raymond stared at the ball of his thumb, not giving Mia the satisfaction.

"Mr. Carter, you published a news piece this morning that contained a message from an active serial killer." Ella this time, deciding to take control of the conversation before Mia said something she might regret.

"Yeah, I did. I gave the go-ahead. Who's asking?"

"We're asking. You need to consult us before publishing anything this person sends to you. You're endangering lives and giving a narcissistic psychopath the attention he craves."

Raymond laughed and tapped his fingers on the desk. "Sorry lady, but I can publish whatever I want, okay? You think I'm going to *not* publish something a murderer asks me to? I'm not stupid. If I do that, he might come for me. Better them than me. And how am I endangering lives? I'm endangering them if I *don't* publish it."

"No, it's just a threat to give him what he wants," Mia said. "This person is going to murder regardless of whether you publish his letters or not. These are pieces of evidence in a murder case and should be treated as such. They're not exploitative fodder to boost your sales."

Raymond waved his hand dismissively. "Well, judging by the clicks we've got, I'd say that's exactly what it is. We've made seven figures from his messages already. They've all been on the phone to me this morning. Coco Chanel, Microsoft, Home Depot, all begging for ad space on the same page. Ka-ching."

"You publish one more of his letters without consulting us first and you'll be arrested," Mia snapped. "And that money won't do you any good in jail, will it?"

"Yeah, whatever," Raymond said and looked out of the window beside him.

"How are these letters arriving to you, Mr. Carter? In the mail?"

Raymond scratched the back of his neck. It was obvious he was reluctant to reveal any further information. "No, actually. There's no stamp on them. The two we've had were both put through our mail slot."

Ella shot a look of surprise at Mia but she didn't return the gesture. Too busy controlling her reactions to this guy, she thought. "He's hand delivering them?" Ella asked. "That means he was here, right outside your building."

"Well, no," Raymond said. "Our mail slot is a big box at the side of the building. It's not on the front door."

"Still, CCTV might have caught him," Ella said.

"Afraid not. Some of our investigative journalists were quick to check that. This story has whipped them into a frenzy. The cameras don't catch the mail slot and whoever did this seems to know that. Pretty crazy, huh?" A smile formed on Raymond's lips but he quickly wiped it away. He seemed to enjoy this game of death.

Mia jumped up out of her chair and for a second, Ella thought she was going to reach across the table and slap the tan right off Raymond's face. Luckily, she didn't.

"We'll be setting up cameras around the mail slot," Mia said. "Discreet ones, from multiple angles. Any more letters arrive, you call us immediately, understand?" Mia threw one of her business cards on the table.

"Yeah okay, sure. Are you finally leaving me now? I'd like to say it was a pleasure."

"Oh no, don't be so optimistic," Mia said. "Agent Dark and I need to see these letters for ourselves."

CHAPTER EIGHTEEN

In the empty office, Ella cast an eye over the objects on the table.

One letter, two ciphers, two envelopes and a piece of bloody clothing in a plastic bag Ella. Mia and Raymond stood around them.

"This is everything we have," Raymond said.

"And you didn't think to immediately give this to the police, no?" Mia asked, pointing towards the bagged piece of clothing.

"I was going to, eventually," Raymond said.

Mia held up her palm in his office as if to say *get out of my face*.

To Ella, it was like being transported back in time. The letters were almost identical to the Zodiac's. A5 paper, slanted handwriting, black text, perfectly symmetrical grids. If they put the Zodiac's letters side-by-side with the now-named Gemini's, it would be difficult to believe they weren't written by the same hand.

"Okay, so what do you make of this, Dark?"

Ella scrutinized the first cipher. A ten-by-sixteen grid that had already been cracked. "His first correspondence was a cryptic message. No direct letter. That means he wanted to get the games off to a start right away."

"That, or he wanted to stand out from the other murder confessions the press get." Mia glanced at Raymond. "You get plenty, right?"

"Oh yes. All fake. Attention seekers."

"What made you pay attention to this one?"

"The lack of a stamp and the fact one of our journalists said he recognized the symbols."

"Another Zodiac nut, Dark. Can you fetch the person?" Mia asked. Raymond left the room without responding.

"But with the second correspondence, he sends a letter in plain English *and* a cipher."

"Well, he's said quite a lot in this written message, so he probably didn't want to slow down his momentum. If someone took a while to crack his code, the frenzy around him might die down. For a guy like this, that would be a real gut punch."

"In this one, he's spelled message as *messege*. In the first letter, he spelled it correctly," Ella said.

"And look at *killed* in the first message. Both times, he only used one *l*. In the new letter, he's spelled it perfectly fine."

"The original Zodiac misspelled words on purpose. He wanted to give the impression he wasn't smart to throw off the police. Could this guy be doing the same?"

"It's a possibility," Mia said.

Ella looked at the new cipher, much smaller than the first. Some of the same symbols were present; the half-colored circle, the triangle, the backward *K* and *P*. But there were some new ones in there too, including half-moons and the killer's own symbol.

"He's not saying much in this one," Mia said.

"I know, but what *is* he saying?"

The office door gently opened and a young gentleman walked in. Jet black hair, thick glasses, drainpipe trousers. He looked all of twenty one years old.

"Yes?" Mia asked. "We're busy."

"Oh, I'm sorry to interrupt. My name's Mike Owen. I'm a journalist here. Raymond sent me up."

Ella reached out and shook his hand so as not to scare him off. "Don't mind my partner. Mr. Carter said you recognized some of these symbols when this letter arrived. Is that true?"

"A little more than that. I was the guy who solved that cryptogram. I've always had a thing for puzzles so that was like crack to me. Don't mind the pun."

"You did? And so quickly too?" Ella asked.

"I had software to help me. All I had to do was plug those characters into the system and run a transposition cipher cracker. I got about six hundred thousand results, then I just filtered down to the ones with more than ten real words in them. That left about three hundred. Then I just went through and read them one-by-one."

"Wow, interesting." Ella was quite impressed. The original Zodiac had used transposition ciphers in his letters but he also added a few extra movements in there too. Sometimes, he would purposely shift words around, not to mention the original Zodiac made a lot of mistakes when transposing. "And it was all clear? No errors?" she asked.

"Nothing," said Mike. "It was all there in full. Oh, and I bagged up that piece of clothing for you. I didn't want anyone else here to get their prints on it."

"Well, thank you. I take you're familiar with the Zodiac killer, then?" Ella asked, more out of personal interest than professional.

"Sure am," Mike said. "Spent my college days trying to solve his messages. Never did though. But whoever's doing this isn't as smart as the original. Well, either that or he's way smarter."

"How do you figure?" Ella asked.

Mike pulled out a folded-up piece of paper from his pocket and waved it in front of her. "Because I solved his new cryptogram too. Same process. The original Zodiac used to throw in a few curveballs but this fella has military precision." He unfolded the paper and laid it on the desk. The agents inspected it.

I just got back from the lake of the dead. This was the most fun yet. I left the scissors with the girl because they will remind her of what she did once she's in the afterlife.

Ella read it over and over, looking for anything that might give a hint into this person's identity or pathology or anything that lead her to him.

There was one thing.

"What's he talking about, scissors?" Mike jumped in.

"We don't know," Ella lied, not wanting to give the journalist any ammunition despite his good intentions.

"Mr. Owen, thank you for this. You've done a fantastic job. Could you leave me and Agent Dark alone for a few minutes? We'll call you if we need anything."

Mike nodded his understanding and reluctantly left the room. Ella knew it must have killed him to not be privy to their conversation.

"So he wrote the letter before he murdered last night's victims, and then wrote the cipher afterward," said Mia.

"Looks that way," Ella said, desperately racking her brain to make sense of the link she'd made. "Lake of the dead. Scissors. He's playing a game with us, I just can't th-," Ella stopped herself mid-sentence.

"What are you thinking?" Mia asked, peering through the glass door to ensure no one was listening to them.

"Holy crap. Of course," she said, clasping her hands together. "He's not talking about the couple at the Dixon lake."

"Huh? He must be."

"Well, he is, but this little reference, *lake of the dead,* it's an old horror film from the fifties."

Mia stared at Ella blankly. "What's that got to do with anything?"

Ella leaned over the materials and scanned them as she explained. "The Zodiac referenced the Exorcist in one of his letters. This guy is also referencing an old horror film, but the question is…"

"It's kind of a stretch, rookie. If you ask me, he's just trying to make the lake murders sound even more sinister."

Another spark. There it was. Undeniable. "Oh my God. I just remembered, in the film the *Lake of the Dead*, a married couple goes camping. The woman goes insane and cuts her husband's throat out. With…"

Mia's suddenly perked up. Now Ella had her attention.

"A pair of scissors," Ella finished, realizing what this revelation suggested. Judging by the contortion on Mia's lips, she realized the same.

"That's why Ava was holding the scissors," Mia said.

Ella didn't want to say it. It was too harrowing a thought to speak aloud. Fortunately, Mia did it for her.

"Our unsub made her cut out her boyfriend's throat."

Both agents let the silence do the talking for a moment. Ella rubbed her eyes, desperately trying to cleanse the image of a hysterical young girl forced to massacre her own lover. "But this film isn't widely available, so we should definitely look into it. He might have watched it recently."

"Alright." Mia pulled her phone out. "I'm gonna call a few officers to bag this evidence up properly. We need to find out who's handled them. Once that's done, you and I are going to watch an old horror movie."

CHAPTER NINETEEN

Both agents returned to the San Diego PD building around midday. In their office, Ella pulled up everything she could about the *Lake of the Dead* movie.

"There's not a whole lot to say about this film," she said. "For a start, it's Norwegian. It came out in 1958. I've got a few screens from it but the full film is pretty difficult to find."

Mia slammed two coffees down on their desk. She collapsed into her chair. "Video stores? Rentals? Maybe there's a store round here that specializes in vintage horror films. California is full of niche shit like that."

Ella stopped scrolling and looked at Mia over her laptop screen. "Video stores? You mean like Blockbuster?"

"Blockbuster, Video Vision, Movie Gallery." Mia brought her coffee to her lips but stopped when she caught Ella's still-life glance. "What?"

"Ripley, those stores haven't existed for years. The last Blockbuster went out of business a decade ago. You're showing your age there."

Mia shrugged it off. "Well, shit. The times they are a-changin'. What do people do these days then?"

"Online streaming. Or piracy. Either way, there's no real way of finding this guy through either of those routes. Besides, I can't find any streaming platform that hosts this film. He either obtained it illegally or he watched the film years ago and remembered the details." Both agents fell quiet for a moment. Ella used the opportunity to pry. "What was the last film you watched?" she asked.

Before she could reply, Officer Denton peered his head around the door and dropped some papers on the desk. "Coroner's report from the recent victims. Fast-tracked," he said. "Thanks for paying a visit to the Tribune. We've butted heads with those guys plenty of times in the past."

"Thanks, officer. Jeez, the last film I watched was *Misery*," Mia said. "In the cinema."

Denton looked confused. "Eh?"

"Never mind," Mia said.

"In one of those classic film cinemas?" Denton asked. "We have loads of those around here."

"No, this was in about 1990," Mia said. "Ex-husband dragged me there against my will. Ironic, considering what the film was about."

Ella quickly perked up. "Whoa, hold on. Classic film cinemas. Why didn't I think of that?" She opened up a webpage and performed a quick search: *San Diego, classic horror, cinema, Lake of the Dead.* Her heart began to pound when she saw the first search result.

The Theatre Bizarre. An independent cinema dedicated to forgotten horror.

Ella clicked into the page and headed to the 'Showings' tab. A list of titles sprung up, some she recognized, most she didn't. *Nightbreed, Gaslight, Spider Baby, L'Inferno, Eyes Without A Face...*

"Shit, no Lake of the Dead," she said.

Mia came round and peered at the screen. "Well, it would be in the old listings, wouldn't it?" she said. "I'm no expert, but I doubt there are a million people clambering to see *Spider Baby,* so surely they just show films once and move on?"

Ella smacked herself on the forehead. "Of course. You're right." She clicked around the screen looking for previous showings but couldn't find a link. "It only shows upcoming films. Crap."

She scrolled down to the bottom of the page and found the contact details. Ella grabbed her phone and punched in the number. It rang three times... four times....

"Theatre Bizarre," a bored voice answered.

"Good afternoon, sir. I just have a quick question if you don't mind."

"Sure."

"Have you ever screened a horror movie called Lake of the Dead?"

The man on the other side laughed. "You missed your chance with that one, sweetheart."

Ella put the voice on speaker phone. "I missed it?"

"Oh yeah. We just played it last night."

Mia rushed to the other side of the desk and grabbed her car keys. "Tell him we're coming," she mouthed.

Ella got that tinge of elation she loved so much. There was no chance this was a coincidence. The killer had been in that cinema last night – she knew it. "Sir, I'm with the FBI. We need to come and speak with you."

***

The Theatre Bizarre was an old building in Cortez Hill, barely noticeable between a café and a liquor store. From the storefront, it looked more like a prop shop than an independent cinema. In the two glass windows on either side of the door were old movie posters for Dracula and Nosferatu.

Mia parked their car on the curb outside. They made their way into a small carpeted foyer with a couple of cheap sofas. At the head of the room was a small desk beside a tunnel leading to what Ella assumed to be the screening room.

"Hello?" Mia called out. Footsteps sounded through the tunnel. A gentleman appeared, looking like he'd come straight from the wilds of the jungle. He was a stocky gent, long curly hair glued to his scalp, a beard that was three months' overgrown. He wore a t-shirt with a huge Jason Voorhees mask printed on the front.

"Feds?" he asked. "Is that you?"

"That's us. I'm Agent Ripley and this is Agent Dark. You are?"

"Derek Riggs, the owner here. What's this about?"

We need to speak with you about a film you screened last night," Ella said.

"Yeah, *Lake of the Dead*," Derek interrupted. "What of it?"

"We're investigating a homicide in the area and we believe the culprit may have been inspired by this particular film. It's possible that whoever carried out this homicide was here last night."

Derek moved behind his counter and rested his elbows on it. "Inspired by *Lake of the Dead*? You know that film is seventy years old? He could have seen it at any point since 1958. It's not exactly a slasher film, either."

"We understand that, Mr. Riggs, but we can't brush this off as a coincidence," Mia said. "At least not yet. Do you have a list of customers who went to see that particular showing last night?"

Derek pushed his hair back with both hands and eyeballed his electronic till. "Afraid not. All of our customers pay in cash, and we don't exactly take roll call. I can tell you there were about fifteen people who came to that showing from what I remember. Your bog-standard horror buffs, one couple on a date, a few regulars. That was it."

"Anyone who stood out?" Ella asked. "Anyone who looked a little suspicious, anxious?" She checked around the room for cameras, seeing none.

"No one, but I wasn't really looking," Derek said. "Times are tough. I just make sure they pay the fee in full. I don't really pay attention to the clientele."

"CCTV?" Ella asked.

"I wish I could afford CCTV."

"Damn it. Will you be screening the film again?"

Derek shook his head and pushed himself to a standing position. "Not anytime soon. We only have one cinema screen and we rotate films daily. We might show it again in few months, but we wouldn't show it more than twice a year, especially a niche title like that."

"Mr. Riggs, could you give us the names of any regulars who attended the screening last night? That could be a great help," asked Mia.

"Totally. I'll note them down. You won't tell them I snitched, will you?"

"We won't," Mia said.

A good lead at last, thought Ella. She felt like the jigsaw pieces were finally revealing the true picture, and when it was all put together she'd be staring at the unsub. This move felt like a leap rather than a small step, and the excitement in her veins was stubborn and immovable. Even if one of the cinema regulars wasn't the killer, there was every chance that one of the regulars had conversed with him.

Derek grabbed a pen and paper and began scribbling. "How is someone *inspired* by this film, anyway? It's not exactly *American Psycho*."

"We can't reveal any more information, unfortunately."

Derek nodded as he wrote. "Fair enough. I hadn't seen it until last night myself. Well, I caught the last half of it."

"You hadn't seen it before screening it?" Ella asked, more out of personal curiosity than anything else.

Derek passed the small slip of paper to Mia. "No. But my projectionist hauled ass during the screening. Said he felt sick or something. He asked me if I could finish swapping the reels over so I caught the last half of it. Still, there's a first time for everything."

Ella and Mia wore the same look. "What time would this have been, Mr. Riggs?" Ella asked.

He chewed the tip of his pen. "Uhm... I wanna say about midnight. Maybe a little bit before. The showing began at ten-thirty, so yeah, probably about a quarter to midnight." Derek froze, the silence confessing Ella's thoughts. "You don't think...? No. No way. Not Matt. He's a diamond."

"We'll need his name and address," Mia said.

"Uh, address? All I've got is his name. I don't know where he lives."

"You don't know where your own employee lives?" Mia asked.

"Not his exact address. I know he's somewhere in East Village but that's pretty much it. Do *you* know your colleague's addresses?" he asked.

"Fair point. Just his name will do," Ella said.

Mia handed the paper back and Derek wrote down the details. Mia took it back and looked over the names. "You've been a great help, Mr. Riggs. One last question, what's this…" she checked the paper again, "Matt Striker like as a person?"

The question seemed to catch him off guard. He wrinkled his nose. "Pretty smart. Used to be in the military. He's got a quick temper but apart from that, he's golden."

"And he works here every night?" Ella asked.

"Oh, no. This is Matt's side job. He's a watchmaker by day."

"Interesting job," Mia said. "We'll check him out."

"Yeah, he works for a company called Gemini."

Before Derek could say any more, Ella had her hand on the door.

CHAPTER TWENTY

Outside the cinema, Ella refreshed her inbox as she waited for Striker's file to come over. Mia had called the FBI field offices in Los Angeles and had all of Striker's information sent to them.

Ella looked up from her phone and leaned against their car. She thought back to the coroner's report. "Time of death for both victims was between one and two AM. That would have given Striker enough time to leave the theatre, head out to the woods and commit these murders."

"It absolutely would," Mia said. "It would be a twenty minute drive, enough time to scope out a potential victim and attack. It's definitely plausible."

"I never asked what you made of his new moniker," Ella said. "The Gemini."

"I'm not surprised. The name itself? Not important. The fact he's assigned himself a nickname is a power move. He wants to control his own narrative. Even if the press or police assign him a different name, he'll always be known as the Gemini from here on out."

"It's got obvious links to the Zodiac too," Ella said. "There's the astrology link and Gemini can mean two or three depending on the context. The Zodiac was reportedly obsessed with both of those numbers."

A new email pinged in her inbox. Ella opened it up. "Got it."

"Same," Mia said. "Christ, this guy looks like a real deviant. Check out his history."

Ella scrolled to the second page. Matt Striker had no arrest history, but there was one thing that stood out on his report. "He was in a psyche ward," Ella said.

"Yup. Well, if that ain't something."

Ella scrolled through and landed on the wall of text. *Matthew James Striker (DOB: March 31, 1987) was arrested on July 14, 2017 and charged with assault and battery on his direct manager Rachel Hogan. Striker reportedly assaulted her as retaliation for her treatment of him during his tenure at Omega Watches Ltd, which he cited as unfair and unreasonable. Hogan pressed charges against Striker who was forced to undergo psychological evaluation at Hawkins Grove Mental Facility.*

"Shit, he attacked a woman because she treated him badly. We know it's the female half of the relationship he really wants during these couples-attacks. Maybe this is where his hatred of women stems from?"

"Could be," said Mia. "I'm just concerned he's got no history of violence prior to that. But still, everyone starts somewhere. Get your dancing shoes on because we're heading to his house right now."

Ella didn't need to get ready. She was always prepared to come face to face with a homicidal psychopath.

***

At the entrance to the Whitechapel apartment complex in East Village, Ella got lucky. As they exited their car and approached the door, one of the residents was on the way out. Ella grabbed the door and nodded her thanks.

"Number 65. Two floors up," Mia said. In the carpeted hallway, there was a lemony odor in the air. Whitechapel complex was quite pleasing to the eye, an unexpected development considering what they knew about Matt Striker so far. On the top floor, there were four doors. Matt's was at the far end of the corridor.

Ella lifted her hand to knock and then stopped herself. She moved her ear closer to the door. "Ripley, you hear that?"

"No, what?"

Ella held up her finger to the air, hoping it would magically silence the traffic coming from the street. "Listen. Sounds like...retching? You can't hear it?"

"Shit," Mia said, "you're right. Could be a struggle. He might have someone in there now. No time to waste." She lifted up her leg and slammed it into the door, sending it rocking on its hinges. She stepped back and did the same again, splitting the wooden frame with a deafening boom. The door burst open as the metal clasp on the lock shot out into the apartment.

They were in. "I'll lead," Mia hoisted her pistol and edged into the room. Ella wasn't licensed to carry a firearm in the field, at least not yet. She knew her way around a pistol but the legalities kept them out of her hands.

"FBI, freeze!" Mia shouted. She checked the corners and Ella followed suit. The apartment was a cozy, plush little place, with a spacious hallway leading into a lounge area. That was their first point of call, but there were no signs of life in there.

Suddenly, coughing, spluttering. Voices came from another room. Ella retreated and found them coming from behind a second door in the hallway. "Ripley, in here," she shouted as she gripped the handle. She nodded one, two...

She pulled it open on the third count. Mia pointed her pistol at the source of the inhuman sounds. Ella let go of the door and peered around.

"Err..." she said. "Hello?"

A man in a blue robe sat on the bathroom floor, his hands shaking as they gripped the toilet seat. His vacant eyes traced the detectives, looking like a terrified deer caught in a snowstorm. His lips glistened with excess vomit, a dark shade of yellow. No words came from his mouth.

"Mr. Striker?" asked Mia.

After loosening his grip on the lavatory, he nodded, still looking as though he was awaiting execution. "Yes. I'm Striker," he said through shaky tones.

"Are you okay?" Ella asked.

"What is this? Why are you in my home?" Striker picked up a towel and wiped his face. Ella didn't address the fact he wiped his vomit and his forehead with the same cloth.

"Uh, this might be a misunderstanding," Ella said. Back came the familiar surge of disappointment, but Ella had to consider that the unsub they were chasing was highly intelligent. Could Striker simply be playing the part of an innocent man?

"I'm ralphing," Striker said. "Did you say FBI? The hell do you want with me?"

"You know what, we're going to wait in the hallway," Mia said. She motioned for Ella to join her and they left Striker to clean up. The two agents didn't say a word while they waited, instead using the opportunity to glance around the man's living quarters. It all seemed quite high brow, with tasteful art decorating most of the walls. Ella had a quick look for a writing table or a computer, finding neither.

Finally, the bathroom door clicked open. Matt Striker stood there, drenched in sweat. He pulled his robe around his naked torso. "Mind explaining?" he asked.

"Mr. Striker, I'm Agent Ripley and this is Agent Dark. We're with the FBI. We'd like to speak to you about an incident last night."

"An incident?"

"A homicide took place near Dixon Reservoir. We're wondering if you know anything about it."

"What? A homicide? Are you out of your mind? Why the hell would you think *I* had anything to do with a homicide?"

Ella watched for the micro-signals. Matt Striker displayed authenticity from top to bottom. The fact he said the word homicide twice suggested he wasn't trying to hide anything. Either that, or he was very confident he could fool her and Mia. He didn't blink rapidly, he didn't put any psychological barriers between them and himself. So far, not good.

"We believe our perpetrator was inspired by a film entitled *Lake of the Dead*. You acted as a projectionist for this film at a local cinema, correct?"

"Yeah, because that's my job. One of my jobs."

"And you left this showing early, just before midnight last night?" Mia asked.

"Because I was about to wretch up my organs, that's why. It didn't have anything to do with no murders. I came straight home last night, onto that toilet and didn't move for about two hours. That good enough for you?"

"Can anyone verify this?"

Matt ran his hand through his hair, soaking it with sweat. His face burnt bright red. "Yes, actually. My neighbor saw me, just after midnight. She was out front walking her dog. We said hello. She lives on the next floor down."

"We'll be checking, Mr. Striker. And we're sorry about your door. We'll arrange a new one to be put in place today."

Ella moved over to the front door, or what remained of it, and did her best to put it back to an acceptable position. It dangled limply in the frame, then slowly swayed open. No luck. She turned back and apologized.

"A couple of things before we leave you," Mia continued. "You're a watchmaker by day, correct?"

"Yes," he said, clearly frustrated at his lack of privacy for the next few hours. "For Gemini Watches. Why?"

"Just curious. And at night you work for the Theatre Bizarre? What hours do you work?"

"I'm a contractor for Gemini. I'm not needed there every day. But I work at the Bizarre every night from eight PM until one AM. I have Sundays and Mondays off."

Ella knew why Mia was asking. This meant that Matt Striker had a solid alibi for all of the murders and Amanda's abduction. The more he spoke, the more clear it was that he wasn't their unsub. And so the stabbing disappointment returned, somersaulting inside Ella's stomach and taking their investigation right back to square one.

"Did anyone stand out in the audience for *Lake of the Dead* last night?" she asked, desperately searching for a lead of any kind. "Anyone who looked a little odd? Maybe someone you've never seen before."

Matt shrugged. "I don't see the patrons. I spend all of my time in the projector office. All I see is the backs of their heads."

Ella had nothing else to ask. "I'm out of questions. Ripley?"

She conceded. "Nope, let's get out of here. Thanks for everything, Mr. Striker."

Dead end. This killer was still out there and they were no closer to finding him. For all they knew, he could have been planning his next attack, and even with all Ella's knowledge of the Zodiac, pinpointing his next move was next to impossible.

CHAPTER TWENTY ONE

Ella looked out of the glass partition in her office at the mass of police officers going about their business. Behind her, Mia shut the window blinds, keeping out the afternoon sun and casting the room a dark shade of orange.

The darkness turned her mind to the recent horrors: Amy Evans's mangled corpse on the roadside, the dead lovers in their vehicle, the forest massacre. It was Ella's job to stop the person who'd committed these atrocities, and so far, all she knew was that he was obsessed with the Zodiac and that he was confident and capable. Nothing more. The frustration was beginning to mount, and she feared that more bodies would come before she could intervene. Even worse was that the killer had displayed an appetite for brutality that was growing with every crime scene.

There's nothing systematic about the act of murder. Killing is the rope across the spiritual abyss, between man and his failed aspirations.

Tobias's comments invading her thoughts again, putting the exclamation point on her failures. She thought about him up in Maine, wondering if he had the information she had, would he have figured out this unsub already? Could he see this killer in his head, understand him, calculate his next move?

She turned to Mia, sitting with the recent coroner's report in her hand. "Ripley, what can we do? This guy is eluding us. We have six victims, one of whom is alive, and we're still no closer than we were when we started."

"Dark, it's barely been two days. Stagnation happens. Cases can go cold for months, years, decades. Things can take time to become clear. We've put a curfew out. We've widened the patrol area. Anyone who's out after dark is going to wind up in the cells."

The curfew was a new idea, and a good one at that. But to a predator like this, Ella doubted it would stop him. "What if he's out there right now? What if he's already got someone in mind? Given how fast this guy is working, it wouldn't surprise me."

"And we're doing everything we can to stop that from happening. And you know what? Fretting about it isn't going to stop him, is it?"

Ella stared at her phone. There was a text from Ben. Again, she'd forgotten to message him the day before.

Hey, just wanted to see how things were going over there. Can't wait to see you when you get back x

And like the explosion of flames, an idea invaded her head. She might not know much about this killer, but there was one person who might.

Could she? Was it crazy? Or was it a constructive tool that she'd be foolish not to use?

"Dark?" Mia asked, jolting her back to life.

"Huh?" she realized she'd been lost in her thoughts. "Sorry. Yeah, you're right. I'm being defeatist. I guess I'm still a little exhausted from everything. God knows how many dead bodies I've seen over the past two weeks. It's all starting to blur, to be honest," she said, half-lying.

"I told you, this stuff takes its toll. You might feel fine one day, but it can all come crashing down on you like a sack of shit the next. Take a break. Take the night off if you want. Go back to the hotel and have phone sex with that boyfriend of yours."

"He's not my boyfriend," Ella replied quickly, "but a quick break could be good. I might go for a walk and get a latte or something."

Mia shut her laptop and grabbed her coat. "Good idea. I could use some air too. There's nothing quite like a walk around the city at rush hour."

The crazy idea vanished as quickly as it arrived. It was stupid to even think it would be an option. She was desperate, but she wasn't *that* desperate.

"You'd be surprised what getting away from it all can do," Mia said. "When you let your mind relax, it makes the connections for you. As is the beauty of the subconscious."

Ella picked up her jacket. "Alright, let's see what we come up with."

***

He crossed the road to avoid a group of youths along Broadway. Usually, he'd curse them under his breath, with their noise and bad language and juvenile capers, but everything was different now. He was on top of the world, a master of life and death, an unstoppable machine that had broken free of society's bonds. No one else he'd passed on his journey to the store even came close to what he was capable of. Now, he found himself studying the people he came into contact with daily, imagining how they'd look as they drew their final breaths. Would they beg? Would they defy his power with a middle finger? Would they accept their fate as pawns in his game of death? He'd discovered that people revealed their true selves when death was imminent. The bitch in the car had fought with might she probably didn't know she had. Meanwhile, the girl in the forest couldn't butcher her boyfriend quick enough in a futile attempt to save herself.

He passed by a hardware store and ogled the hammers and saws in the window. Just the sight of them was enough to get his blood pumping, imagining the kinds of torment he could inflict with such sturdy equipment.

But no, the knife was enough. If it was good enough for Zodiac, it was good enough for him. And besides, the knife was a substitute for sexual organs, or so they believed. As far as he was concerned, they could carry on believing it.

Those poor police, how frustrating must it be for them. He pictured a bunch of uniformed officers, sitting at their desks brushing up on Zodiac lore, and that just made everything so much easier. He knew where they were looking and what they believed might happen next, so all he had to do was do the opposite. He wished he could have seen their faces when they first discovered the young couple at the lake.

Did they really think they could put a halt to his activities by setting up a curfew? Did they honestly believe that taking down his cipher off the Tribune site would do anything? Short of capture and execution, it was foolish to believe that they could do anything to stop him now. He was too far gone into this game of death, too involved. The next victim would come when the stars aligned, and unluckily for that poor bitch, that night would come soon.

She was an easy target. He already knew everything about her. He knew her name, address, workplace, relationship history, social security number, even her favorite clothing stores. The only hardship was making it look like it was all random.

Nothing was random; it was chaos theory gone rogue.

Along Broadway, he came to a coffee shop. An adorable little establishment with a cute canopy beneath which the filth and the vermin drank and gossiped. He had no doubt that at some point in the past few days, his name had cropped up in conversations amongst the rabble. There, he saw a couple of women exit the store with drinks in hand. One older, one younger. The older one was a little too tall, too muscular. She looked like she could put up a fight.

But the younger girl, with her cute glasses and white sneakers, she looked like a treat. What he wouldn't give to run into her alone one night. No doubt she'd beg for mercy right before he thrust a knife into her abdomen. A pleasurable kill in every sense.

Inches away from her, she didn't even look in his direction. She walked right past, chatting to her friend about God knows what. He watched them disappear down the street, enjoying the brief high his daydream provided.

Oh well, there would always be others. Behind the coffee shop, he watched the sun descend. Nightfall was only a heartbeat away and that meant hunting time grew closer. But before that, it was time to contact the press again. He'd already drafted up the next letter in his head. He just needed to get home and put pen to paper.

And since they'd disrespected him by removing all mention of the cipher off their website, he needed to take things to the next level.

CHAPTER TWENTY TWO

Ella felt better after getting away from the stuffy office. She'd texted Ben back and loaded up on high quality caffeine. A few thoughts came to her during her time out, but as she sat back at her laptop, she realized they were futile.

Organize another showing of *Lake of the Dead* at the cinema? No, it was too obvious. Their unsub would see right through it.

A press conference to state they *weren't* dealing with a Zodiac copycat? An attempt to diminish his comparisons to the infamous killer, possibly drawing him out of the woodwork? No, it could put innocent lives in danger. Ella was happy to put herself at risk, but there was no guarantee he'd come for her. Instead, he might take his frustrations out on a proxy.

Everything was no different than before she left, only staler. She dropped her head into her hands and peered at Mia through the cracks in her fingers. "Ripley, what do we do when the trail goes cold? What do *you* do?"

Mia was leaning against the window typing on her phone. "I fend off questions from Edis, just like I am now. Aside from that, I drink. But that's just me. And it hasn't gone *cold,* so stop saying that. We have the CCTV cameras being set up around the Tribune and the theatre. We have officers checking out the names Derek gave us. We have forensics checking for prints on the piece of clothing, okay?"

As if on cue, one of the officers knocked on their office door. Ella didn't recognize him. Or at least, she hadn't spoken to him since her arrival here. She waved him to come in, praying it was good news.

"Agents, I've got something you might want to see," the officer said.

"Oh?" Mia asked.

"Yeah. Well, I'm not on your case but I just ran across this. It popped up online literally a few minutes ago." The officer walked between the agents and held out his phone screen. "This is your guy, right?"

"That son of a *bitch,*" Mia shouted, slamming her hand against the wall.

***

Ella really didn't want to get in the car with Mia, and judging by how she was driving, she'd been right.

Mia commandeered a police cruiser to cover the ten miles between the precinct and the San Diego Union Tribune building. Vehicles parted for them, and even so, Mia sped through the swarm like a comet through the sky. It took less than fifteen minutes to get there, even in early evening traffic.

They abandoned the car outside the building and rushed inside, Ella doing her best to keep with Mia's inhuman pace. Into the blinding foyer, there was no receptionist to open the security door. The only soul in there was a sweeping janitor.

"Buddy, open this door for me," Mia shouted.

The janitor looked up from his duties and lowered his cap. "Can't do that, missy. Not allowed to let strangers through there."

Mia breathed out heavily. In one hand, she pulled out her badge. In the other, her pistol. "Buddy, I'm a Fed, and I'm about five seconds away from shooting this door to pieces. Either let me through, or you'll have a lot more shit to clean up."

The janitor dropped his brush and scuttled over. "Well, why didn't you say you were the fuzz?" he said. He pulled up his lanyard from his pants and scanned them in. The red tag beside the door switched to green.

"Thank you," Ella said as Mia stormed through. "Do you know where Mr. Carter is?"

"Third floor, but I didn't tell you that."

"Gotcha. Thanks." Ella caught up with Mia. "Third floor."

They ascended a staircase wider than an ocean, taking three steps at a time and reaching the third floor in a matter of seconds.

"Carter," Mia shouted. "Where the fuck are you?"

Fortunately, the offices were mostly deserted save for a few late-night workers. Ella saw a few faces peering out of the doors to see who was making such an intrusion.

Then Ella saw him, his olive skin unmissable in the fluorescent light. He retreated back upon sight, but it was too late. "Ripley, in here," Ella called. They turned the opposite direction along the corridor and came to a vast, lavish office with a mahogany desk. Standing at the window was Raymond Carter, fumbling as he tried to shut the window blinds.

"Not so fast, buddy." Mia thrust open the door so hard it bounced off the wall. "You did it again? What did we tell you this morning?"

Raymond escaped behind his desk, wrongly believing it might give him an ounce of protection from the oncoming onslaught. "I'm the editor. I can do what I like."

"No, you can't. You've committed a serious offense, and endangered the lives of everyone in this city."

On Raymond's desk, Ella spotted it. The new letter. She rushed over and grabbed it, pushing away Raymond's hands as he tried to stop her. She stepped away from the altercation.

Dear Editor, this is the Gemini speaking. You have disrespected my honour by removing my last letter from your page. This behaviour is unacceptable and your city will be punished accordingly. My kill rampage must continue.

Below them was another cipher, only three lines long.

Ella laid it down on a nearby bookshelf while Mia and Raymond's voices mingled behind her. She zoned them out and focused on the letter contents. The killer must have been keeping an eye on the news cycle to know that his piece had been removed. He was clearly a narcissist, basking in the attention of a worldwide audience. And here was Raymond, willingly giving it to him.

Disrespected my honour.

Strange choice of words, especially as, until now, the killer had displayed no signs of craving respect. He was committing these murders because he enjoyed the sexual thrill and the sensation of power from terrorizing a city. If anything, he wanted the people to despise him. It only made the hunt better.

But then Ella noticed something else.

Honour.

She scanned everything again, noticing a pattern.

Behaviour.

Behind her, Mia was threatening to arrest Mr. Carter, and was probably searching for some kind of legal grounds to do so, Ella thought. But she ignored them and returned to the note. She grabbed her phone and pulled up a picture of the previous letter. She compared them side-by-side. The handwriting was similar, but a few of the letters looked a little off. The pen used to write this new letter was thin, ball-point, whereas the last had been closer to a felt-tip.

Something was off.

She checked for spelling errors, finding none. In a note that contained the words *disrespected, behaviour, unacceptable, punished* and *accordingly,* this killer would have at least spelled something wrong on purpose to throw them off.

And then there was the cryptogram. Not only was it badly-drawn, but it was attached to the same piece of paper as the English message. The Zodiac only did that once in his whole reign, and even then it was a very short cipher.

"You can't arrest me. You have no grounds to do so," Raymond screamed. Ella turned around to find him backed up against the far wall with Mia leaning over his desk.

"Yes we can," Ella said, waving the note at him. "Ripley, who do you know spells honor with a *u*?"

"Huh?"

"Look at this." She showed Mia the contents. "*Honour. Behaviour.* They aren't the American variations of the words. Who spells these words with a *u* in them?" she asked again.

Mia caught her eye. "British people," she said.

Right then, Raymond Carter fled from behind his desk, out of the office and into the corridor. His blurry figure passed by the glass panels, followed closely by Mia's. Footsteps thundered down the corridor as Ella joined the chase, and by the time she was halfway down the hallway, both runners had turned the far corner. Ella followed the sounds and found Mia standing alone.

"Where's he gone?" Ella asked.

"Shit knows, but he can't have got far. Keep looking. I'm going to guard the stairway."

There were a row of office doors, all with their window blinds closed. Ella tried the first door. Locked. She moved on down the row, finding the next door open. Inside was a woman sitting behind her desk, clutching it in fright.

Ella didn't quite know what to say. "Raymond. Seen him?" she asked.

The woman shook her head rapidly. Ella returned to the corridor and continued onward. Suddenly, something rattled from another room. She pursued it, narrowing the sound down to two doors to her left. She pulled at the first and heard the metal bolt clink against the lock.

But as she did, there was another boom from inside. She rattled the door again to alert the occupant of her presence. "Raymond, you're not getting out of here without us noticing," she shouted. "Ripley, in here," she called up the hallway.

No response from either, so Ella did the only thing she could. She took a few steps back, put her weight on her leg, then kicked the door with all her might. The high ceilings above nurtured a satisfying echo upon impact, but the door remained in place. Two more kicks followed, the sheer force sending a shockwave of pain through her leg.

For reasons unknown to her, she suddenly pictures Tobias Campbell's face. She heard those slimy tones again, navigating her way through her ear canals against her will. The invasion summoned a newfound power, injecting her with new life and new fortitude. The next kick collapsed the door, disintegrating the lock and bringing a small storage cupboard into view.

And up in front of her was Raymond Carter, half of his body hanging out of a tiny window, gradually shimmying lower. Before Ella could rush inside, Ripley appeared beside her and took over. Ella followed and both agents grabbed what remained of Raymond. The window offered only a tiny opening, and no doubt Raymond had to contort himself to make any headway. Ella clutched one arm, Ripley the other, while Raymond kicked in a lame attempt to free himself.

"Buddy, you want to fall three floors to your death?" Mia shouted as she grappled with him.

Muted grunts came in response. Raymond began to slip from their grip, and the best case scenario was that he landed on his feet and shattered his legs to dust. Worst was that he died, taking his answers with him.

In panic, Ella grabbed the raised window and slammed it down, trapping Raymond against the ledge. Raymond screeched in what Ella assumed to be agony given the impact on his spine, but it kept him in place nonetheless. Mia wrapped her arm around Raymond's head and furiously hauled him in with Ella's assistance. His wriggling body reached the cupboard and he and Mia landed on the ground. Ella slammed the window shut and joined Mia in standing over their new suspect.

Raymond Carter remained silent, breathing heavily like a wounded animal. Ella didn't have the time or energy to stand on ceremony. Mia snapped the handcuffs on him in a swift motion.

"Mr. Carter, you wrote that letter, didn't you?" Ella asked.

CHAPTER TWENTY THREE

Ella kept a watchful eye on Raymond Carter through the two-way mirror. He'd been sitting alone inside one of the interrogation rooms for almost half an hour. His hands were cuffed together by a foot-long chain that ran through a loop at the center of the metal table in front of him. The table and the chair he was sitting on were both bolted to the floor.

Leaving a suspect waiting in an interrogation room was a common psychological technique that offered two advantages to the agents. The first was that it made the suspect anxious, meaning they'd be more likely to make mistakes during their interrogation. Secondly, it gave them a chance to observe their movements and body language. Sometimes, law enforcement got lucky and the suspect, when left alone for any significant amount of time, would say something to themselves. Guilty and nervous suspects tended to rehearse what to say.

Mia and Denton appeared beside her. "He's been pretty calm since he got in there, no?" Denton asked.

"Yeah, but he's not our killer. He's just a scumbag. But he knows something we don't and we need to extract it from him," Mia said.

"What gave it away?" Denton asked.

Ella pulled the 'new' letter from her pocket and showed it Denton. "He's used Britishisms. He's spelled *honor* and *behavior* with a *u* in them. Ironic, considering he's a freaking newspaper editor."

"Old habits die hard," Mia said.

"Carter's a new guy in town," Denton said. "He just came over from working at some newspaper in England. He's only been in America a year or so."

"You can tell. He's the only person in California who uses fake tan," Mia said. "Anyway, let's see what he knows. Denton, keep an eye on him from here, will you?"

"Will do."

Ella and Mia entered the stone cold interrogation room. Raymond Carter did his best to inspect his fingernails but the shackles made it difficult. The two agents took a seat opposite him.

"Mr. Carter, you know why you're here," Mia said. "Do you have anything to say for yourself?"

Raymond said nothing. He tapped his fingers on the table in a rhythmic fashion.

"Let me guess, you're pleading the fifth," said Mia. "Very well, we'll get this over with quickly." She dropped a brown folder on the desk.

"I'm not saying anything until my lawyer gets here," Raymond interrupted. "And I've got one of the best around."

"Good, because you'll need that lawyer when we detain you on suspicion of murder. If you didn't forge this note, then I'm inclined to believe that *you* are our perpetrator, Mr. Carter."

Ella saw a brief flicker of worry on Raymond's face. His eyes twitched, his nose wriggled. She knew it was very unlikely that Raymond was responsible for these murders and that Mia was just baiting him to reveal the truth.

Mia opened up her folder and threw a photo across to Raymond. "See that? Amy Evans, 23-years-old. Butchered and left on a roadside. Amy and her mom were about to move out of the slums to somewhere nicer, but you took that away from her. Now, her mom has to stay put, and with a dead child to boot. How do you feel about that?"

Raymond said nothing. He kept his stare down.

"What about this couple right here?" Mia continued, placing the next picture beneath Raymond's nose. "Max and Zoe. Two young lovers just looking to spend some time together, now they're fertilizing daisies because some loser couldn't keep his urges in check. Did you have anything to do with this?"

No response. Ella was trying to gauge Raymond's body language but he seemed to keep himself calm, even with the images of mutilated bodies in front of him. It was only when the threatened with the possibility of imprisonment did he show a hint of concern.

"No? Then take a look at these pictures, Mr. Carter." Mia pulled out the crime scene photos of the lake murders. "Ava and Peter. Another young couple. They went camping in the woods last night. Ava woke up with her large intestine leaking out of her stomach. Peter had his throat extracted while he was still alive." She hammered her finger on the pictures. For the first time, Raymond glanced at them, but then turned away in disgust.

"I don't want to see that."

Mia laughed. "Don't want to see it? Raymond, you *did* this. Just admit it and you'll save yourself a lot of hassle."

Raymond shuffled in his chair, clinking the metal chains at his feet. "You really think I committed these murders?"

Mia turned to Ella, prompting her to take over. She improvised.

"Yes, Mr. Carter. You certainly fit the criteria. Judging by what little reaction you've had to these crime scene photos, chances are you're high on the psychopathy scale. No remorse, no guilt, reckless, selfish. A lot of psychopaths tend to hold positions of power too. Like newspaper editors."

"That's it? That's all you got?" Raymond asked.

"Oh no," Ella continued. "That poor woman you abducted, Amanda Huber. She's outside the room right now." Ella pointed to the two-way glass.

"And? I just ran the story. I've never seen her in my life."

"That's not what she said. She said she recognized you. Same height, same accent as the man who abducted her. That's why you shouldn't leave a living witness, right? Because they've seen your true nature."

Tobias's words again. Ella suddenly felt dirty, like she needed to spit.

"And if that wasn't enough," Mia jumped in, "there are the letters. The first two didn't have any British spelling variations in there because there were no words that differed from American. But in the most recent one, you've slipped up twice. I'm afraid your heritage has been your undoing."

"And you couldn't be looking for *another* person of British origin, no? That thought never crossed your mind?"

"Of course it did," said Ella, "but we believe in statistical probabilities. A British serial killer in California, passing letters to another British person in California? Pretty unlikely, isn't it?"

Mia waved her hand at the two-way glass. She gave a thumbs-up. "Looks like we've got everything we need. This seems pretty open and shut to me. Mr. Carter, you might want to tell Apple that your little deal is off." Mia slid her phone across the table. "Better tell them yourself before they read about your arrest in a newspaper. A better newspaper."

Only then did Raymond's mask begin to slip. Ella saw him weighing the options in his head. Any second now, the cracks would show, and they could get their claws in and rip them open. Raymond leaned his head forward and scratched his nose on his shoulder. "Fine, but I want impunity," he said.

Mia looked nonchalant. "Impunity from what?"

"Any punishment. Give me impunity and I'll tell you everything, as long as my name is kept out of everything."

"That depends on what you're going to tell us, buddy. If you confess to murder, we can't exactly waive a prison sentence. We could exempt you from death row, maybe."

"Look, I didn't murder those people, alright? I had absolutely nothing to do with this…"

Ella suspected more was forthcoming. Both she and Mia remained silent, waiting for Raymond to fill the uncomfortable silence himself.

"I did one thing. One stupid thing. That was all. I swear to God."

"And that was?" Mia asked.

"The new letter. I wrote it. This is a media sensation and I'm capitalizing on it."

Mia dropped back in her seat and shook her head in despair. She looked at Ella as if to say *can you believe this guy?*

"You put lives in danger, Mr. Carter. How do you think the real killer will react to a forgery?" Ella yelled. "Once he sees this, he's going to be pissed, then he's going to take his frustrations out on a stranger. You did that."

Raymond raised his shoulders, looking like he was about to raise his hands up in a *what you gonna do?* motion. The chains kept him from doing so. "I'm sorry, but this is too good an opportunity to pass up. This lunatic chose my newspaper as his podium and I want to milk it dry. The clicks have never been this high. We're making hundreds of thousands by the hour."

Ella had to think soothing thoughts. She imagined herself back in Virginia, sitting near the river on a winter morning with the birds singing and the ducks quacking. Anything to stop her from reaching across the table and rearranging Raymond Carter's face. No doubt the real killer had seen the fake message by now. He was probably planning his retaliation as they spoke.

"I'm disappointed," uttered Mia. "Just when I think humans can't get any more stupid, or desperate, or pitiable, you come along and lower the bar even further."

Raymond didn't seem to take kindly to the criticism, but Ella saw he held himself back from rebutting. Probably to ease his punishment.

"So, am I off the hook?" he asked.

Mia considered it. "We should charge you on forgery, but providing you're completely honest with us, and we mean *completely* honest, we can overlook it. Is there anything else?"

"Promise me that there won't be any mention of my arrest anywhere, and I have one other thing for you."

Ella wondered where this would end. How much did this guy actually know?

"Done," Mia said.

Raymond took in a deep breath before confessing. "The letters. They didn't arrive in the Tribune mailbox."

Ella and Mia both paused. Ella certainly wasn't expecting to hear that.

"Then how did the letters arrive to you?" asked Mia.

"My assistant. He brought them to me. He said they appeared in his mailbox. His home mailbox."

Ella arched her eyebrows in shock. "Are you kidding? And that didn't raise suspicions?"

"No. My assistant's address is easy to find. A lot of my mail goes directly to him."

Mia jumped out of her seat. "I wish you'd have told us this earlier, buddy. You could have saved yourself a lot of trouble. We need his name and address. Now."

"Stefan Redburn. 10 Springfield Way in Point Loma. I don't know the zip."

"Describe him," Ella said.

"Brown hair. About five-eleven. Well-built. California born and bred."

Ella grabbed the photos from the table and made her way to the door. She and Mia exited without comment. Outside, Denton was waiting for them.

"You checking this new guy out?" Denton asked.

"Immediately. Keep Carter in the cells overnight. Tell him that if this fake letter isn't removed from his website in the next ten minutes then we'll charge him on forgery and obstruction of justice," Mia said.

"Consider it done. If he refuses, we can have our tech team take down the page," said Denton.

"Good. Come on, Dark. Something is going on here and we need to find out what."

CHAPTER TWENTY FOUR

He stared at his computer screen in shock. He couldn't believe what he was seeing.

This wasn't his handwriting, or his writing style, or his tone. The symbols were completely incorrect. It was amateurish from start to finish, and the cipher didn't even spell a single word when cracked. It wasn't even the correct pen or paper. It wasn't *him.*

Jumping from his wooden stool, he clenched his fist and slammed it into the wall. His framed newspaper clippings shook, one of them dropping and cracking on the floor. Wooden splinters invaded his knuckles but the rage stopped him from feeling any pain at all.

It was obvious what had happened. The scum at the newspaper had faked the letter for publicity. How dare they be so bold as to use his name to make money? It was sickening, maddening, and someone was going to pay dearly for it.

Did they not think he'd notice? And what did they think was going to happen? He could just send another letter claiming that the previous one was inauthentic. Then he could remove the black mark off his record and continue onwards and upwards to true divinity.

He picked up the cracked picture and scanned the words. It was a Zodiac letter from 1969.

I hope you are having lots of fun in trying to catch me. That wasn't me on the T.V. show, which brings up a point about me. I am not afraid of the gas chamber because it will send me to paradise all the sooner.

That wasn't him on the T.V. show, his idol had said. The Zodiac had his own copycats and predators who tried to use his name for notoriety, so in a way, it was a fitting tribute that he did too.

But even so, history would say that this letter was written by him. Maybe when he was long gone, somewhere in his own paradise, the facts would blur and people would believe this note was a genuine Gemini article.

He couldn't let that happen. So far, his record was impeccable. Five dead and no traces left behind. The police were chasing their tails and he was living the life he'd dreamt of for years. No one was going to take this away from him, not the police and certainly not some vermin journalist.

Death would have to come sooner than originally planned. Whoever forged this note needed to understand that actions had consequences. The blood of the next victim would be on their hands, not his, and when it was over, he'd write another note – maybe to a national newspaper like the New York Times or USA Today – revealing the true events.

The police would be out in full force on this night. There was a 9pm curfew within a 30 mile-radius, so that meant one of two things. He'd either have to go outside the curfew zone or take the risk regardless. Given that he already had the next victim scouted, it would have to be the latter.

The man fell back into his chair and composed himself. He was a phantom, invisible, uncatchable. His idol had never been caught and he wouldn't either. Fate had brought him here and the shadows would guide him. No matter what he did, he couldn't get caught. It simply wasn't possible.

Outside, dusk was only a breath away. That meant he didn't have much time if he wanted to strike tonight. He needed to reach the hiding place before dark so he could lie in wait.

From his collection, he pulled out the necessary items to remind him of her. Her purse, still with her ID cards and photos inside.

And more importantly, her address.

She might have escaped him once, but that would all be rectified in a matter of hours. Tonight would be Amanda Huber's last night alive.

CHAPTER TWENTY FIVE

Ella stepped out of their car on Springfield Way. "This is only a mile away from where Amy Evans was murdered," she said. Springfield Way was a neighborhood in Point Loma, well-maintained and well-presented. Mia parked their vehicle away from the suspect's home so as not to raise suspicion.

"I know. That makes things look very good for this guy. Most killers start out close to home because they need the familiarity."

It was 7pm now and gray clouds had appeared overhead. The temperature had dropped to a manageable sixty-six degrees, but the sweat on Ella's palms told a different story. They kept themselves as discreet as possible as they approached number 10. Every house on the street was a single-story building, which meant their suspect had limited places to hide should he try and flee.

"Why would this killer send messages to the editor's assistant?" Ella asked. "It doesn't make sense to me."

"Agreed. It's too personal. Either this Stefan person is our killer or he has a connection to the killer. There are no two ways about it."

The pathway sloped down, leading to number 10's front door. The home was small but decent to look at, with a pristine front garden and a red Vauxhall parked on the driveway. "Someone's in," Ella said, "but no sign of a silver Volkswagen."

"That car's long gone, Dark. Forget about it. We go in, and if he tries to run, we grab him. Clear?"

"Crystal," Ella said. Raymond's description of Stefan had matched Amanda's description of her attacker to a tee. And as a detective, she wasn't allowed to believe in coincidences.

They moved to the door and Mia knocked. Ella stood to Mia's side so if Stefan peered out of the window, he'd only see a lone woman. One person knocking on your door could mean anything, two meant you were in trouble.

But there was no peering. Shuffling sounded behind the door. In the small glass window, Ella saw a figure dressed in yellow. The door opened.

"Hi?" the man said.

There was a second or two of silence as both agents glanced the man up and down. Ella was certain Mia was thinking the same thing. This guy didn't resemble Raymond or Amanda's descriptions at all.

He was short, blonde, scrawny as they come, dressed in a Brazilian football shirt.

"Stefan?" Mia asked. "Stefan Redburn?"

"No," the man said, prolonging the *o* sound. "That's my roommate. He's not here right now. Can I help?"

"Do you know when he'll be back?" Ella asked.

"I'm not too sure. He's probably at work. I can give him a message that you dropped by?"

"No, it's very important we speak to him now."

Ella saw the worry creep up on the man's face. "Is everything okay? Is he in trouble?"

"We can't say anything," Mia said, "it's just vital that we talk to him tonight."

"Is this about the electricity bill? Because I assure you it was a total accident."

"Could you call him for us?" Mia asked. "Could you ask him to come home?"

The guy shrugged. "I can try. Give me a sec." He retreated into the house but left the door ajar.

Ella was a little shocked at Mia's proposal. To her, telling this guy there were two women at his doorstep was a total red flag. Just out of the man's earshot, Ella whispered to Mia. "Call him? Are you sure? What if it just scares him off?"

"Our killer has escalated with every crime," Mia whispered back. "He said in his last real letter that his nightly bloodlust is overflowing into his days, meaning he might be tempted to kill during the day or early evening now. What if he has a victim right this second? This is our best chance at saving a life."

The man in the football shirt pulled the door open again. "He's already on his way home. He's about two minutes away. You want to wait inside? Looks like it's about to pour down."

The agents accepted and entered the home, straight into the lounge. They sat on the sofa staring at a gigantic television, but that wasn't what Ella was focused on. In the corner of the spacious lounge was a writing desk, and in the pen holder was a bunch of black felt pens. Beside the desk was a bookshelf, where Ella spotted a number of true crime classics. Charles Manson, Edmund Kemper, and interestingly, *Zodiac: The Shocking True Story*.

Ella glanced at Mia who nodded at her, noticing the same thing already. From beside the sofa, Mia pulled out a pile of magazines. *Codebreakers, Puzzle Mysteries, CodeWords.* From the kitchen, they heard Stefan's roommate making coffee.

"Do you want a drink?" the man shouted.

"No thanks," Ella called back. She knew that as soon as this man entered the room they had to pounce. This was all too much of a coincidence for it to be a misfire.

Ella assessed the likelihood of this Stefan individual being responsible for the gruesome events they'd seen over the past few days, and the odds were something akin to a coin flip. Until she saw the man, she couldn't say for sure, but the circumstantial evidence staring back at her said this guy was involved somehow. Could he have been allured by the possibility of worldwide recognition? He had the contacts, he had the resources, and maybe this could have been his way to fame? Or perhaps it was all a shadow-step towards promotion or advancement in the ranks of the Tribune? Manufacturing the killings, then become a podium for the killer by somehow obtaining the killer's correspondence?

She'd seen corporations do some shady things during her law enforcement years, so maybe something like this was the final step in abhorrent corporate marketing? God knows, she wouldn't put it past some of them.

And sitting here now, with a writing desk, true crime books and puzzle magazines surrounding her, the feeling in her gut said that whoever walked through that door in the next few minutes had secrets she needed to unearth. There was a stern confidence in her that victory was a heartbeat away, and despite all the times that victory had been pulled from under her feet, there was something here now that told her she was in the right place at the right time. And when that victory came, not only would it save future lives and put a million minds at ease, but she could shove it right into Tobias Campbell's mouth and vanquish his constant presence in her head.

A key sounded in the lock. Ella glanced out the lounge window and saw a new car had parked across the driveway. A black Volkswagen. Not silver. Could Amanda's memory be a little hazy, maybe?

The front door opened and a new soul entered the room. Both agents looked him up and down, and for Ella's money, he matched Amanda's description perfectly. He was about thirty-two, five-eleven with a stocky build. He wore a grey hoodie above black jeans and had dark hair that was long overdue a wash.

"Mr. Redburn?" Mia asked, standing up the moment he walked in the room.

"Yeah, that's me. Who might you be?"

Mia pulled her badge out of her jacket. "I'm Agent Ripley and this is Agent Dark. We're with the FBI."

And as quick as he arrived, Stefan Redburn was gone, leaving only his backpack behind. The door slammed shut and his glassy outline vanished into the street.

CHAPTER TWENTY SIX

Mia was out the door fast enough to see Stefan vanish beyond the houses on the opposite side of the street. She and Mia followed to the spot where he disappeared.

"Dark, you head left. I'm going straight ahead. He's gonna go around a few corners. Try and block him off."

Ella was gone before Mia even finished her instruction. Behind the houses there was another street, leading into an adjacent neighborhood. Mia fled forward, narrowing avoiding a collision with a taxi. The driver shouted something from the window but Mia was too far gone to notice.

She sped into the neighborhood, seeing rows of townhouses stretching beyond her vision. There were multiple turns, meaning Stefan had multiple options available. When pursued, it was human nature to turn corners rather than continue on a straight path. The rational brain believed it made the runner more concealed, but it wasn't always the case.

Mia took the first turning, arriving at another housing estate, a small, private park. Given the street layout, it was a cul-de-sac up ahead, so there was no way Stefan would have escaped here, assuming he was familiar with the surrounding area.

But then she saw a small path just behind the park area. Mia put herself in the runner's head and came to the conclusion that if she was trying to escape someone, she'd head there. Mia followed the path and found herself on a long patch of grass stretching in both directions. She could see about a hundred feet both ways.

To her left, nothing.

To her right, a figure.

There he was, leaning against a tree about fifty feet away, struggling for breath.

Even from so far, Mia saw him shoot back up once he realized he hadn't yet acquired freedom. He darted down the grassy strip, amongst the trees. Mia wasn't sure, but she thought he took a right turn.

She followed anyway, unsure of herself. She quickly came round to the idea that Stefan might have evaded her, but even so, she knew his name and location and what he looked like. Surely, he couldn't stay hidden for long.

Mia came to the end of the strip and turned right back onto the road. Another residential area; one she didn't recognize. She paused for breath. In through the nose, out through the mouth for maximum intake. Mia suddenly had a flashback to the days when she could run for miles without pausing for breath. She saw herself acing the assault course in the FBI training grounds, over the ten-foot wall, across twenty monkey bars and up that net that nearly touched the clouds. Back then, easy. Now, the years of double-whiskeys had quenched a lot of that physical fire.

After rejuvenating herself, she continued to follow the snaking pathways. The houses were rowed, so there was no place for Stefan to hide amongst them. It would be unlikely he'd jump a fence too, considering he'd be cornered. All his primal urges would tell him to stay on an open road.

Mia suddenly had doubts. Why had Stefan been so quick to bail? Surely, he must be guilty, or at the very least be involved with these murders. An innocent person never ran.

And if he *was* their killer, surely someone so organized would have a game plan, an exit strategy, a way out. What if his plans involved escaping to another state, another country? If they didn't catch this killer eventually, God knows where he might end up. He wasn't some disorganized sociopath taking chances and hoping for the best. He was as organized as they come, methodical, a forward-thinker. A risk taker, sure, but she'd seen plenty of similar unsubs over the years who'd disappeared in similar fashions. Nothing was stopping this killer from going the same route.

Mia found herself back on the main road, opposite Springfield Way.

"Shit. He's gone," she said aloud. Hands on her knees, gasping for air.

She surveyed the road up and down, hoping to catch a glimpse of him far in the distance. Nothing. She turned her attention back to the suspect's street.

Movement.

A gray sweatshirt, its hood flapping in the wind.

There was Stefan Redburn, running with the longest strides she'd ever seen.

He was heading back home.

No, to his car. Of course. "God damn it," she screamed.

Mia chased in pursuit but her mind quickly did the calculations. Stefan was too far gone, already within touching distance of his black Volkswagen. She saw its flashlights blink on and off to signal the doors had opened.

Mia stopped, thinking maybe she could throw herself in front of the car to stop him?

No, it was a death wish. He'd already killed five people. What was another one to him?

But then Mia saw something else. She squinted to make out the scene up ahead of her.

Another figure appeared, seemingly from out of nowhere. Suddenly, Stefan's entire body was hauled into the air. Mia had to wince at the point of impact.

Thud.

She heard the hood dent from a hundred yards away.

***

At the San Diego precinct, Stefan sat in chains. All of the interrogation rooms were in use, so they carried out the proceedings in their office. Ella rotated her shoulder blades to release some of the tension. The body slam onto Stefan's car had pulled a muscle there.

Stefan looked a sorry sight. He fit the physical description perfectly, and the fact he was so eager to run meant he had something to hide. Ella was desperate to get to the bottom of it, but more than anything, she wanted to wipe that woe-is-me look off his face with the bottom of her boot.

"So, what? You just went back to the car?" Mia asked, in full view of the suspect no less.

"Yeah. I assumed he'd go back there." She nodded at Stefan. "A coward like this. Of course he's going to go back to his vehicle. He obviously can't fight a fair fight."

Stefan's eyes jumped between both agents, then back to the shackles on his wrist.

"Good call, Dark. Nice drop too."

"Thanks. I didn't mean to damage your car, Mr. Redburn."

"Well, you did," he said. His first words since their arrival here.

"Sorry about that. Really, I only wanted to break your spine. Call it retaliation for what you did to her." Ella threw Amy Evans's crime scene photo at Stefan. "And her, and this couple, and these two." Ella launched every photo at him one by one with venom. "Now, you better start talking or we've got a very cold, damp prison cell downstairs which I'll happily throw you in myself."

"I don't know what you're talking about. I haven't murdered anyone," he said, referring to the photos in front of him.

"Then why did you run away like a scalded dog?" Mia asked.

"I thought this was about the letter. It is, right?"

"No," Ella snapped, "it's about five dead people, and we have reason to believe that you killed them."

Stefan shook his head frantically. Now, there was grief in his eyes. His bottom lip stuck out like a kid being scolded. "I never killed anyone. I swear it."

"What about the letter, Mr. Redburn?" Mia asked.

"We faked it. Me and Mr. Carter. We wrote it together in his office this morning. It was his idea. I wanted nothing to do with it because I thought it was crazy. But that's the extent of it. Honestly."

Ella didn't like his brutal honesty. It meant that he might have been telling the truth. So far, everything pointed to Stefan Redburn as the guilty party. The physical description, the letter handling, the fact he fled so suddenly, even the Zodiac book on his shelf. But this little outburst went against the grain.

"What about the other letters? Mr. Carter said the real ones were delivered to your mailbox at home, yes?"

"Uh huh." Stefan nodded continuously, to the point that he resembled a bobblehead.

"Bit of a coincidence, isn't it?" Ella asked. "Why would a murderer send letters to *you* specifically? Why not the Tribune office? Or directly to Mr. Carter? Things don't add up for me."

"A lot of Mr. Carter's mail arrives to me directly. The office receives literally thousands of letters every day. Any letters with Mr. Carter's name are automatically redirected to me by the U.S. post office."

"What? Why?" Ella asked.

"It means the Tribune doesn't have to employ someone to sift through the mail every day. The post office does the hard work for us."

"Christ," Mia said. "Cheap bastards. All that money and you can't even afford a sorting assistant."

Stefan seemed to agree. "I know, right? I don't agree with it. But that could be why the letters came to my door. They weren't addressed to Mr. Carter but they said 'for the attention of the editor' on the front.

Ella still wasn't buying it. "And what did you think when the first letter arrived? Your first thought was to give it to Carter and not tell the police?"

"Because I thought it was fake. At that point, we didn't know anyone had been murdered. I showed Mr. Carter and he got real excited. He published it straight away. I told him not to because it was unfair and disrespectful but he ignored me. He said it would bring in crazy money."

"And the second letter?" Mia asked.

"Exactly the same. Appeared in my mailbox this morning and I took it straight to Mr. Carter. But this time, I freaked out because it had bloody clothing in it. I went to call you guys straight away but he stopped me and told me to wait."

Ella couldn't quite make out the truth. Stefan spoke like a frightened kid, but even so, the person they were hunting understood how humans operated. He surely knew that emotion was the key to successful manipulation. She looked for signs that Stefan might have recently been in a struggle. Broken fingernails, bruises, cuts, band-aids, blood beneath his fingertips.

Other than the invisible damage to his spine that her body slam had undoubtedly caused, there was nothing. He was a relatively healthy individual, much to Ella's dismay.

"And the supposed fake letter?" Mia asked. "Tell us about it."

Stefan turned his gaze to the ceiling. He instinctively went to rub his eyes but the cuffs kept him still. "Mr. Carter's idea. He wrote it. I just sourced the pen and paper that resembled the previous letters. As far as I know, only he and I knew that it was fake."

Ella laughed. "Are you kidding? There's someone else who knows it's fake. Use your brain."

It took Stefan a second. "The actual killer."

"Bingo. Your boss will have really pissed this killer off, and I won't be surprised if he goes after him next," Mia said.

"Mr. Redburn, we'll need to verify your whereabouts for the past two nights. Where were you?"

"At home. Asleep," Stefan said quickly.

"Your roommate can verify, I assume?" Ella asked.

Stefan hesitated. His eyes wandered around the room before settling on the door. Nervousness, worry, anxiety Ella thought. "Uhm… no. Not exactly."

"No?"

"He works the night shift. Ten 'til six."

Ella glanced over at her partner. Judging by the look in Mia's face, she was in the same two minds as Ella was. Stefan fit the bill in some ways but not all of them.

"Nice collection of true crime books you had back there. Puzzle magazines too. You know what our killer loves? The Zodiac killer and puzzles," Ella said. Mia would probably caution her later for revealing case intricacies like that, but she was past caring.

"My what? Books? I wish I had time to read. If I'm not working, I'm watching ships down the docks. I don't do much else. Me and Alex got those books just to look good on our shelf. We've never read them. Alex is the puzzle guy."

Ella took her glasses off and dropped them on her lap. On paper, Stefan Redburn could very well be their killer. Certain things matched, and circumstantial evidence made a solid case.

But her gut told her the opposite. It told her that Stefan was an innocent man, a blameless party who had been unwillingly pulled into this game by his despicable employer. She didn't know what to think, and as nightfall set in overhead, she was certain that this killer was going to strike again in the next few hours. She looked up at the ceiling and wanted to scream in frustration.

"Dark, let's go outside," Mia said. "We need to speak to Officer Denton."

CHAPTER TWENTY SEVEN

Outside of their office, the agents reconvened with Officer Denton. Ella kept her eye on Stefan through the window, looking for even the vaguest signs of guilt. Now left alone, he looked a pitiful sight, fixating his stare on his trembling hands in front of him.

"Is there any solid evidence against this guy?" Denton asked the agents.

"No. At least not yet," Mia said. "Plenty of circumstantial but nothing hard."

"His story about the letters just seems too unbelievable. Too convenient," Ella added.

"Well, I checked him out and as far as I can tell, he's completely clean. A golden kid. Not even a parking ticket."

Mia scratched her cheek and glanced at Stefan through the glass. "No criminal history and jumping straight to premeditated homicide? Doesn't add up."

"What's for the best, then? Keep him here?"

"Yes. We can hold him on a forgery charge for twenty-four hours. Hold him here for now until we've made some headway with this," Mia said.

Ella picked up on Mia's line of thinking. There was every chance that the killer would strike that same night given the little stunt that Raymond and Stefan pulled. So, if Stefan was in custody during another murder, that would cement his innocence – at least in part.

"Alright, I'll take him to the cells," Denton said. He went and fetched Stefan from the room and escorted him out, past the agents and past the rest of the officers on duty. The whole time, Stefan refrained from eye contact with everyone, keeping his otherwise athletic frame low and slumped. At Denton's desk, he stopped and spoke with Stefan about something. Probably telling him how the next 24 hours were going to play out.

"You see that?" Mia said. "Total submission. If this was our killer, he'd be holding himself high. He would look right at those cops' faces and revel in the pain he'd caused. I just don't see it."

Ella leaned her shoulder against the wall. Her minor injury – now all for nothing – flared up a little on impact. She bent her neck to crack it. "I know. He seemed to me like he was telling the truth. I'm no expert on body language but he didn't seem like he had anything to hide."

"Yeah, well I *am* an expert on body language and his micro-signals were all on point. Nothing that suggested he was hiding anything. His feet were pointed at us the whole time. He didn't put up any barriers between us. When he recalled the stuff about the letters, he looked up and to the right."

"Visual recollection. It all happened exactly as he described."

"I can't say for sure, but it looks that way," Mia said.

Ella's phone pinged. A text from Ben.

Hey, how are things over there? Any idea when you're coming back? x

She began to type a reply but deleted it. Right now, she didn't know what to tell him, and the last thing she wanted was to give him hope that she might be heading home any time soon. She'd see what tonight brought, she told herself, then if there were no advancements in the case she could tell him she'd be home within two weeks.

But still, two weeks? Was it fair to keep him waiting like that?

"I just wish I could get into this guy's head," Mia interrupted. "What's he thinking? What's his next step?"

"Yeah, I know what you mean. I can't figure him out," Ella said.

"If there's another incident tonight, it means Stefan is off the hook. I'm going to get a picture of him across to Amanda and see if she recognizes him. Maybe I'll send her a voice sample too. But still, it's a long shot."

"I'm not going to get my hopes up. Not again. Every time we get close to the finish line it just gets pushed back even further," Ella said. "How long are we staying out here for?"

"Two weeks in the field, usually. Then we can resume the case back at HQ. But what usually happens is another case comes in, then you have to find time to work on them both. The same thing happens again and again, and before you know it you're juggling ten active cases. It's inevitable at some point, Dark."

Ella sank further into the wall. She breathed out a heavy sigh, her motivation dispersing along with the warm air. Fatigue numbed her legs and sent her a little dizzy, rousing up all of the injuries she'd suffered over the past few weeks. She was stuck here in this precinct while a psychopath was hunting through the city for his next kill. That fact alone brought a wave of dread, knowing that tomorrow morning she'd probably wake up to that dreaded line: 'There's been another murder.'

"It's all too varied. Where would someone like this strike next? Especially with the curfew. Is he bold enough to risk hitting the streets after dark? Normally, I could predict a guy like this down to his clothing, but I have no idea how this person thinks. We know he's getting a sexual kick out of these kills, but he's also getting off on the terrorism aspect of it too." Mia held her palms towards the ceiling. "Nothing's coming."

Ella looked down the office and saw Stefan and Denton disappear down the distant staircase. That was their prime suspect, now vanishing and taking all hopes of a successful capture with him. They could interrogate him further, Ella thought, but she knew there was nothing else to learn from him. He was just a pawn in this deathly game of chess.

Just a pawn.

Ella stared at the phone in her hand.

Neither she nor Mia understood this killer, but there was someone out there who might.

"Ripley, I just need to make a call."

***

Ella stood outside the precinct with the number already punched into her phone. It was dark now, with a cold breeze that soothed her and flared her injuries simultaneously. She walked past the smokers' area, predictably deserted given the health-conscious nature of the police profession. It was quiet here, with enough open space to maneuver should any wandering souls intrude.

Every fiber of her being told her that this was a bad idea.

But was there another option? What was the cost of saving lives? Her own feelings were unimportant now that she'd entered the world of law enforcement. Seven years ago on her first day as an analyst for the Virginia PD, she took an oath to protect the public with fairness, integrity, diligence and impartiality. Now more than ever, she needed to remember that.

The phone rang once then cut out.

There was a beeping sound, like an old dial-up modem from the nineties.

"Maine State Prison Department of Corrections," the voice said. No more.

"Hello. My name's Agent Dark with the FBI Washington office, I was-,"

"ID Number please," the voice interrupted. Ella gave him the details and heard him typing something on the other end. "Thank you, Miss Dark. What can we help you with?"

"I was at your prison on Saturday to visit inmate number two-seven-six-one. I was wondering if it would be possible to speak with him again."

"Over the phone?"

"Yes, please," Ella said.

More typing on the other end. "Campbell? You want to speak with Tobias Campbell?"

"I do." Suddenly, Ella felt out of place. Who was she to make such a request? Wanting immediate access to one of the most high-profile prisoners in the country was a bold move. Hearing the voice on the other end made it all a bit too real.

"That's a big ask. It could take a while," the man said. "Hold the line please."

Ella was greeted by a beeping sound. Looking around the yard area, her whole body began to tremble. She felt like she was violating something she shouldn't be, like she was trespassing in alien terrain. It wasn't right. There was no way this would work, and who knew how what legal issues she might get the Bureau into.

Ella silenced the beeps and hung up immediately. She breathed in the night air and was instantly back in San Diego, back in the real world. Jesus Christ, what the hell was she thinking? Every single phone call to prisons was recorded. Somewhere in Maine right now, a prison official was verifying Ella's details with the FBI office. They'd know she called. She'd be surprised if the director didn't call her phone right away to ask what the hell was going through her stupid head.

And then there was Mia. Of course she'd hear about it. After that, she could kiss goodbye to her career in the field. Mia would put in a request for a new partner; some other lucky S.O.B. plucked from a desk job to live the life Ella had dreamed of. She'd have thrown her perfect job away all for the sake of a mistake that she could have easily avoided.

Ella passed the smoking shelter and made her way to the precinct's rear door. She pulled the bar and the warm air from inside hit her like a speeding truck. Inside, she reached the staircase and prepared her excuses for Mia.

She was calling Ben, maybe. Or her roommate. Either one would work.

But she had to stop halfway up the stairwell to ensure she wasn't imagining it. To ensure it wasn't her anxious mind playing tricks on her.

The jingle echoed throughout the stairwell, bouncing off the walls and steel handrails.

Her phone was ringing.

Worry crippled her instantly, preventing her from peering down and looking at the caller ID.

One ring. Two rings.

With trembling hands, she reached into her pocket and reluctantly brought the screen around.

UNKNOWN CALLER.

Three and four.

After six, they were gone.

Was it William Edis, about to demand she return to Washington at once?

Or was it someone else?

Five. Ella took a deep breath and pushed the ANSWER button. "Hello?"

Silence. Then shuffling.

And while she couldn't see the person on the other end, she just knew that he was beaming that crooked smile of his right that second.

"Hello, Miss Dark. So nice to hear your voice again."

Ella went back outside, away from prying ears. This time, she didn't feel the chill at all. Every inch of skin burnt with trepidation.

"Tobias? Is that you?"

"It is me. You wanted me?"

"How are you calling me?" Ella asked, frantically scanning the outside for signs of life. Still no one present.

"They bring a telephone to me, you see. I'm not allowed to mingle with the plebs in the visitation area."

His voice was low and calm but it penetrated her regardless, each word slithering down her ear canal like a noxious viper. "Oh. I see. Tobias, this was a mistake. I didn't mean to call you."

"Nonsense," he hissed, articulating the *s*'s. "You called me because of that naughty boy down in California. He's got the police chasing their tails like demented dogs. You want to be one to pin him down, look him in the eye and tell him he couldn't compete with the FBI.

Then you want to convince yourself you were one step ahead from day one, don't you?"

She remembered her dream. How this man made her feel. She pictured him now, in his cell, perhaps sitting on his bed and relishing in the delight that the FBI wanted his help. The thought of it made her sick, but if it saved a life, it was worth the suffering.

"Yes. I do." She wasn't sure how Tobias knew of the case but she wasn't going to ask. The less she revealed herself, the better.

"Tell me about him," Tobias said. "I've heard the news but the details elude me."

Ella decided to give him the short version. Divulging confidential details like she was about to, especially to a high-profile criminal and manipulator like Tobias was instant dismissal and a blacklist from working for any law enforcement outfit in the country. But she was here now. No turning back. Either way, the FBI higher-ups were going to hear about this.

"Victim number one was a lone woman. 23-years-old. Stabbed 42 times on a roadside. Victims two and three were a teenage couple, stabbed in a lovers' lane in their car. After that, he abducted an older woman in his car but she escaped. And last night, he killed another couple camping in the woods. He made the female kill the male and then mutilated them both. He's been taunting the press with letters and puzzles too."

Tobias inhaled deeply and satisfyingly, like he'd taken in a deep hit of nicotine. "Interesting. We have a Zodiac copycat."

When Tobias said *we,* she again fought the urge to hang up. The idea that they were working together was a nauseating thought. She swallowed her pride. "Yes, that's correct."

"Tell me, Miss Dark, what have *you* done? You and your little band of soldiers up there. How have you tried to stop this perpetrator?"

Ella looked around again to ensure no one had snuck outside. She kept her eyes on the door. No signs of life. "How do you mean?"

"Much like the Zodiac, this man wants the media and the police to play a part in his story. You are as important to him as the murders he's committing. Without you, his murders lose a certain sense of prestige. He surely enjoys the sexual gratification his kills provide, but fooling around in class is more fun when the teacher is aware. It's a power play to him. Children don't just want one toy car, they want the whole set. Maximum tragedy means a more intense thrill. You and his victims are toys to be meddled and manipulated."

"Okay, and? How do I stop him? We've put a curfew out within a thirty-mile radius. No one should be out after dark unless they have a good reason."

She heard that smirk again.

"Oh dear. And given the time difference, that should be right now, correct?"

Ella glanced at her watch, unaware of how fast the hours were flying. "Yes, that's now."

"Well, I'm afraid you've sealed the fate of an unlucky soul already. This man sees your curfew as a challenge to his predatory abilities. You must remember, Miss Dark, this man doesn't see the world as you do. Rules and policies are simply a way to prove his mastery by besting them and in the process, besting you too. But I will tell you one thing, Agent."

"Yes? Please do."

"Tonight is your best chance of catching him. Perhaps your *only* chance to catch him."

Ella kept herself calm, trying not to think about the hours ticking away. "How? Why?"

"Much like the Zodiac did, this man will make his mark and then vanish. He's smart enough to understand that you can't go higher than the pinnacle. Once he's drenched the city in blood and cemented his name in annals of history, he will simply disappear from view, using only the memories of his reign to relive that high for the rest of his life."

"Okay, but if that's the case, how should I catch him? Where will he be? What's he thinking?"

"Tell me this, Miss Dark. Why should I help you?"

Ella went to speak but no words came out. It felt like a question she should have an answer to, but now that she thought about it, Tobias had no reason to help her.

"I can get you things. I'm in the FBI. I can send you-,"

"No. Please stop talking," Tobias interrupted. "I can already get whatever I want. However, you do have one thing that no one else can provide."

Ella didn't like the sound of this. "What's that?"

"If you promise to grant me this wish, I'll tell you the exact location your unknown subject will be tonight."

"Yes. Whatever you want," Ella said, the excitement clouding her rational thought for a moment. After the words escaped her throat, she suddenly regretted it.

"Agent Ripley," Tobias said. "I want her."

Ella almost dropped the phone from her hand. "What? You want me to put you in contact with her?"

Tobias laughed so hard the line crackled. "No, Miss Dark. I want you to kill her for me."

At that moment, everything felt surreal. Ella thought that maybe this was another dream and that any second now she'd wake up in her dim hotel room with sweat dripping off her forehead. "What? Are you kidding me? I'm not going to do that. Obviously I'm not."

"Tut tut. Well, I'm afraid I'll be leaving you now."

"No, please, you have to tell me. I'll do anything else. I can get you transferred to a nicer prison, a bigger cell."

"Oh, Miss Dark. How sad it must be for you. Spending your life researching the disordered mind and still being so far away from it. Trying to fathom something unknowable, it's enough to drive a sane person mad. The irony."

"Just this one thing, then I'll come to visit you again. I'll talk to Agent Ripley about coming to see you too. You know she talks about you too?"

"This is the last thing I'm going to tell you, then I'm going back to my books." Tobias lowered his voice a little. "To your unknown subject, his victims are objects. Every kill makes them so, stripping away what once made them human. They belong to the killer now, and they will forever. Now Miss Dark, think about what you told me earlier. Think about the details. I've told you where this killer will be tonight already, you just have to figure it for yourself. I have no doubt that you and I will speak again someday."

"But where does-,"

And the line went dead.

CHAPTER TWENTY EIGHT

At her desk, Mia checked the time on her laptop. 9:23. Where the hell had Ella got to? Mia hoped she hadn't got lost in the labyrinth that was the San Diego PD building.

The door opened and Officer Denton walked in. He grabbed one of the spare chairs and took a seat. "Had some of my guys look into Stefan Redburn. I mean a real deep look."

"Oh yes?" There was a glimmer of hope in Mia's voice.

"One of the officers checked his computer and they found he'd played a few files at about one AM on Friday morning. Meaning..."

"Meaning he was at home during the Black's Beach murders."

"'Fraid so," Denton said. "But if you ask me, that doesn't exclude him entirely. Myself, I think it *could* be him. Just because his computer played a couple of movies doesn't mean he was at home. It's all a bit fishy to me."

"There's not enough evidence. Almost zero evidence."

"His prints were all over those letters. We're getting a handwriting sample as we speak. Plenty of my guys have looked over the details and seem pretty sure Stefan is your guy."

The door opened again. Ella returned to the office, her hair scraggly, her arms red with cold. She sat down without addressing Mia or Denton.

"You okay, Dark? Thought you'd got lost."

Ella pulled her laptop closer and remained fixed on the screen. "I'm fine. Just called Ben and he kept me talking for ages."

She didn't look like her usual self. Relationship problems? Maybe Ella had just given him the elbow? By the looks of her, she didn't want to talk about it so Mia let it rest.

"Dark, some of the guys here think Stefan is the guilty man. What say you?"

Ella typed something and stared at the screen for a few moments. "I don't think so," she said eventually. "And neither do you, Ripley."

"You're absolutely right. My gut tells me he's an innocent man, but I can't ignore some of the circumstantial evidence we have for him. Not to mention he seems a little *too* clean. Everything we throw at him he has an answer for. Like he's prepared for it."

Ella tied back her hair and scratched her neck. "No, there has to be something we're missing. And for every second we waste trying to convince ourselves it was Stefan, the more chances someone else out there gets slaughtered tonight."

"We've got patrols out in full force," Denton offered. "Anyone who's out on the streets will be stopped and questioned."

Ella closed her laptop screen with force. An unexpected move. What was wrong with this girl?

"And what's stopping them lying?" Ella asked, her voice a little higher than usual. "Our unsub has run rings around us, and we think a curfew is gonna stop him? He probably has his excuses already prepared in case he gets stopped. Probably fake identification too."

Mia thought Ella was probably right. A curfew wouldn't do a whole lot to stop someone as determined as their killer. It was a band aid on a bullet wound. "So, what's your suggestion, Dark? We go stalk out every single beach in San Diego? Every lake, every woods, every secluded lane? And then what if he doesn't strike at any of them? What if he completely adjusts his M.O. again?"

Ella stood up and paced up and down near the far wall. Something had gotten into her, Mia thought. Something had rattled her. But what Mia had learned from their past two cases was that whenever Ella reached those unfathomable levels of desperation, that was when she came into her element. Urgency brought out the best in her, just like it did for so many. When she was against the wall, she fought back hard.

"This unsub sees our curfew as a challenge to his abilities," Ella said. "He doesn't see the world like we do. This curfew is just a way for him to prove his dominance."

"Correct," Mia said. "But that doesn't indicate where he might strike next."

Ella placed her forehead against the office window and spoke into it.

"Maybe it does," she said.

Mia thought about it, unable to arrive at any conclusion. "No, it doesn't. I can't see how a curfew will help us predict his movements."

Ella still stood with her back to her and Denton, observing the night skyline through the glass. To Mia, Ella's thoughts were coming across as stream-of-consciousness and not through any kind of rational deductions. Maybe it was her exhaustion talking.

"These victims are objects to him. Once he's attacked them, they belong to him forever," Ella continued. "Like how the original Zodiac killed because he wanted slaves for the afterlife. He killed because he wanted to go to some kind of eternal paradise. In his last letter, our unsub mentioned something about an afterlife, so he probably shares the same beliefs."

Mia ran through the victims one by one. She put herself in this killer's head and tried to imagine what he would do when confronted with these odds. The general public would be in their homes and while he might get lucky finding a few stragglers on the streets, it would be a long shot for him. And would this unsub risk hunting only to return home without a successful kill?

No, he needed to slaughter tonight. He would be determined to show the letter-fakers who was really in charge. There was no chance someone this strong-willed was going to let it slide even for a night.

Ella's words still lingered in the air. Mia turned to her, realizing that she'd said something incredibly revealing. Maybe the rookie wasn't even aware of it.

"Dark, what was that?"

Ella turned around with that solemn look on her face. There was heartbreak there, certainly.

"He believes in some kind of afterlife, like the original Zodiac."

Mia shook her head. "No, no. The other thing. About the objectification."

"Oh. He sees these people as objects after he attacks them. They're his possessions. He's like a child with toys."

Mia slammed her hands on the desk and sprung to her feet. "Holy *shit*. Of course. That's it! Dark, you're a genius. Why didn't you say this sooner?"

Ella looked like she'd just won the lottery but was stuck in the initial state of disbelief. "What? What are you thinking?"

"He won't strike anywhere public because of the curfew. That's too risky, even for him. He knows we'll have eyes and ears on the streets. Last time, when we thought he was going to strike at the carnival, what did he do?" Mia asked.

"Misdirected us," Ella said, phrasing it like a question.

"Exactly, he lured us somewhere and in a completely different place. Tonight, he *wants* us to think he's going to hit the secluded areas again, but I don't think he is."

"No?" Denton jumped in.

"No. Like Dark says, his victims are his possessions and he can play with them whenever he wants. He's going to strike someone he knows he can't fail. Somewhere safe and secure away from the watchful eyes of the police."

Ella's expression changed from disbelief to understanding. "Oh crap, you're right. That's exactly where he's going to hit. Let's go," she shouted.

The agents grabbed their jackets. "Denton, you monitor the patrol. If we're wrong then it's even more important that we have plenty of officers out on the streets."

"Wait, where are you going?" Denton asked.

"Somewhere in La Mesa," Mia said. "I'll text you the details in a second. If we need backup, I'll call you."

***

Ella did her best to vanquish the thoughts of Campbell as they tore through the streets of La Mesa. Mia's driving awarded them precious seconds, but time was not their ally. It was 9:42pm and nightfall had already set in. There was every chance that they were already too late.

The San Diego streets blurred past her, barely a soul present thanks to the curfew. Ella's heart pumped like a thousand drums at the thought of what they might uncover up ahead. Would she come face to face with this killer, or had he thrown them off yet again? The one thing she was certain about was that he'd strike again tonight. It all made sense, even though it was Tobias who'd planted the seeds of the idea in her head.

"What are the chances?" Ella asked.

Mia took a corner so sharply Ella nearly slammed into the door. "Chances of what?" she asked. "Chances that we're about to meet this guy? Pretty high. I'm rarely certain of anything in this game, but of this, I'd bet my life on it."

"Really?"

"Hundred percent. The curfew, the letters, the payback. If I was him, this is exactly what I'd do. Unfinished business."

If it was good enough for Ripley, it was good enough for her. Was this what Tobias Campbell had meant? When Ella fit the pieces together, it was all there right in front of her. Their curfew had protected the citizens of San Diego, but it also meant that this killer knew exactly where any potential victims would be – at their home. All he needed to know was the address of someone who fit his victim type, and given the evidence, he definitely had it.

Think about what you told me earlier. Think about the details. I've told you where this killer will be tonight already, you just have to figure it for yourself.

Where else could have meant? There was no other place than their destination. They were all in on this, and if they were wrong, then another life would be lost at their hands. Ella wasn't sure if she could live with another defeat.

The GPS said their destination was two streets away. Mia took a sharp right, shot to the end of the road and slammed the brakes on hard. "Go," she shouted.

Both agents jumped out of the car and took cover behind the parked cars along the street. They crept down, out of sight, until they found number 4 Ravenscourt Avenue. It was a decent sized townhouse backing onto the woods, and from what Ella could see, all lights in the home were off. But the car in the driveway suggested that the occupant was inside.

"Come on," Ella said, taking the lead. They pressed on towards the door and Ella hammered on it with her fists. "FBI. Please open up."

Please don't be too late, she begged silently. *Please answer the door.*

A few seconds passed. Ella knocked again, but the silence spoke volumes.

She peered in through the window, seeing a darkened lounge and not much else. Panic became her primary emotion. She grabbed the door handle and yanked down hard but the handle barely moved. Locked.

"I don't have a good feeling about this."

Ella went back to the window, this time banging on the glass. Their intrusion would probably draw the attention of the surrounding neighbors but Ella wasn't concerned. In fact, it would be a good thing. More eyes, more ears.

Then in the darkness, she saw movement.

Adrenaline came in overwhelming waves, the rush feeling as if it had elevated her off the ground.

The movement came closer. The outline of a figure appeared, staring right at her with its glimmering eyeballs. "Ripley, someone's in here," Ella shouted, not sure if this was a success or failure yet.

"FBI. Answer your God damn door," Ripley shouted.

Ella saw the figure stop, clearly startled by the command. It waited still like a mannequin, and for a second Ella wondered if that wasn't exactly what she was looking at.

But then, to Ella's horror, the figure disappeared out of sight.

CHAPTER TWENTY NINE

The curfew was in full effect, but the man was already ready and waiting in position. His destination was a townhouse on Ravenscourt Avenue, and from his hiding spot, he had eyes exactly where he needed them.

At the end of the street was a small church, long since abandoned judging by the crumbly exterior. Outside the church was a graveyard, similarly deserted given the knee-high grass and beer cans and discarded needles. From here, he could see the whole street through the wrought iron gate and could retreat into the shadows if any passers-by became aware of his presence.

Unbeknownst to the police, the curfew just made things easier. They'd be checking the lakes, the woods, the make-out points. They'd be wasting their time looking in the wrong places. They'd never suspect that this time, he'd do something the Zodiac never did. Tonight was the night he elevated himself above the Zodiac, proving that he could adapt his operation whenever the situation called for it. The Zodiac relied on guns, sneak-attacks, blitzes. He shot when his victims' backs were turned, and worst of all, he never went back to finish the job. Three of the Zodiac's victims survived his attacks, and not once did he try and rectify his mistakes.

This man idolized the Zodiac and had done so for decades, but there were a few aspects of his crimes that left a sour taste in his mouth. He had a love for him, a respect that he had for no other human being. But there was also some contention there. History proved that imitation only got a person so far. If he quit now, he'd be forever known as the *Zodiac copycat*. They'd mention his name in true crime discussions for years to come, but someone would always be quick to mention the similarities to his original inspiration.

Only by going above and beyond what the Zodiac did could he ascend to new heights and become legendary. That's why tonight was so important. By killing this bitch, he was achieving two things. He was showing the world he was much more than a Zodiac copycat, and he was giving a middle finger to the scummy reporters at the Tribune who thought they could fake his letters and get away with it. After tonight, the entire residents of San Diego would know they weren't safe. The reporters would get the blame for provoking him, as they should, and with all the luck in the world, the guilt would drive them to madness.

Engines in the distance. He heard it faintly, gradually amplifying as the vehicle came into view. He peered through the iron gate to observe, seeing a police patrol car cruise by. The driver lazily glanced out of the window then began to drive on. He veiled himself behind the wall until the sounds of the engine faded.

This was it. His chance. This was the longest time before another patrol came by. By his calculations, that gave him fifteen minutes to get in, then as long as he wanted to get out.

He made his way to the rear of the cemetery and stepped through the gap in the metal fence. Out on the street, he walked down a side alley to the back of the houses. They all backed onto a tiny piece of woodland. There was no pathway there, only bushes and shrubs and nettles. With his jacket hood over his face, he quietly made his way through the foliage. He passed a woman smoking in her garden, completely oblivious to his presence. Lights were on in the second house along, but the silhouettes inside told him no one had spotted his movements. The shadows guided him to where he needed to be, just like he knew they would. He was as invisible as always. Too smart to fail, too capable to fumble at the last hurdle.

Then he came to house number four in the row. He looked inside and saw absolute darkness. No lights were on, but he knew someone was home. Her vehicle was in the driveway. Hers and hers alone. She had no boyfriend, no husband, no life partner. Inside was just her and her baby daughter.

One would die, the other would live. And in twenty years, when that little girl was old enough to understand what had happened, he'd write her a personal letter. Maybe even send her a package with her mother's heart inside. Now that would be a thrill.

There was a gate leading directly into the garden, but he couldn't risk the metal clanging, giving his location away. Instead, he hopped the fence, landing on a dirt patch. He landed silently, then crouched down below the fence height and moved behind a tree. He waited for the dust to settle, scanning the nearby windows to make sure no eyes were upon him.

They weren't. Under the cover of darkness, he moved to the back door, checking for any signs of an alarm system. He hated to generalize, but this area wasn't particularly affluent. People around here barely had locks on their doors, let alone alarm systems.

Beside the back door was a window overlooking the kitchen. Closing in on 10pm now, the woman was no doubt sleeping, or catching what sleep she could before her child woke her up at an ungodly hour. That worked greatly in his favor.

From his jacket, he pulled out his first item. His knife that had already consumed enough blood to fill the elevator from *The Shining*, he thought. He chuckled at the metaphor before sliding the blade between the door and frame. There, he felt resistance in the form of one lock and one latch. He didn't want to risk tugging on the door handle in case it alerted the woman inside.

Next, he pulled out his small flathead screwdriver. He gently pressed it into the lock and searched around for a ridge in the tumbler. With the blade tip pressed against the lock, he gently pushed it to the right as he turned the screwdriver.

The momentum was enough to bring the tumbler to life. Once the lock had moved a few millimeters, he used the blade to brute force it out of place. The lock snapped open with a tiny thud. Not enough to arouse attention, he thought.

And he was inside.

***

He had to rest a few minutes before continuing. He stood in the kitchen, inhaling cold air in the pitch blackness. This was new territory for him and he wanted to make sure it was done right. Even with his confidence and callousness, he was still a little anxious about pulling this off correctly. The woman knew this house better than he did, so he was the one at a disadvantage this time. Not to mention there were people in the houses on either side, and the slightest noise could summon law enforcement here.

But the challenging odds were what made this so perfect. He imagined the looks on the faces of the press and police tomorrow when they found a flawless suburban murder during a city-wide curfew. They'd be in awe of how he pulled it off, how he invaded the home with such mastery. Some people would start to believe he was some kind of phantom, maybe a supernatural entity that could disappear at will.

He applied his gloves, making sure not to bring his skin into contact with any surfaces. He'd remained still for an unknowable amount of time now. It could have been two minutes or ten. What he'd found was that time either sped up or slowed down during the act of murder. But no one had stirred in the house, no rogue footsteps from upstairs. Everyone in this house was sound asleep.

Into the lounge, he used his senses to navigate. No lights, minimal touching. He couldn't quite see everything as he'd hoped but his eyes gradually adjusted to the darkness. He accidentally kicked a sofa, then stepped on a child's teddy bear. He decided to slow his pace and whenever something hit his foot, he reconvened. He found himself in the hallway at the foot of the stairs within a few seconds.

This was going to be the hardest part, he thought. The stairs were the creakiest part of any house, and while he'd practiced on his own steps to obsessive levels, there were still factors he couldn't account for. He stepped onto the first one, keeping his feet as close to the exterior wall as he could. That was where the creaks were less likely to occur.

And he was up. Halfway there, he heard movement from one of the rooms. He salivated at the thought that only a few feet up ahead, his victim lay there, completely unaware that her bringer of death was within spitting distance. He stood still, imagining himself one with the darkness. Once the sounds died out, he continued on.

The landing area was a small strip of carpet with three doorways branching off. Two were open, one was not. He saw the bathroom by the moonlight coming in through the window. The same light illuminated the closed door, displaying a cartoon princess. Beneath that read CHLOE'S CRIB.

The third door was his destination. Suddenly, the outside world felt like it was a million miles away. It had been less than thirty minutes ago he was in the graveyard, but it felt like he'd ventured across oceans and desert plains to get here.

Into the master bedroom he went. The woman's curtains were slightly open, bringing in the briefest flicker of moonlight. He saw the figure in the bed, one arm hanging out of the covers. He recognized her scent from last time; that combination of sweat and perfume. She was a little shorter than he remembered but the hair was the same.

His hand reached for his blade almost by instinct. It was like something else was guiding him, perhaps the omnipotent force that had kept him safe and secure so far. He stepped quietly towards her and raised the blade high.

Should he wake her first? Should he savor the terror in her eyes?

Or should he just get it over with quickly and cleanly?

His heart wanted the former, but the logical side of him told him otherwise. If she screamed, that could alert others. Maybe wake the little girl and have to endure her cries too.

Still, this was good enough.

He gripped the knife with both hands and brought it down with relenting force. Into the fleshy tissue of her neck.

It felt tough, rigid, not like the others.

There was no blood.

The woman didn't even move.

He withdrew the knife, tapped the woman's skull.

Then his world came crashing down. The light above him suddenly burned brighter than a thousand suns. He was visible, exposed. He barely had time to register the new events when a voice behind him screamed, deafening, sending him into a rage-induced panic.

"Stay right there," the voice shouted. Delicate and feminine but determined. "If you move, I'll put a bullet in your head. Do you understand?"

This wasn't meant to happen. This couldn't be how his story ended. He raised his hands in surrender and slowly turned around.

Her. He'd seen her before.

CHAPTER THIRTY

Ella didn't have time to quake or shudder. She kept her pistol trained firmly on the intruder. On his forehead. She wanted nothing more than to pull the trigger and rid the world of this monster for good, but death would be a last resort. She needed him behind bars. She needed his victims' families to see him rot in jail. And who was this man? She couldn't fully see his face but wasn't anyone she recognized. None of the suspects. He was someone completely off their radar. A distressing fact, but the important part was that they were now sharing the same airspace.

"Drop your weapon. Do it now," Ella demanded.

"Where's the woman?" he grunted. "Where is she? I need her."

His voice was gruff and gravelly. There was desperation in there. Here was someone pointing a gun at his head and he was asking about his intended victim.

"She's gone. Safe. So is her daughter. It's over. Drop your weapon or I'll shoot."

Only minutes before, Mia had escorted Amanda and Chloe Huber out of the front of the house. Truth be told, they both thought Amanda and Chloe would be living elsewhere for the time being, but Amanda had made the decision to return home. According to her, she'd bought 'protection' and stashed them around the house. In the bedroom and in the bathrooms. Mia said she'd meet Amanda and Chloe somewhere safe and send backup immediately.

But Ella didn't want backup. She wanted some alone time with this scumbag. This was the culmination of everything she'd worked for, not just in the past few days but all her life. This is what made all the doubts and disappointments worth the torment, because this was what saving lives felt like. This was what changing the world for the better felt like. Running through her veins was terror and conviction in equal measures, and it was the rush she chased so badly. Her whole body shook with a sensation that no other experience on earth could measure up to. This was a moment she'd remember for the rest of her days, however long that might be.

"Gone? No, she can't be gone," his voice booming. His whole body writhed as he screamed, and every movement made Ella pull that trigger just a little bit more.

"She's safe from you. You'll never see her, mister...? What's your name? Or should I call you Gemini?"

The man ignored her question. He violently rotated his body, staring at the doll in the bed. Ella had picked the biggest one from Chloe's collection.

"You replaced her with a doll?" the man shouted, the frustration building in his voice. "You thought you could fool me?"

"Yes. Then I waited for you in this corner. Misdirection, you see. You know all about that, don't you? Now, I'll ask you one final time. If you don't drop that weapon in the next five seconds, I'll put a bullet between your eyes."

Ella saw his hands trembling. He was now coming to terms with reality. He looked her up and down like she was an artifact in a museum.

"I've seen you before. I saw you today. This afternoon."

The breath left her lungs in a sudden heave. How could this man have seen her? Was this some kind of mind game? Ella didn't believe him. "What? Where?" she asked.

"Outside a coffee shop on the Boulevard. You were with a redhead woman. I looked at you and imagined how much fun it would be to slaughter you."

Ella's stomach twisted into knots. Yes, that had been her. She walked right past this son of a bitch, plain as day. This piece of trash who'd made her wretch and worry more times than she could count in the past two days alone had been right there beside her. She was one more comment away from pulling the trigger. Screw a jail sentence, this asshole deserved to die for everything he'd done.

"That won't be happening. What's going to happen is you're going to put that knife on the floor. Then you're going to turn around and I'm going to cuff you. Do you understand?"

"No."

A simple defiance of orders. It was not a word many people said when they had a gun pointed at them.

"No?"

"I refuse to go out like this. This isn't how it ends. I simply cannot be caught. I'm a phantom in the night. I'm a ghost of death. Uncatchable, impalpable. Do you really think a tiny woman like you is going to stop me? I've run the police around in circles for three days. I assume you're a police officer?"

"I'm an FBI agent. I have an entire task force on their way here right now. There's no way out of this house for you. You're not the Zodiac killer, you're a sham."

"No, I'm not the Zodiac killer. I'm better than him. He would never be able to pull off what I have."

Ella laughed. She was in two minds about what to do. She wanted to talk to this man, but she also wanted him in chains. Was there anything stopping her doing both?

"The Zodiac never got caught, did he? He went uncaptured. Fifty years and counting. But poor Gemini got caught after a few days. That must really sting."

"No!" he screamed. He turned around and kicked the bedframe. He plunged his knife into the mattress. Anxiety burnt her from head to toe. Her hands trembled. She knew she'd have to shoot this man to keep him down. He clearly wasn't listening to rationale.

"I was going to be *better* than him, you see?" He pulled the knife back from the mattress and held it close to his chest. "The Zodiac killed thirty-seven people. I was going to kill thirty-eight, all across the country. I was going to move from city to city, reaching my number and then retiring into the shadows. *You've* ruined that."

Ella felt confused. Was this person deluded or did he really think that? "Thirty-seven? The Zodiac killed five people. You've killed five people. You're equal. But the difference is, you've been caught."

The Gemini's rage overflowed. Ella tried to keep her crosshairs on his torso but he was too erratic. *There's no use in this,* she told you herself. *You have to shoot.*

With one long stride, the man was upon her. His gleaming blade was right in front of her, and Ella had no choice but to pull the trigger. Her Glock exploded with deafening gunfire, the recoil jolting her shoulders for the briefest of moments. When the blast subsided, returning their senses to normal, Ella realized the man was still standing.

Behind him was a splintered hole in the wall.

Then she felt his whole body on her, crashing them into the cupboards and sending them sprawling to the floor. Ella desperately maneuvered to get into a clear firing position, but he was too sturdy. He held her down, holding her shooting hand by the wrist and raised his blade with the other.

Ella's vision went black. The next thing she heard was her blood leaking into the floorboards.

CHAPTER THIRTY ONE

She was out for a couple of seconds, but it felt like a lifetime. The pain paralyzed her, distorted her vision, and in the yawning blackness she saw things that only existed in her mind now.

Mutilated corpses, grieving parents, her dead father, young love ravaged by bloodshed, Tobias Campbell sitting in his cell with that yellow grin.

Ella's eyes shot open, erasing the flurry of images and replacing them with a single shot. A shot of the man who'd pushed her down and stabbed her in the shoulder. His blade was high again, and the promise of death was enough to bring her back to life for a final attempt at survival. She brought her knees up into the man's spine, then wrapped them either side of his ribs and squeezed. It brought her enough time to reach out, clutch his wrist and hold him at bay.

His strength was adequate, but not so much she couldn't match it. Ella rolled herself forward with her knees digging into his ribs, using the momentum to spring the Gemini off and send him sprawling across the floorboards. Ella jumped to her feet, suddenly feeling the extent of her injury. Blood streamed from her shoulder across her neck and down her arm. A warm, uncomfortable, gooey sensation. She couldn't see the wound through her clothing, but she knew that blood was leaving her body fast. Ella kept herself upright by using the cupboards, and only now realized that her pistol had fallen from her grip.

She reached down to grab it but the Gemini got there first. He slid towards it, kicking it out of the bedroom and leaving Ella unarmed. A sick smile spread across the man's face as he realized his advantage, but something in his posture told Ella that he wasn't a fighter.

"Not used to fighting one-on-one, are you?" Ella asked as she assumed the square fighting stance. The Gemini would no doubt swipe his blade at her, so she needed a solid defensive position. Attacking was no good if he could just cut her down.

Without responding, the Gemini did exactly that. He swung his butcher's knife ferociously and without aim, probably hoping that random cuts would be enough to subdue her. Ella jumped back and hurried to the other side of the bed. She reached down and lifted up the metal frame, sending the whole thing toppling against her attacker. It smashed against him, burying him against the cupboards and smashing some furniture in the process.

Ella escaped the room and searched the landing area for her pistol. The light was minimal, and all she found was kids' toys and junk. Footsteps thundered behind her and the Gemini appeared from the darkness, clutching his arm around her neck from behind. He pulled up to a standing position, and Ella's instinct told her to clutch his wrists so he couldn't maneuver the blade.

She caught it but his position gave him the advantage. He moved the blade closer to her stomach, and all Ella could do was watch. No air would reach her lungs. He'd blocked off her respiratory trackt, and the lack of new oxygen made her gradually weaker.

"Those kids in the woods. They'll be nothing compared to what I'm gonna do to you," he whispered.

Now Ella saw her pistol, mere inches from her feet. She moved her foot to grip it but her efforts were in vain. The Gemini realized her intentions, stepped around and kicked the gun down the stairs.

Helpless now.

This was how she died, she thought.

Her hands around the man's wrist weren't enough. His knife inched closer to her abdomen, threatening rupture at any second. Her thoughts were of Mia and Ben and her roommate. She thought of her father and wondered if he'd be proud that his daughter died in combat.

How far away was backup? Mia said it would take around eight minutes. That was five minutes ago.

Could she buy time? What could she say or do that might keep her alive for a few more minutes?

There were a few things she could say, but talking was impossible. As the life drained from her, she found herself considering the idea that had occurred to her the moment this man clutched her. The idea that could very easily kill one or both considering there was a butcher's knife between them.

A desperation maneuver, but if she was going to die anyway, she might as well spin the wheel. Ella lifted up her leg, the movement bringing the tip of the knife into her flesh. She ignored the pain, told herself it was a flesh wound and continued with her plan. With her foot against the landing wall, she pushed back with the last ounce of strength her body had left.

The Gemini toppled back, taking her along with him. One step.

Two steps.

She felt him struggle to keep his balance, and less than a second after her push, the Gemini's foot tripped on the stairs. The lack of visibility helped, because while she felt herself spiraling along with the man, she didn't see the world turning as they fell. Ella suddenly thought of her first ever rollercoaster ride as a kid, when she fixed her eyes shut as the loops came.

Ella felt her skull crack off the wall twice, three times. Her feet dragged along the opposite wall, but it felt as though the Gemini's torso cushioned her blow. Since she couldn't control the fall, she only prayed that gravity was in her favor and the Gemini's blade wouldn't find its way into her flesh.

Then everything stopped. Oxygen returned to her lungs and she took in a series of panicked breaths. Ella pushed herself up off the wooden floor, feeling light-headed, bruised and stung, but ultimately alive.

More concerning, the Gemini was nowhere to be seen.

She'd felt his torso against hers when they landed. He couldn't have gone far. How did he rise up and disappear so suddenly?

Ella scrambled along the floor for her gun. He'd kicked it down here so it must be here somewhere. There was nothing, and every second she searched was a second this man had to escape.

She checked the front door, still deadbolted. He couldn't have gone out there. That meant he was in the house. She hadn't heard any other door open or shut, but the layout of the bottom floor was a mystery. She'd come in through the front and gone straight upstairs.

Into the lounge, Ella stepped cautiously. She stopped and listened for any signs of life but could only hear the sound of her beating heart. Blood oozed from her shoulder, worse now following her plunge from the top step. She ignored the pain. Now wasn't the time to die.

Ella quickly scanned the room and the adjoining kitchen but saw nothing, no one. Her hands found her phone in her pocket. She pulled it out and turned on her flashlight. It illuminated the room, and the radiance stirred something in the shadows. From behind the far sofa against the wall, the figure rose once more.

Right then, Ella felt more helpless than she ever had in her life. The Gemini had her pistol clutched in his hands. There were five live rounds in there. Her flashlight threw his shadow against the wall behind him.

"No escaping now," he said. "Keep that light on me. Move and I'll shoot."

Left led back to the stairs. Right to a closed door. She could flee and hope for the best, but even for an unskilled marksman, her chances of survival were low.

Were backup nearly there? They couldn't be more than a minute away now. And what would happen when they burst through the door? He'd fire at her, taking her down as a final middle finger to the police.

Was there any way out of this alive? Ella began talking without any direction, hoping that she'd find her footing.

"A gun? Why use a gun now?" she asked.

"I don't care. You don't count as one of my victims."

"No. The whole world will know. This is how your legacy ends. Trying to shoot your way out of a backed corner. Do you really want that?"

"Shut up," he shouted. He moved away from the sofa and blocked the lounge exit. No escape. "This is my story and I'll tell it how *I* want."

"Why did you do it?" Ella asked. "Why kill those innocent people?"

"Because I was always better than everyone else," he said confidently.

"How so?"

The Gemini took a few steps closer to her. For a second, she thought he was about to fire.

"Smarter. More capable. Harder working. But society kept me at the bottom. I decided I'd had enough. That's when I decided to start doing things my way."

From the room to her right, Ella could smell chemicals. Bleach.

What had Amanda said earlier?

She got an idea. It might be sealing her fate, but it was better than dying with her hands surrendered. All she needed was a distraction.

"What did you think of *Lake of the Dead*?" she asked. "You saw it, right?"

The Gemini looked confused, even impressed. "You caught that?" he asked, and for the briefest of moments, he lowered his weapon by an inch.

Ella darted.

She sheathed the phone-turned-flashlight into her pocket to darken the room again and flew towards the door to her left. As she grabbed the handle, two bullets pierced the wall behind her, sending her momentarily deaf.

And she was in the room. A downstairs toilet, the room barely wider than a cupboard. She frantically searched for a light switch and found a pull cord. The room lit up. Outside, the Gemini's footsteps rumbled the floor. Ella sat on the toilet and rammed her feet against the door. The Gemini pulled on the handle, then rammed the door with his full weight. The impact sent shockwaves of pain through her feet and ankles, but she was so close to survival.

"I've locked it, you idiot," Ella screamed.

The ramming stopped, giving Ella a few seconds of freedom. She knew what was about to come. If he had any sense, he'd just shoot through the door.

She reached down to the floor and searched for Amanda's so-called protection.

There was nothing there.

Shit, where else it could be?

"Fine," he said. "I'd like to see the look on your face when you die, but this will be enough."

Ella knew she had about five seconds before the hail of bullets came ripping. She stood up and scanned every inch of the room. Finally, as her last resort, she lifted up the toilet cistern.

A zip-locked bag.

With trembling hands, she fished it out and pulled out what lay inside. She felt the weight, about three pounds, she guessed.

Loaded.

There was a tap against the door. Ella couldn't see the other side, but she was certain that was the Gemini putting the pistol head right up against it.

There no time to think, no time to even aim. She pointed Amanda's newly-purchased Springfield XD at the door and pulled the trigger.

Then again.

Four more times until the barrels were empty.

Smoke filled the tiny room. Ella's eardrums had all but ruptured to pieces. Her wrist burnt from the explosive recoil. She sat half on the lavatory, half on the floor, listening, waiting for a sign that her plan hadn't worked.

It took a short eternity. There was a constant ringing in her ears, like a busy telephone line. She couldn't be sure, but she thought she heard floorboards creaking, the unmistakable sound of another soul in the home.

That was her last shot. She was now defenseless. If the Gemini had avoided her attack, it was game over.

Then she saw something.

Between the wounds and the terror, her heart almost stopped beating.

At one of the bullet holes in the door, an eyeball appeared.

Ella dropped her head into her hands and did her best to conceal her cries.

"Agent Dark, are you alright in there?"

A tsunami of relief swept away the horror. For the first time in as long as she could remember, she exhaled a full breath.

It was over.

CHAPTER THIRTY TWO

Ella sat on the curb outside Ravenscourt Avenue, now truly suffering, at least physically. Her shoulder continued to ooze blood, which had since smeared across her face and neck. Even ten minutes later, it still felt like there was an alarm ringing in her head. A medical official looked her over, bandaged up her shoulder and gave her some painkillers.

Every resident in the street had come out to observe the proceedings. A couple of uniformed officers did their best to keep them away, but their smartphone cameras bested the officers' abilities.

She could hear the stirs from inside the house. Officers came in and out, but there was no sign of the killer's body yet. She wanted to take a look at his face, imagine him at the crime scenes, see the wounds she'd inflicted. But at the same time, she didn't want to do any of that. Now that the battle was over, finality brought a clear head. The adrenaline high was diminishing, and she saw the world in plain view. Ella realized that she really had done everything she could to find this perpetrator, and she realized that she wasn't far off all along. It was the longing for that rush, she thought, that brought the doubts in with it.

"Amazing job," a voice said. Agent Ripley appeared and took a seat beside her. "How did it all happen?"

Ella rotated her shoulder, feeling the blood squelch beneath the wraps. She ran through the events in her head, not really sure where to start. Since she pounced on the Gemini in the bedroom, all events that followed blurred into one.

"I threw him down the stairs," Ella said. It was the first thing that came to mind, and the only part of their battle she remembered in detail.

"You're not kidding," Mia said. "There's blood all over the staircase."

"That would be mine."

From her pocket, Mia pulled out her Glock 19. The same Glock 19 she'd lent Ella before leaving. "I guess this was no use, then?"

Ella let out a subtle laugh. "No. He knocked it out of my hand. I feel so stupid for that."

"Ha. Don't. It's happened to me a hundred times too. All it takes is a moment of weakness."

Ella sighed. "Luckily, I found another one. In the toilet."

"You what?"

"Amanda said she'd hidden some guns around her house. Said she'd hidden them in her bathrooms. The killer cornered me, and I ran into the downstairs bath. Found a Springfield in there. If it wasn't for Amanda, I'd probably be dead."

Mia shook her head. "No, you adapted. You thought on your feet. That's the mark of a good agent. You should hold your head up high."

Ella reluctantly accepted her praise, at least on the surface. Inside, she felt much differently. Unlike this killer's victims, Ella had just been in the right place at the right time. Others had helped her on this journey; she was just the vehicle that executed everything. Tobias had told her how to find this man. Amanda's forward-thinking had put the gun in her hands. If she'd been left to her own devices, she'd still be chasing this phantom.

"Is he dead?" she asked, the question that plagued her since the officers arrived. Since that eyeball at the door which she mistook for the killer's. It was actually one of the arriving officers'.

"Not sure," Mia said. "He was breathing when we got there. You hit him in the chest but didn't hit the heart. He was bleeding pretty badly."

Ella wasn't sure whether she wanted him alive or dead. As long as he couldn't take any more lives, that was what mattered the most. "I just unloaded," Ella said. "I just pulled the trigger until there was nothing left. I had no idea if I hit him or not. I just remember thinking that it was my last chance at survival."

Mia tapped her on the back. The impact hurt but she didn't show it. "Don't overthink it. Don't play the *what if* game," Mia said. "If you weren't here, this guy would still be out there right now. You caught a killer. Very few people in the world can say that. Stop analyzing everything and just enjoy the moment."

Ella nodded. "Thank you."

Instantly, the whole street went quiet. All eyes, including that of the guarding officers, jumped to the scene at the front door of 4 Ravenscourt Avenue.

Officer Denton emerged from the house. But he wasn't alone. The suspect, the Gemini killer, was cuffed to high heaven. His wrists were bound, his feet were shackled. His movements were slow, accompanied by the lifting power of the officers to keep him on his feet. If they let go, it looked like he'd collapse in a heap under the weight of his injures. His shirt and jacket had been removed, exposing the bullet wound in his chest. He looked a lot less threatening in chains.

"Well, that's him. Doesn't look like much, does he?" Mia said.

It wasn't the first time she looked him up and down, but it was the first time she really saw him. The man couldn't have been older than thirty-five, dark hair glued to his forehead by sweat and blood. Wide eyes, black as coals. A beard long overdue grooming. His figure was sturdy but athletic with strong shoulders that screamed manual worker. Even in his slumped position, he looked like he could put up a fight. Ella had found that out the hard way.

Ella said nothing to Mia. She watched Denton escort the Gemini to a waiting cruiser, purposely avoiding any close proximity to Ella.

"Wait," she shouted. She rose to her feet and approached them beside Denton's car. Ella had a question she wanted to ask. Since beginning this case, Ella was so focused on the man's obsession with the Zodiac that she didn't for a second think there was a rivalry there. She always imagined he wants to be *as* good as him, but not better.

"Agent Dark, you don't need to be here," Denton said. "Please go home and rest. This is over."

"No. I need to know something."

The Gemini kept his head low. He didn't want the attention, not this way. He narrowed his eyes at her. "I won't talk to you. You don't know me. You got lucky."

"I might have got lucky, but I realized something back there," Ella said. "Amanda Huber. You let her escape your car on purpose, didn't you?"

Something on the Gemini's face told her that she was right. He didn't acknowledge her comment.

"You orchestrated a scenario where you could best the Zodiac. Do something he never did. You had no intentions of murdering Amanda on the night you abducted her, did you?"

The Gemini looked down at the hole in his chest. He coughed up a globule of blood and spat it at Ella's feet. "No, I didn't."

She let the moment hang between them. Maybe she *could* see into the criminal mind as good as the criminals themselves. But still, she had her doubts. She needed the Gemini's prompt to plant the theory, but she got there eventually.

"Get him out of here," she said and walked back to Mia. Ella took a final look at the house where it had all played out. From the outside, it looked nothing special. But the interior had been torn to shreds.

"Good deduction, Dark. That never crossed my mind. Is that he told you?"

"He said he was going to be better than the Zodiac. That's when I realized we'd missed something. All this time, we thought he was just copying the Zodiac. Maybe because the Mimicker in Louisiana did exactly that. The Mimicker just wanted to match what his heroes did, but this guy wanted to go above and beyond."

Ella rotated her shoulders to shake off some of the pain. Even without the pumping adrenaline to numb the hurt, it didn't phase her as much as it would under other circumstances. The successful capture felt too good. Should she have waited for Mia to get back before battling this unsub? She could have, but she was glad she didn't. She didn't need Mia to hold her hand, nor did she want her to.

Mia put her arm around Ella. "Excellent work. You cracked this one open, but right now you need a break. Go home, seen that boyfriend of yours."

"He's not my boyfriend," Ella said.

"Whatever. Come on, Amanda is back at the precinct. We need to apologize to her. Well, you do."

"I do?"

"Yeah. It wasn't me that wrecked her house."

CHAPTER THIRTY THREE

Just after midnight, Ella and Mia sat in the San Diego PD precinct with Amanda. Chloe was asleep in her stroller, cuddling the plush bumblebee she'd stolen from the toy box.

"How are you feeling?" Ella asked Amanda. Despite the redness around her eyes, Ella saw that Amanda's worry had been lifted. A smile hung on her lips, one that suggested relief and optimism.

"Better than you," Amanda said. "I'm just glad he's behind bars now. What do you think will happen to him?"

"Based on tonight alone, life imprisonment," Mia offered. "Once they confirm he was responsible for five murders, which won't be too difficult given the evidence we have, I'd say he's looking at death row. This is California after all. Judges round here throw out the death penalty like it's confetti."

"As long as he can't hurt me or my girl, I'm fine with that."

"No chance," Ella said. "About your house... I'm sorry."

"What's wrong with it?" Amanda asked, barely a note of concern in her voice.

"I wrecked it. I smashed your cupboards, broke your staircase, shot some holes in your walls."

Amanda just laughed. "Sounds like a good time. Don't worry, I needed to redecorate anyway."

"I was only joking, Dark," Mia said. "Your home will be good as new in a few days, Miss Huber. All expenses paid. Choose whatever interior you want."

"Well, thank you. At least something good has come from all of this."

"You could say that," Mia said. "Now please, go and stay in a hotel until it's all done. Will little Chloe be able to sleep in a hotel? We'll get you a travel cot."

"Oh, don't worry about this devil. She'll sleep anywhere."

"Must be nice," Mia said.

Amanda picked herself up and moved to the door with the stroller. She pulled it open. "Thank you, agents. If you hadn't have shown up at my doorstep tonight, I could be dead now. And God knows what might have happened to my little girl."

"No, thank you for putting that gun in your cistern," Ella said. "If you didn't do that, I'd be dead too."

Amanda smiled, pulled open the door, and maneuvered the stroller out.

"And he wouldn't have hurt Chloe," Ella said. "He told me."

She stopped. Ella knew that Amanda didn't know what to say. And what could she say? There was really no appropriate response.

"Take care, agents. If you need anything, I'll be available."

They nodded their thanks and Amanda left. She disappeared through the precinct, on her way to a better life.

"That wasn't true, was it?" Mia asked.

Ella decided to just be honest. "No. It wasn't. I have no idea what his intentions were with Chloe." She expected Mia to give her a scolding, a lesson in morality. None was forthcoming.

"You said that because you didn't want her worrying for the rest of her life. I get that. Good choice."

"Exactly. Like you said, the *what if* game is a bad one. It can drive you mad. I seem to play it a lot and I wouldn't wish that mental stress on anyone."

Mia collected her belongings. She wound the cords around her laptop and put it into her bag. "Honestly, fantastic work, rookie. Although I might have to stop calling you rookie now. If you hadn't figured out he was seeing his victims as possessions, we would never have got here."

Ella collected her own belongings. She neatly collected her case file back together and slotted them into her backpack. "Yeah, I suppose."

"Not suppose. Definitely. You figured that out and then worked backward. You got into his head and that's what this job is about. This morning, you were doubting you could do it. Fifteen hours later, you'd done it. That's pretty remarkable if I do say so myself."

Ella didn't feel worthy of the praise. It wasn't her revelation; it came from the mind of Tobias Campbell. Not only was he the person Mia despised the most, but her conversation with him was still a guarded secret.

Was now the time to tell her? If not now, then when? She'd never be as receptive to her as she was now. She had to.

"Ripley, I did something and I'm not sure you're going to like it."

"Oh?" Mia said, stuffing the rest of her possessions into her bag. "Right now, I don't care what you did. This case is over and we can get the hell out of California."

"I'm being serious. I arranged a visit with someone."

Mia quickly perked up. Ella had her attention now. "Who? Who did you arrange a visit with?"

Just the look on her face was enough to send Ella into an anxiety overload. It was clear that Mia guessed who she was referring to.

No. She couldn't say it. She couldn't tell her, ever. It would have to stay a secret for the rest of their time together. Ella told herself this, and for a second she naïvely believed it was possible. She cursed herself for being so wildly optimistic.

"That woman. The one who wrote the letters to my dad. I'm going to meet her in person."

"Huh? Why wouldn't I like that?" Mia asked. "That's fantastic!"

Ella back peddled. "Oh, really? I thought you said it was a bad idea. Maybe I'm misremembering. Sorry, I'm still a mess. I've been through the wars."

"You certainly have. How're your eardrums?"

"Bad. Constant ringing. Is my hearing screwed forever now?"

Mia laughed again and hoisted her bag over her shoulder. "No, but it lasts a few days. See one of the FBI medics when you get back. It's painful but it goes away. Just don't make a habit of listening to gun blasts without protection."

"I won't. Are we going?"

"One AM flight to D.C. Let's say our goodbyes and get out of here."

Time to go home. While the weight of the case was off Ella's consciousness, there were still a number of issues bringing her down. When they got back to D.C., she had to address them.

All of them. No matter how hard they might be.

CHAPTER THIRTY FOUR

Ella woke up in her apartment around 7pm the next night. After getting off the plane around daybreak, her first stop was Virginia Hospital for a check-up. Her condition was stable, her red blood cells had rapidly reproduced and bandages would keep away any infections. She got lucky, they said. If her lacerations were a few inches to the left, things could have ended much differently.

By 2pm she was home, where she collapsed onto the bed and slept away the events of the past few days. Or tried to, at least. When she woke up, it all suddenly came hurtling back. The dead bodies, the Gemini, Tobias Campbell, her deceit. The pain was all still there too.

According to a message from Mia, the Gemini's real name was Ramsey Coolidge. He worked as a janitor at a local school, and that was everything they could find on him. He had no criminal history, no previous incidents of sexual assault. He was a nobody who revered the Zodiac and that was all there was to it.

Ella picked herself up off her bed, making sure not to put unnecessary stress on her shoulder. She grabbed her phone from her bedside table. Three new messages. All from Ben. The panic hit her. She'd completely forgotten she was meant to meet him tonight.

Hey, you back from home? x

What time tonight, sugar? x

Oi, you still there? Don't say you've given up on me already! x

It was dark outside already, and her body told her that it wanted breakfast despite the evening hour. She didn't plan on sleeping this long. Now, her body clock would be messed up for the next few days.

But more concerning was her lack of desire to meet up with Ben. She really liked him, but there was something there that didn't click for her. She thought that maybe her desire to meet him would change when she got back to Virginia, but nothing had changed on the airplane ride or the taxi home.

It was like they were from two different worlds. He was a performer, someone who played a character for the entertainment of others. But when it was over, he could go back to being his real self, and everyone simply accepted that his in-ring persona was an act. In Ella's world, she sometimes played a character too, but she had to keep it to herself. When she came off the job, she couldn't be someone else. The events that happened in her professional life spilled over into her personal one, and no amount of character detachment could stop it from being so. She didn't really expect Ben to understand, nor was he required to.

Beside her bed sat her father's letters: the ones sent to him by a mystery woman over twenty years ago. Now, with her identity and location uncovered, all Ella wanted to do was pay her a visit now that she was back home. The desire burned brighter than any other, engulfing any longing to see Ben.

She began to type a reply, not really sure what to say. She'd hadn't done this once in her 29 years of life.

Ben, I'm sorry. I can't make tonight. I hate to say this, but I think you and I should cool things off. I wanted to say this to your face but I didn't want to waste your time. With me being away so often, I don't think it would work. I hope you understand. You're a great guy and you'll easily find someone who makes you happy.

With a reluctant finger, she pressed *send*.

Ella collapsed back on her bed and closed her eyes, waiting for that inevitable reply. Somewhere out there, Ben was going through that crushing disappointment she'd felt herself enough times in the past.

She found herself falling back to sleep, thinking of the letters and the mystery writer. Ben's reply never came.

***

The next morning, Ella drove the fifty miles to Richmond to meet a woman named Samantha Hawkins. Ella had her name and address, and Samantha wasn't aware of Ella's upcoming arrival.

Only two weeks before, Ella had discovered the letters among her father's possessions in her lockup. After he'd died in ninety-seven, Ella had taken his belongings from place to place, always finding somewhere to store them. Only recently had she summoned the courage to sort them out in full. She couldn't keep them forever, she knew, and some of the bigger items had to be thrown away.

Among the tattered playing cards and the rusted ornaments, Ella had found a series of letters written to her dad, all of which were signed off as *Samantha*. The letters were dated from ninety-five to ninety-seven, and the contents were casual and spirited. Samantha spoke to Ken like he was a close friend, maybe a lover, but it was difficult to determine from written words alone.

Ella had taken one of the letters she found among her father's stuff and ran the signature through the graphology software at HQ. She'd found the signature matched a number of bills and legal documents, and they all declared the same address in Richmond, Virginia.

Ella didn't know what to expect, or whether this Samantha person would even remember her father at all. But there was a chance that they shared some of the same memories, and there was something in that idea that called Ella towards this mystery woman. She might have some stories, or some pictures, or anything that could resurrect her dad for the briefest of moments in her mind.

Ella parked about twenty feet away and stared at the house. It looked to her like a split-level house, a relic from the eighties. It was a nice house, immaculately presented, if not a little small. There was a red Toyota on the narrow driveway.

Exactly what she was going to say, Ella didn't know. Would the woman even remember her dad? It could have been just a brief affair, a kiss in the dark. Maybe she'd long since moved on and had banished Ken Dark to the depths of her memory? And how would this woman react to a stranger appearing on her doorstep in the middle of the day?

Ella gripped the key in the ignition, thinking that this was all a silly idea. But something up ahead changed her mind. A woman emerged from the house and put a trash bag into her bin. She was dressed up, like she was about to leave. Ella saw the woman's Toyota blink to life.

Almost unconsciously, Ella leaped from her vehicle and hurried over to the house. The woman, short in stature, light blonde hair, no doubt dyed to conceal the grays, got into the driver's seat. Assuming she was around the same age as her father would be now, she'd aged considerably well.

Ella stood beside the driveway. The Toyota's engine started up and the woman waved Ella in a *you go first* gesture. Ella didn't move.

The woman rolled her window down. "Go on, darling."

Ella decided to just get it over with. This woman might not even be the right person, she thought. "Are you Samantha Hawkins?" Ella asked.

The woman looked a little scared. Ella had come to learn that people of a certain age naturally grew suspicious when someone knew details that weren't clear on the surface.

"I might be. And you are?"

"Samantha, I'm so sorry to scare you like this, but my name's Ella Dark. Do you remember me?"

The woman pushed the automatic locking button. "Ella?" She scanned her memory, pursed her lips and slowly shook her head. "Sorry, it doesn't ring a bell. Can I help you with something? Are you trying to sell me something? Because I can tell you right now I'm not buying."

Ella panicked and held up her palms, trying to reassure Samantha she wasn't a salesperson. "No, I'm not selling anything. I could be wrong, but I think you used to know my father. A long time ago. Ken Dark."

The woman's face was blank. "Are you sure you've got the right person?" she asked. "Sorry, but I don't know anyone by that name."

Another layer of grief to Ella's amassing pile. If this woman wasn't being serious, she was a very good actor. But how could Ella have gotten this wrong? She had the signature, the name, the address.

"Sorry, miss, but I need to get going. I'm sorry I couldn't help you." The woman put the car in reverse and checked her rear mirror.

One last shot, Ella thought. She couldn't yet face the drive back home. "So you don't remember writing this?" Ella asked. She pulled out one of her letters, unfolded it and passed it to the woman through the car window.

She scrutinized it with a thorough eye, as though she was looking at an alien contraption. Ella kept a watchful stare on her micro-signals, looking for any sign of familiarity.

Ella didn't have to look hard.

The woman lowered the letter to her lap and pressed her fingers into her eyes. She shook her head rapidly from side to side.

"I've done everything I can to forget about this," she said.

Ella could hardly believe it. Even after everything, it didn't seem real. "You wrote it?" Ella asked, desperately.

"Yes, I wrote this."

This was her.

"I'm so sorry about what happened," she continued. "But please, don't blame me for it."

Ella hadn't expected that. "Huh? Blame you? For my dad's death?"

The woman turned off the car engine and reluctantly stepped out of the car.

"You better come in."

CHAPTER THIRTY FIVE

Ella was impressed with the tidiness of Samantha's house. It was small but well-kept, polished to perfection, cleaner than a ship's whistle. They sat at Samantha's kitchen table, a coffee for Ella and a glass of wine for Samantha. Ken's letter sat in between them.

"I had no idea these letters still existed. I thought I'd destroyed them all."

"No," Ella said, "there are quite a few."

Samantha took a sip of her white wine. Ella thought it best not to mention that it had barely gone midday yet.

"How did you find me?" Samantha asked, only moving her gaze between the letter and her alcohol.

"You put your signature on them. I ran them through handwriting recognition software at work."

"Smart," Samantha laughed. "Where do you work?"

"At the FBI."

The comment caught Samantha off-guard. "Oh, hell. That's amazing. Ken would have been so proud."

"Would he?" Ella asked, genuinely not knowing the answer.

"Of course. You were his whole world. Last time I saw you, he was teaching you to play chess out on your porch. You must have been, what, five years old?"

Ella recalled the memory with clarity. Out on their beaten up porch, playing games and watching the vehicles go past. "About that."

"You used to love the tractors," Samantha laughed, finally raising her eyes to meet Ella's. "There was a farm down the road and the tractors would come and go. You'd chase the ones that had animals in it and me and Ken had to run after you."

Ella remembered it all too well. "What was he like? I only knew him as my dad, but there must have been other sides to him."

Samantha took a gulp of wine and blinked the memories to life. "No, you were everything. After your mom vanished, you became his world. He was always a man's man, working class to the bone but he had a heart of gold. He could build a shed in record time and he'd do anything for anyone. That was Ken."

174

Ella already knew that, but it was elating to hear it from another mouth. She always thought that maybe she idealized the memories of her father, but Samantha's claims told her otherwise. That thought alone was comforting. Something she'd been waiting over twenty years to hear.

"Were you and he an item?"

Samantha shook her head. "Not quite. I'm not sure what you kids call it these days, but we courted for a few months. It was nothing official. I met him at your karate lessons, believe it or not."

It was bojutsu, Ella thought, but she let it slide. "You had kids that went to those lessons too?"

"Oh no. I don't have children. I took my nephew. Me and Ken got talking and I took to him immediately. Unfortunately, I worked away a lot during the week, so I didn't have time to see Ken very often."

"That's why I don't remember you," Ella said. She held her hands against the coffee mug to warm them.

"Pretty much. I probably saw you three, four times max. Your dad had quite a few close friends, so you probably just thought I was one of them."

Ella subtly glanced around the kitchen, looking for something that could glimpse into Samantha's current life. She didn't want to be rude and ask. There were four cups and four glasses positioned above the sink. Cutlery was minimal. A few plaques dotted around. There were two cat bowls and a litter tray on the floor. From what Ella could tell, Samantha lived alone.

"What did you mean by *blame you*?" Ella asked.

Samantha finished her drink and poured another one. "I'm sorry. I spoke too soon. I instantly thought that if you found me, you'd researched me too."

Ella had no idea what she was talking about. "No, all I know is your name and address. I didn't look into your past."

Samantha placed both hands palm-down on the table. It was a gesture that said *I'm about to tell you the truth now.*

"When I met Ken, I had a husband," Samantha said.

Ella was a little shocked at the revelation. "You and dad were having an affair?"

"Not exactly. I was separated. The divorce was going through but it wasn't finalized. At the time, I didn't tell Ken any of this. I didn't want to scare him off."

"Right," Ella said. She remembered that her dad always pushed her to be honest, even as a child. She guessed that he wouldn't have taken kindly to this deceit.

"After a couple of months, my ex-husband found out I was seeing someone new. He wasn't happy about it. The divorce wasn't amicable, you see. He thought I was seeing Ken while he and I were together. And that same day, Ken found out I was married too."

Ella quickly made a connection and it brought her to the point of tears. "Please don't say…" she began.

"No. Well, I don't know," Samantha said. "That day, my ex, Richie, went round to Ken's house and gave him a piece of his mind. Richie was a real sleaze. A troublemaker. Always in and out of jail. He and Ken got into a fight. Neither would back down. I wasn't there to see it, but apparently it wasn't pretty."

Ella had no idea her father ever fought with anyone. If it happened, she wasn't aware of it. "Okay. And then?"

"Richie backed down and drove off."

Ella didn't want to ask the question. "What date was this?"

"March sixteenth. Ninety-seven."

Ella clasped her hand around her mouth.

Only two days later, her dad had been murdered as he slept.

Memories flooded back and Ella felt the tears extinguish her burning eyes. She knew everything about her dad's death that was possible to know, from both memory and police report. God knows she'd replayed the events over and over in her head, constantly trying to make connections and deduce names of her dad's potential killer. But this Richie person? She hadn't come across that name at all in her research.

"Richie? And his surname?"

Samantha scratched her cheek. "Richard Cassidy."

Ella didn't need to note it down. The name was already etched in her mind. "And you know nothing else about him? Where he might be?"

Samantha held up her hands in surrender. "I swear it. I haven't seen or heard from him since that year. Our divorce came through not long after Ken died. Richie disappeared. No one heard from him. I've even asked mutual friends since then and he's just completely vanished off the grid."

Ella pushed back her hair and shut her eyes to block the tears. It didn't work. There was a name attached to her father's death, and it somehow made the whole group of events realer than they'd been for twenty years.

She clasped her hands around the table and realized she was rising to her feet. "And you *swear* that you haven't heard from him at all? Even during your divorce? He just fought with my dad and then… disappeared?"

Her voice was raised. She calmed herself, realizing that Samantha had done nothing wrong. She held up her palms in an apologetic gesture. She felt Samantha move away from her, a slight lean to the left.

"God's honest truth," Samantha said. "I've got no reason to protect him. For all I know, he might not even be alive. He was a heavy drinker, big-time smoker. Violent outbursts. I wouldn't be surprised to find someone had took matters into their own hands when it came to Richie."

Ella had questions and lots of them. So many that she didn't know where to start. They all converged into one giant flurry of words and thoughts, hammering against her temples with wanton fury. But what became clear was that she had a suspect, a suspect with a motive and a history of violence. The profiler in her naturally applied the same thought process as she would to any murder scenario, but doing it to such a personal case felt like a violation.

But she couldn't stop herself. The pieces fell into place and created a very clear picture.

This Richard Cassidy person *had* to be the man who killed her father.

And it was at that moment, sitting in this woman's kitchen with tears in her eyes and rage in her veins, that she vowed to find him.

EPILOGUE

Thank God she hadn't driven to the bar, because she could barely see straight once the cool night air hit her. She walked the three miles home, stopping along the way to admire the Shenandoah River. She thought of the Gemini's victims, who could now be put to rest peacefully. By now, their families would have been alerted of the killer's capture, so they could begin the grieving process in full.

Ella got back to her apartment complex just after midnight. At the main door, she stumbled around for her keys in her bag and came up short. *Damn it.* Since she didn't drive, she must have forgotten to bring her keys at all. She pushed the buzzer to her apartment and hoped that Jenna was still awake. She usually was at this hour.

"Jennaaaaa," she said, thinking it might magically summon her awake. There was no response. "Pish. The one time I need her and she's nowhere to be found. Typical."

Luckily, someone came through the other side of the door and let her in. A man in a beanie hat who'd she'd never seen in the building before. Must be a newbie. He smiled at her as they passed.

"Don't worry. I'm not a burglar," she said. "I live at number 35."

"Yeah well, maybe I am," he laughed and continued on his way.

Ella trudged up the stairs to the top floor and prayed her door was still open. If it wasn't, God knows what she'd do. Maybe she'd sleep in the hallway or hit a hotel – if she managed to make it that far.

When she turned the corner to her row, she froze in absolute shock. All of the alcohol in her system suddenly disappeared, replaced by a fear she knew all too well by now.

Outside her door was a pool of red liquid.

And there was something else.

Ella grasped the hallway door for support, not wanting to venture any closer for fear of discovering the truth. She squinted her eyes to make it out.

An animal?

What the hell?

Slowly, she made her way closer, every inch animating the horror a little bit more. She stopped a few feet from her doorstep, the full scene now plainly in view.

A cat hung from her door, a noose tied firmly around its neck.

It was a huge black thing, certainly not one of the residents' pets. There was a cut along its stomach, dripping blood onto the crème floor.

Ella stepped back and pulled out her phone. The police needed to check this. She went to dial 911, but she rested her eyes on her recent calls list. The last one she'd made was to Maine State Prison.

Then there was that familiar spark that lit up whenever she thought of historical murder incidents. But this time, it involved her.

What had she said to Tobias Campbell only a few days ago? How had their conversation gone?

"Do you like horses, Agent Dark? You look the type. I could see you in an equestrian getup; a sleeveless jacket and riding boots."

"Never had the interest. I was always a cat person."

No. It couldn't be.

Ella felt an ice cold rush numb her whole body. Crippling dread tied her stomach in knots. Her knees trembled to the point she had to grab the wall for support, trying to tell herself this was all a dream or hallucination. Breathless, clutching her face as though she was trying to undo what she'd just seen.

But it was no use.

She swore she could hear Tobias's laughter all the way from his prison cell.

GIRL, SILENCED
(An Ella Dark FBI Suspense Thriller—Book 4)

"A MASTERPIECE OF THRILLER AND MYSTERY. Blake Pierce did a magnificent job developing characters with a psychological side so well described that we feel inside their minds, follow their fears and cheer for their success. Full of twists, this book will keep you awake until the turn of the last page."
--Books and Movie Reviews, Roberto Mattos (re Once Gone)

GIRL, SILENCED (An Ella Dark FBI Suspense Thriller) is book #4 in a long-anticipated new series by #1 bestseller and USA Today bestselling author Blake Pierce, whose bestseller Once Gone (a free download) has received over 1,000 five star reviews.

FBI Agent Ella Dark, 29, is given her big chance to achieve her life's dream: to join the Behavorial Crimes Unit. Ella has a hidden obsession: she has studied serial killers from the time she could read, devastated by the murder of her own sister. With her photographic memory, she has obtained an encyclopedic knowledge of every serial killer, every victim and every case. Singled out for her brilliant mind, Ella is invited to join the big leagues.

When johns are found murdered in their cars, it appears to be a jilted prostitute morphing into a serial killer. Ella sees echoes of it in many past cases, and feels sure she understands this killer's M.O.

But when the killer strikes again and surprises her, Ella realizes that everything she thought she knew was wrong.

Can Ella save the next victim before it's too late? And can she learn to throw out everything she knows and trust her budding instincts?

A page-turning and harrowing crime thriller featuring a brilliant and tortured FBI agent, the ELLA DARK series is a riveting mystery, packed with suspense, twists and turns, revelations, and driven by a breakneck pace that will keep you flipping pages late into the night.

Book #5 (GIRL, VANISHED) and Book #6 (GIRL, ERASED) in the series are now also available.

Blake Pierce

Blake Pierce is the USA Today bestselling author of the RILEY PAGE mystery series, which includes seventeen books. Blake Pierce is also the author of the MACKENZIE WHITE mystery series, comprising fourteen books; of the AVERY BLACK mystery series, comprising six books; of the KERI LOCKE mystery series, comprising five books; of the MAKING OF RILEY PAIGE mystery series, comprising six books; of the KATE WISE mystery series, comprising seven books; of the CHLOE FINE psychological suspense mystery, comprising six books; of the JESSIE HUNT psychological suspense thriller series, comprising nineteen books; of the AU PAIR psychological suspense thriller series, comprising three books; of the ZOE PRIME mystery series, comprising six books; of the ADELE SHARP mystery series, comprising thirteen books; of the EUROPEAN VOYAGE cozy mystery series, comprising six books (and counting); of the new LAURA FROST FBI suspense thriller, comprising five books (and counting); of the new ELLA DARK FBI suspense thriller, comprising six books (and counting); of the A YEAR IN EUROPE cozy mystery series, comprising nine books (and counting); of the AVA GOLD mystery series, comprising three books (and counting); and of the RACHEL GIFT mystery series, comprising three books (and counting).

An avid reader and lifelong fan of the mystery and thriller genres, Blake loves to hear from you, so please feel free to visit www.blakepierceauthor.com to learn more and stay in touch.

BOOKS BY BLAKE PIERCE

RACHEL GIFT MYSTERY SERIES
HER LAST WISH (Book #1)
HER LAST CHANCE (Book #2)
HER LAST HOPE (Book #3)

AVA GOLD MYSTERY SERIES
CITY OF PREY (Book #1)
CITY OF FEAR (Book #2)
CITY OF BONES (Book #3)

A YEAR IN EUROPE
A MURDER IN PARIS (Book #1)
DEATH IN FLORENCE (Book #2)
VENGEANCE IN VIENNA (Book #3)
A FATALITY IN SPAIN (Book #4)
SCANDAL IN LONDON (Book #5)
AN IMPOSTOR IN DUBLIN (Book #6)
SEDUCTION IN BORDEAUX (Book #7)
JEALOUSY IN SWITZERLAND (Book #8)
A DEBACLE IN PRAGUE (Book #9)

ELLA DARK FBI SUSPENSE THRILLER
GIRL, ALONE (Book #1)
GIRL, TAKEN (Book #2)
GIRL, HUNTED (Book #3)
GIRL, SILENCED (Book #4)
GIRL, VANISHED (Book 5)
GIRL ERASED (Book #6)

LAURA FROST FBI SUSPENSE THRILLER
ALREADY GONE (Book #1)
ALREADY SEEN (Book #2)
ALREADY TRAPPED (Book #3)
ALREADY MISSING (Book #4)
ALREADY DEAD (Book #5)

EUROPEAN VOYAGE COZY MYSTERY SERIES
MURDER (AND BAKLAVA) (Book #1)
DEATH (AND APPLE STRUDEL) (Book #2)
CRIME (AND LAGER) (Book #3)
MISFORTUNE (AND GOUDA) (Book #4)
CALAMITY (AND A DANISH) (Book #5)
MAYHEM (AND HERRING) (Book #6)

ADELE SHARP MYSTERY SERIES
LEFT TO DIE (Book #1)
LEFT TO RUN (Book #2)
LEFT TO HIDE (Book #3)
LEFT TO KILL (Book #4)
LEFT TO MURDER (Book #5)
LEFT TO ENVY (Book #6)
LEFT TO LAPSE (Book #7)
LEFT TO VANISH (Book #8)
LEFT TO HUNT (Book #9)
LEFT TO FEAR (Book #10)
LEFT TO PREY (Book #11)
LEFT TO LURE (Book #12)
LEFT TO CRAVE (Book #13)

THE AU PAIR SERIES
ALMOST GONE (Book#1)
ALMOST LOST (Book #2)
ALMOST DEAD (Book #3)

ZOE PRIME MYSTERY SERIES
FACE OF DEATH (Book#1)
FACE OF MURDER (Book #2)
FACE OF FEAR (Book #3)
FACE OF MADNESS (Book #4)
FACE OF FURY (Book #5)
FACE OF DARKNESS (Book #6)

A JESSIE HUNT PSYCHOLOGICAL SUSPENSE SERIES
THE PERFECT WIFE (Book #1)
THE PERFECT BLOCK (Book #2)
THE PERFECT HOUSE (Book #3)

THE PERFECT SMILE (Book #4)
THE PERFECT LIE (Book #5)
THE PERFECT LOOK (Book #6)
THE PERFECT AFFAIR (Book #7)
THE PERFECT ALIBI (Book #8)
THE PERFECT NEIGHBOR (Book #9)
THE PERFECT DISGUISE (Book #10)
THE PERFECT SECRET (Book #11)
THE PERFECT FAÇADE (Book #12)
THE PERFECT IMPRESSION (Book #13)
THE PERFECT DECEIT (Book #14)
THE PERFECT MISTRESS (Book #15)
THE PERFECT IMAGE (Book #16)
THE PERFECT VEIL (Book #17)
THE PERFECT INDISCRETION (Book #18)
THE PERFECT RUMOR (Book #19)

CHLOE FINE PSYCHOLOGICAL SUSPENSE SERIES
NEXT DOOR (Book #1)
A NEIGHBOR'S LIE (Book #2)
CUL DE SAC (Book #3)
SILENT NEIGHBOR (Book #4)
HOMECOMING (Book #5)
TINTED WINDOWS (Book #6)

KATE WISE MYSTERY SERIES
IF SHE KNEW (Book #1)
IF SHE SAW (Book #2)
IF SHE RAN (Book #3)
IF SHE HID (Book #4)
IF SHE FLED (Book #5)
IF SHE FEARED (Book #6)
IF SHE HEARD (Book #7)

THE MAKING OF RILEY PAIGE SERIES
WATCHING (Book #1)
WAITING (Book #2)
LURING (Book #3)
TAKING (Book #4)
STALKING (Book #5)

KILLING (Book #6)

RILEY PAIGE MYSTERY SERIES
ONCE GONE (Book #1)
ONCE TAKEN (Book #2)
ONCE CRAVED (Book #3)
ONCE LURED (Book #4)
ONCE HUNTED (Book #5)
ONCE PINED (Book #6)
ONCE FORSAKEN (Book #7)
ONCE COLD (Book #8)
ONCE STALKED (Book #9)
ONCE LOST (Book #10)
ONCE BURIED (Book #11)
ONCE BOUND (Book #12)
ONCE TRAPPED (Book #13)
ONCE DORMANT (Book #14)
ONCE SHUNNED (Book #15)
ONCE MISSED (Book #16)
ONCE CHOSEN (Book #17)

MACKENZIE WHITE MYSTERY SERIES
BEFORE HE KILLS (Book #1)
BEFORE HE SEES (Book #2)
BEFORE HE COVETS (Book #3)
BEFORE HE TAKES (Book #4)
BEFORE HE NEEDS (Book #5)
BEFORE HE FEELS (Book #6)
BEFORE HE SINS (Book #7)
BEFORE HE HUNTS (Book #8)
BEFORE HE PREYS (Book #9)
BEFORE HE LONGS (Book #10)
BEFORE HE LAPSES (Book #11)
BEFORE HE ENVIES (Book #12)
BEFORE HE STALKS (Book #13)
BEFORE HE HARMS (Book #14)

AVERY BLACK MYSTERY SERIES
CAUSE TO KILL (Book #1)
CAUSE TO RUN (Book #2)

CAUSE TO HIDE (Book #3)
CAUSE TO FEAR (Book #4)
CAUSE TO SAVE (Book #5)
CAUSE TO DREAD (Book #6)

KERI LOCKE MYSTERY SERIES
A TRACE OF DEATH (Book #1)
A TRACE OF MURDER (Book #2)
A TRACE OF VICE (Book #3)
A TRACE OF CRIME (Book #4)
A TRACE OF HOPE (Book #5)